MW01286001

THE VERMILION STRAIN
POST-APOCALYPTIC EXTINCTION

S.A. ISON

The Vermilion Strain Post-Apocalyptic Extinction
Copyright © 2019 by S.A. Ison All rights reserved.

Book Design by Elizabeth Mackey
Book Edited by Felicia A. Sullivan
Book Edited by Boyd Editing Ent.

All rights Reserved. Except as under the U.S. Copyright Act of 1976, no part of this publication may be reproduced, distributed or transmitted in any form or by any means, or stored in a data base or retrieval system, without prior written permission of S.A. Ison.

This is a work of fiction. Names, characters, places and incidents either are the production of the author's imagination or used fictitiously, and any resemblance to locales, events, business establishments, or actual persons–living or dead—is entirely coincidental.

OTHER BOOKS BY S.A. ISON

BLACK SOUL RISING From the Taldano Files

INOCULATION ZERO Welcome to the Stone Age
Book 1
INOCULATION ZERO Welcome to the Age of War
Book 2

EMP ANTEDILUVIAN PURGE
Book 1

EMP ANTEDILUVIAN FEAR
Book 2
EMP ANTEDILUVIAN COURAGE
Book 3

POSEIDON RUSSIAN DOOMSDAY
Book 1

POSEIDON RUBBLE AND ASH
Book 2

EMP PRIMEVAL

PUSHED BACK A TIME TRAVELER'S JOURNAL
Book 1

PUSHED BACK THE TIME TRAVELER'S DAUGHTERS
Book 2

THE RECALCITRANT ASSASSIN

BREAKING NEWS

THE LONG WALK HOME

EMP DESOLATION
THE HIVE A POST-APOCOLYPIC LIFE

The Vermilion Strain
Post-Apocalyptic Extinction   S.A. Ison

THE MAD DOG EVENT

MY NAME IS MARY A Reincarnation

DISTURBANCE IN THE WAKE

OUT OF TIME AN OLD FASHION WESTERN

YESTERDAY'S WARRIOR

NO TIME FOR WITCHES

NO ONE'S TIME

A BONE TO PICK
THE WILDER SIDE OF Z
THE WILDER SIDE RAGE
THE WILDER SIDE OF FURY
THE WILDER SIDE OF WAR
THE WILDER SIDE OF HELL

ANCIENT DEATH

For Billie Jo,
Thank you for reading my works and your enthusiasm

♥

ONE

Brian Philips held his dying wife, Christa, in his arms. She was drenched in sweat and blood. He smoothed her hair. The scent of sour death was near, mixed with the coppery stench of diarrhea. Christa's eyes were black with blood and she was blind. Brian knew she wasn't cognizant of his presence. It was god-awful; their bed was saturated with blood and bloody diarrhea. She'd beaten breast cancer, only to be struck down by this egregious virus. EV-01-H. The designation was just handed down by the CDC in Atlanta, so swift was this bio-weapon.

Brian was certain the virus had to be a bio-weapon. Be it China, North Korea, Russia, or the Middle East, it didn't matter to him, with his wife limp and cold in his arms.

Christa was bleeding out and there was nothing to stop it. The hospitals had closed their doors; Lancaster was a ghost town at this point. He contemplated how the Amish had fared and wondered if they'd closed ranks. Since it was still unknown how the virus was spreading, the Amish had a fifty-fifty chance of staying clear of it since they were a closed community. Then again, they didn't use most modern medicines. Not that medicine helped anyone who'd contracted the virus.

He'd gone out yesterday attempting to gather supplies. The stores were empty of people, the shelves full of product. Brian knew the power would eventually go. The power stations and electrical grids were likely running on auto at this point. When it came time, even that would stop. He owned a whole house generator, but that would only last so long. If he used it a few hours a day, it would last longer. His mind was clicking away at all the scenarios ahead. He'd had nothing but time to think as he held his dying wife.

Brian had driven his extended bed RAM truck to take advantage of the ample storage room in the truck bed. He'd stopped at several gas stations, confiscating the five-gallon gas cans, and filled them up. He'd loaded the bed of his truck with the cans, and topped off his tank. He'd added fuel additive to extend the life of the gas, though he was confident he'd go through it quickly enough. He was a firefighter, or had been only weeks before, and he knew how to be prepared. Well, he thought he did…until the Vermilion Strain.

Christa's chest suddenly stopped moving, the wet, rattling sound of her lungs ceased. The room was eerily quiet, his harsh breathing the only sound. Brian wanted to weep but his face was oddly numb. His brain was numb. He smoothed the bloody hair from Christa's face, her eyes unseeing and vacant. A void where wonderful animation had once been. Christa's face was densely speckled with petechial hemorrhaging, as was the rest of her body. His wife was what his mother called high yellow, with very fair skin for a black woman. Her skin was now nearly as dark as his own. It was now the color of vermilion, hence the unofficial name of the EV-01-H virus. He imagined that someone white would be a crimson color or a deeper shade of vermilion.

Warm tears slid down Brian's face. He sighed heavily and laid his wife down, gently shutting her eyes with his large hand. He stood up from the bed, using his forearm to wipe his face, and walked through the quiet house into the attached garage. He found a shovel and headed out to the backyard.

He paused by the row of roses his wife had planted years before. Pumpkin roses, she'd called them. The color of pumpkins, the roses were her pride and joy. A quiet, sad smile creased his face. He wiped absently at the tears. A shuddering exhalation rippled through him and he bent to the task of digging a grave by the roses, knowing Christa would want to rest there. It was mid-morning and the day was already heating up. The world was silent, only his loud breathing keeping him company. Shoveling the loamy ground, he was able to make a respectable grave for his wife. He set the shovel aside and returned to the cool and silent house.

When the power eventually went out, the house would be like an oven. He went to the linen closet and pulled out primrose sheets. Christa would like them. Brian wrapped his wife tenderly in her burial shroud, lifted her slender form, and carried her out into the yard. He placed her on the ground and then jumped down into the grave. Carefully gathering her in his arms for the last time, he hugged her close to his body, rocking. His sobs saturating the yard, he laid her into the grave, reluctant and aggrieved to let her go this last time.

"This is the best I can do, honey. I'm sorry it isn't normal, with a casket and all. But you'll be safe here."

He choked and wiped his face. He wanted desperately to lay down with her.

Climbing out of the grave, Brian snatched the shovel and filled the hole. It was faster filling the thing than it was to dig. After he finished, Brian went into the house and stood at the sink. He washed his face, arms, and hands, then grabbed a beer and his Glock 17. Walking out to the yard, he sat by the patio table sipping his beer. He and Christa had spent many happy hours here in the large yard, tending her roses and landscaping. It became a sanctuary during her recovery from cancer and chemo.

They threw many parties with neighbors and his beloved grill. A tremulous grimace creased his features at the remembrance. Christa was the perfect hostess. With her wonderful laughter and beautiful heart, she made everyone feel welcome.

He wondered idly if he should dig himself a grave, then thought, who would fill it in? Why waste the energy? The Glock was cool in his hand and he idly stroked the weapon as he sipped his beer. He squinted into the clear blue sky, his eyes watering against the glare. He tracked sparrows gliding on the wind above him. There was a nest nearby. Was his wife's soul even now ascending to heaven?

At the squeak of the gate door opening, he swiveled his head and spied Cooper, his next-door neighbor's four-year-old son. He was surprised. The child appeared disheveled and dirty, his clothing badly wrinkled. Brian set the beer aside on the table, along with the Glock.

"Come here, Coop." He waved the boy to him. The child walked to him and climbed up into Brian's lap and that startled Brian. Coop was normally a shy and quiet child. He'd always given Brian shy smiles behind his parents' legs, peeking around.

"I'm hungry," the child said timidly, his pint-sized hands fingering the buttons that ran down Brian's shirt. The boy appeared thin, and Brian felt Cooper's ribs under the bright orange T-shirt. Cooper smelled horrible. Apparently the boy hadn't been bathed nor had he wiped his behind very well. Brian gazed at his cornflower blue eyes and noted his eyes were dull. He ran a hand through Cooper's stiff blond hair.

"Where's your mommy and daddy, Coop?"

"Sleeping. I'm hungry," he said, his voice plaintive.

Brian grunted and got up. He carried the boy into his kitchen and set Cooper on the quartz countertop. He washed his hands then found a clean washcloth and lathered it up with soap and warm water. He went to Cooper and wiped the child's face and hands. The boy sat quietly while Brian did this, his eyes closing when Brian smoothed the cloth across his face. He glanced down at the child and then went to the refrigerator and pulled out bacon and eggs. He found a loaf of bread. For the next ten minutes Cooper sat patiently on the kitchen counter scrutinizing Brian's every move. Brian raked the scrambled eggs and bacon onto a plate and then carried Cooper into the dining room, the child's thin arms encircling Brian's neck. He set the boy down at the table and then went for orange juice.

"I'm going to check on your parents. You sit here and eat. Don't leave, okay, Coop?"

"Okay." Cooper's cheeks were bulging with scrambled eggs.

Brian went out to the backyard to retrieve his Glock. Going through the gate, he headed to Cooper Lane's home. The kitchen door was standing wide open and Brian detected the pungent scent of decomp. He held his hand over his mouth and nose and walked in, scanning the room. There was canned food, empty boxes of cereal, and an empty carton of milk on the floor.

Brian walked into the living room. The TV was on, but there was only static and snow. It had been that way for two days. He'd lost the satellite signal then. There had only been a warning banner before that. It was a little over three and a half weeks since the virus had hit the United States with such devastating efficiency. He'd tried to use his cell phone to Facetime, call, and text his parents and Christa's folks, but there was no service. He'd given up all attempts to contact the outside world when Christa began to show the first symptoms of the Vermilion Strain.

Brian made his way to Shafer and Jillian's bedroom. The door was open and the stench that issued forth almost sent him to his knees. He gagged and stumbled away. He viewed two forms on the bed and hundreds of flies buzzing over them. The room hummed ominously, loud and relentless. The sheets that covered the couple were black. A large white mass of maggots wriggled and writhed on the heads of his friends. He quickly looked away, swallowing hard, trying to push that image from his brain. It was too late. He bent at the waist and vomited on the carpeted hall floor. He stumbled and hit the door jamb of Coop's room. He peered in, wiping ferociously at his tearing eyes. He wiped his mouth and spat out the foulness.

Marching to Coop's bed, Brian ripped the dinosaur pillowcase off the pillow and went to Cooper's brightly painted dresser. He pulled out socks and underwear from one drawer, shirts of all colors and designs from the next. From the third drawer, he pulled out shorts and jeans, shoving it all carelessly into the pillowcase. From the child's closet, he selected shoes, then some toys and piled it on top of all the rest.

He returned to the living room where he spotted an old blue blanket on the couch. He knew the blanket was Cooper's lovey, so he grabbed that. He sighted a family photo and grabbed that too. Cooper would not return here.

With resolve, Brian marched from the house with Cooper's belongings. He'd return later tonight and take all the supplies and food to his place, as well as a few more photographs for Cooper. Coop was now his responsibility. All thoughts of suicide vanished from his consciousness, his concern was now for the diminutive four-year-old eating scrambled eggs in his dining room.

Emma Prichard pushed the shopping cart along the sidewalk. She sported a deep blue checkered bandana tied across her face, Vicks VapoRub smeared across the fabric. It was to keep the stench of the rotting bodies away, along with the bloated flies that continually bounced off her face. She wore sunglasses and latex gloves. The whole city was an open wound, suppurating with noxious and toxic biomatter. Emma was becoming used to the grisly sights on the streets. She hadn't seen another living soul for over a week. Though Boston was a very large city, she was in Jamaica Plain, located on the outskirts of Boston proper. Her apartment was situated near Johnson Park, which was designated a massive dumping ground for the dead.

During the first days of the EV-01-H, she'd been in the thick of it. Scores of victims pouring into the ER, dying within hours. The morgue had overflowed, and when the staff, doctors, and nurses started displaying the petechial splotches on their skin, Emma knew it was the beginning of the end. After a week, she realized there was nothing to be done and headed home and stayed there. Locked behind her doors, she surveilled from the windows and viewed the news as the grim facts and numbers danced across the screen. This was an extinction level virus and there wasn't a damned thing to do but wait it out or die. She was a nurse, not God.

The victims writhed in agony, their skin tone mutating to vermilion as the virus overwhelmed their bodies. Near the end, blood leaked from their ears, eyes, nose, mouth, and their bowels. She hoped their brains were so damaged by the virus the victims were oblivious of their impending death. The husks left behind were gruesome.

Bodies were piled in grotesque monuments outside the doors of Massachusetts General. Before she'd gone home that last day, the trains stopped running, as had the buses. She'd found a taxi driver willing to take her. She'd had to show him her skin, proving she wasn't infected. His face was hidden behind a white surgical mask, his eyes wide and frightened. She was lucky to make it home.

She was uncertain if there were people still alive and hiding or if everyone was dead. The drone of the buzzing echoed from her apartment; the flies were so thick as to be a substantial dark fog. The sound of buzzing was the only noise these days. It was strange that such a large city was so quiet. No sounds of cars or mechanized droning. Sometimes her ears pricked at the calling of birds or she'd see a murder of crows rising from a large heap of bodies. She avoided the windows at those times. It sent shivers through her; it was the harbinger of the end of days.

She'd stayed in her apartment as long as possible, terrified to leave. The smell from the halls and outside her window guaranteed her confinement. When she was down to her last can of peaches, she'd have to go out and search for food and water. Every bowl, bottle, jar, and bathtub were filled with water. The power had died yesterday. She'd kept the receptacles full, knowing at some point the power would go out. The apartment had heated up quickly and she'd had to open the windows. Emma lost her lunch at the foulness that wafted her way. She'd put a dab of the Vicks she used for chest colds under her nose. She'd been a nurse for six years, but nothing had prepared her for this wholesale slaughter.

Emma had only been in Boston three years, having left Lancaster, Pennsylvania after a bitter divorce. She loved the vibrant city, but it was all different now. Sinister. There were fires in the sprawling city and smoke hung low in the sky, and she suspected the smoke was toxic.

She stopped short when gunshots erupted in the distance. So someone *was* alive. It sounded like automatic gunfire. Not the single shot kind, but a rapid tattoo. That didn't bode well for her.

She was making stops to gather up supplies. Her long brown hair was pulled up and covered by a ball cap. She'd gone to Whole Foods and filled a cart, then stopped by CVS for medical supplies to add to her already extensive medical provisions. For her upcoming trip, Emma wanted to ensure she'd have plenty. There were no shortages. With hardly anyone alive, there was plenty of food, water, plenty of everything. She'd found an abandoned ambulance and retrieved the supplies, sterile bandages, saline IVs, and anything and everything. You could never have too much. The less replenishing, the better.

It was never established if EV-01-H was an airborne virus, spread by physical contact, body fluids, or a cough or sneeze. The virus was virulent, and Emma suspected a ninety-eight percent extinction rate, if not more. The extermination of the human race, an extinction event. She'd seen a segment on the news in the first week about the primates at the zoos. Those animals were dying, the large primates, gorillas, chimps, and orangutans.

So rapid was the spread that it had never been discovered which country had unleashed this plague, if any had. The death toll on TV was grim, fast, and prolific. She was fairly certain the strain hadn't been natural, but created by madmen, a government perhaps. They'd done their job too well and had all but wiped out the human population.

She needed to get out of the city because all these decomposing bodies would lead to cholera or typhoid. Although she'd lived through the Vermilion Strain she doubted she'd live through cholera. It would take planning, but mostly it would take figuring out where the hell to go. Her first thought was Lancaster, where her parents and ex-husband lived, but it would be just as bad as Boston. She could not live in or near a city, too dangerous. Definitely away from the city. Out in the countryside? She'd have to commandeer a truck and pack it with supplies, water, and food. She wondered how the Amish were doing and wondered if they'd take her in. Did she even want to stay in a restrictive community?

Shoving the cart, she headed up the final stretch of sidewalk to her apartment building, strolling along Amory Street. She was thankful she lived on the first floor; she'd hate to have to haul all the groceries up the stairs. There was more gunfire, this time closer. That wasn't good. Who was shooting? And at what?

Ahead of her, she spotted a dog. It was thin and dirty, with large, liquid brown eyes. Sad and compelling, the animal melted her heart instantly. It was a tan and brown short haired dog of medium build, with a sweet, dark face. His tail wagged tentatively.

Emma wasn't a dog person—that was her ex-husband's wheelhouse—but she was so lonely that talking to a dog had to be better than not talking at all.

"Hey you. You lost? Your people parents die? I don't have dog food, but I got some canned meats," she cooed. Her smile broadened when the tail thumped harder.

"Well, come on, dog," she said, and the dog followed behind her. Coming up to her apartment building, she stopped, surveying the area. She avoided the bodies littering the street. Opening the door to her apartment, she coaxed the dog in and followed after. She made several trips, bringing the bags of food in. The water was the heaviest and she had to break it down to even more trips. In the kitchen, she pulled out two bowls, poured a bottle of water into one, and placed it on the floor for the dog. She rifled in a drawer for a can opener and opened a can of meat, dumped that into the other bowl, and set it before the dog. The animal wolfed down the food, then licked the bowl.

"I'll give you more later, pooch, I don't want you to get the shits. Besides, I'm guessing your tummy has shrunk a bit, buddy. We'll swing over to Whole Foods later for a few big bags of dog food," she promised.

Emma went to the living room. On the coffee table were several stacks of books. She'd ransacked the local

17

library and a bookstore, choosing books which might help her and her quest for surviving alone in a hostile world. One book, *Mini Farming*, written by Brett Markham, would help her start a garden. She knew nothing about gardening, nor plants. Her mother had a green thumb, but she didn't. She'd have to learn. She had a book on wild edible plants, survival living, *Survival Hacks* by Creek Stewart, and a few other odds and ends, including one about canning food and food preservation.

She'd been amassing supplies over the past few days, gearing up for the big relocation. She knew she was dragging her feet about leaving. Although here was death and disease, here was the known. Out there was the unknown. It was a start to a new life, a life alone in a world where there were very few humans. She didn't know how many people were out there, but they wouldn't all be nice. The gunshot Emma heard earlier bothered her. She didn't own a gun but had found several in the other apartments. If and when she ran into other people, she'd want to be armed. A woman alone was in a dangerous situation. She'd seen enough post-apocalyptic movies to know that. At least there were no zombies, she was thankful for small mercies.

On her kitchen table was a Sig Sauer, or at least that was what the box said. She'd found it in Mr. Willard's home on the third floor. Mr. Willard was the first to die at the apartment building. He'd gone to the emergency room and never returned. She had three boxes of 9mm shells. She carried a .38 special and had two boxes of shells for that. That gun she'd found at an apartment down her hall. She'd gone into every apartment on the block. The ones with bodies, she simply investigated and shut the door. It wasn't worth going in, especially after she'd found the first two weapons. She figured she'd better start carrying one of the weapons on her now. The gunshots earlier caused her great concern.

She would practice shooting once away from the city. Her ex, Dick, had harassed her into going to the gun range. As a nurse, she'd seen her share of gunshot wounds and wanted no part of the weapons her ex-husband so loved. Now, however, she was glad for the knowledge. She didn't know a lot about the different weapons, but she did know how to fire them and how to figure them out safely.

She glanced at the dog. At least she now had a companion. She'd have to give the dog a name. There was no collar or tags. She sighed and caressed the dog's muzzle. She dreaded leaving this place for the great unknown, but she had to.

She eyed the road atlas and flipped it open. There were literally thousands of choices. Her mind kept going to a place she was familiar with. A place she'd been loved and safe. Raymond B. Winter State Park in Pennsylvania. It was roughly seven hundred acres of wilderness, but had trails, fishing, and hunting. It had cottages and plenty of camping sites. She and her parents traveled to the park every year since she held a memory. It was a place she loved. Laughing aloud at the idea, the dog gazed at her questioningly.

"I guess I knew all along where I was going, pooch. And with you here now, I think it's safe to say I'm ready to leave. Tomorrow, I'm going to find us a truck. There are a few in the neighborhood, it's just a matter of finding the keys that go to it." Emma scratched the dog behind the ears. "That shouldn't be a problem, I'll just have to search every apartment for truck keys."

Emma shook her head at the monumental task of locating keys to a vehicle. She had her eye on a beauty, a blue Silverado. It was a quad cab, with plenty of packing room to store lots of food and supplies inside, not to mention the truck bed. She'd need a lot, and once she got to the park, she'd have to see what else she needed to set up her future there.

She'd swing by her parents' home. She knew they were dead, having lost contact with them the first week. Her mother called to say that her father was sick, and her mother hadn't sounded that good either. Two days later, neither parent answered the phone. She grieved for them. She wanted to swing by her old home and select a few personal and sentimental things. There was no more procrastinating. She had to leave this place.

She picked up the .38 and tucked it into her waistband, planning to make another run to the store for dog food, seed packets—she'd have to start a garden fast—and to nab some packs of canning jars.

"Come on, dog, let's go find you some chow."

Flynn Kellerman clicked the remote. Nothing happened. His face was pale with fear and horror. All the channels reported the same thing: the Vermilion Strain was spreading with ferocious speed across the world. Then there was the steady warning banner, and now nothing. The power was out. Shit, when had that happened? It had only been three weeks since the first cases were reported. Or was it five weeks?

Flynn was losing track of time. The virus started in several large cities all over the world, including Philadelphia. South Korea claimed the first victim, but it was a vague report and then all the other countries jumped in. It was a virus Atlanta CDC identified as EV-01-H, a mutated hemorrhagic virus, origins unknown.

China was rampaging and screaming that the U.S. let loose this plague. The United States alleged China, in fact, was the culprit that allowed the deadly virus to run amok. Nations were pointing fingers, nuclear launches were threatened, and Flynn was terrified that a bomb would drop on Philly any moment.

And now the power was out. He was so isolated and alone. The accusations went on for days, yet millions were dying, no matter the architect of the virus, and no cure in sight.

"End of days," Flynn breathed. His mouth was dry with terror. He wasn't a high-strung doomsday fanatic, but Christ in heaven, so many were dying so *fast*. He looked around his apartment and wondered if this would be his tomb. At twenty-three, he'd only just begun to live his life. He'd signed the lease for this apartment only six months ago, he'd just met a great girl, Xandra, and his unwavering belief she was already dead kept him from seeking her out. His whole world was crashing on top of him, all because of this Vermilion virus. He was alone in the world. His father died last year from a heart attack after smoking for a lifetime. His mother was long dead. Flynn had no one.

The Vermilion Strain was aptly named. The virus caused its victims to bleed out of every orifice, their skin transitioning to a deep shade of scarlet or vermilion from the burst capillaries and blood vessels all over their bodies. Even at this very moment, Flynn detected the foul stench from his neighbors' apartments in the six-story building. He'd called in sick three days after the first reports, though he wasn't sick at all. After the first five hundred thousand deaths, Flynn figured he'd keep his head down, job be damned. Stocking shelves in the big box store and dealing with possibly infected customers wasn't worth his life. As it was, two days later, most of the employees of the store died. So, home Flynn remained, following along as the death toll rose across the world. He stood by his window and surveyed the street below littered with bodies.

Bodies for Hell's sake! Just laying everywhere and no one coming to take them away. He hadn't seen the police, any of the National Guard, no one. Random people walked or staggered in the streets below. Packs of dogs fought over the bodies, jerking and yanking them in grotesque ways. He gagged, forcing himself away from the window. An hour later he was back at the window again, witnessing the madness.

"What in the hell?" he cried when he saw a streak of orange and black run across the street into the alley. Was that a tiger?

"A tiger for Christ's sake? Who let the tigers out?" he screamed at the window, pounding his fists on the window frame.

If the virus wasn't bad enough, some dumbass had let out the animals from the zoo! Lions, tigers, bears, all of those predators loose in the city?

My god.

He needed a weapon. Where was he going to get a gun? He'd have to locate a gun store and acquire a few weapons.

Flynn's brain was in overload with the virus, possible starvation, and now predator animals loose on the street. He wanted to shrink down and just disappear. From the window, he searched the streets for wild and dangerous animals. Sometimes a car passed by. The vehicles mostly swerved to miss the bodies, though sometimes he'd see a car bounce and knew it had run over one of the bodies. It was all too grisly. Too surreal.

Flynn had texted his friends, afraid to leave his apartment. He'd urged Cramer Appleton, his best friend and drinking buddy, to quit work or at least take a vacation. Cramer hemmed and hawed. That was three weeks ago, Flynn texted him five days ago and he'd received no response. He'd called and left messages, called Cramer's job, and no one answered.

Flynn then texted Roger Lower, who didn't answer. He went through his list of contacts one by one. No one answered or texted back. No one. Clutching the TV remote to his chest, he went to the couch and sat down. Bending over at the waist, he rocked and tried to breathe. He was having a panic attack and was helpless to stop it. He got up from the couch and walked to the window. He was wearing a groove in the carpet.

This was bullshit. Why wasn't anyone answering?

Flynn wove his fingers through his dirty blond hair and pulled. He was beginning to go crazy, cooped up in his apartment with the reek seeping through the walls. He had to get out of there, but knew it was a very bad idea.

Five minutes later he walked out his front door with his car keys in hand. He went to the elevator, pushed the call button, and cursed when it didn't work. He forgot the power was out. He went to the stairwell and opened the door. It was dark.

Pulling out his lighter, he lit it and quickly made his way down the four flights of stairs. He opened the door to the outside, bent over, and vomited. The stench outside was horrendous, oppressive, and cloying. Though it was only April, the warm spring sun was heating up the dead.

Flynn gripped his stomach, ropes of saliva hanging from his mouth. His body shuddered violently. Hot tears flowed freely from his eyes. The smell was beyond anything he'd ever experienced before. It seared his throat and bit deep down into his gut. With a shaky hand, he wiped his mouth and headed back into the building. He hurried up the stairs to his floor, staggering and tripping. Stumbling to his door, he burst through, slammed it, and locked it. Sliding down with his back against the door, tears falling down his face,

Flynn screamed in anguish, rage, self-pity, and a healthy dose of fear.

Ж

The lights flickered off and then on. His generator started up. Brian was pleased. That was the best investment he ever made. The generator would run for approximately a week before the fuel was out, giving him time to plan and get his shit together. Staying here was out of the question, as much as he wished to. He'd spent the last few days going over YouTube videos, knowing at some point that too would die, and it had. He'd lost his internet yesterday evening, though not before he'd amassed a large amount of knowledge on "how to" and "DIY" videos.

He'd been getting to know Cooper, who'd begun to come out of his shell. The child hadn't asked to go home after the first day living with Brian. Brian gave the boy a bath and dressed him in clean clothing. He'd put Coop into the spare bedroom, Brian slept on the couch, his bed too soiled to be useable. He was unable to bring himself to sleep in the bed without his wife. The child had slept the rest of that day and night. He was clear eyed the next morning, and from then on Brian had taken Coop with him on his forays out into town. Thankfully, the child wasn't big enough to see out of the windows, and missed the dead that littered the roads.

Cooper was now on the floor, coloring with the crayons and few coloring books Brian had picked up their last time out. The child was humming softly as he colored.

That morning, Brian's heart was shattered when Cooper called him Daddy. Coop hadn't noticed the slip. Brian's eyes stung with tears at the remembrance. He and Christa had thought about having children but their lives were busy ones. Then she'd gotten cancer, and they didn't think it was a good idea. Now he had a child by way of a pandemic. Each day, Cooper became more resilient.

Brian had gathered propane bottles along with a camping cook stove. He figured he'd need it. Once he got to where he was going, he planned to gather more propane. It would at least last him a good while. He'd started scavenging dry goods, TP, plastic sheeting rolls, duct tape, nails, screws, and other odds and ends. He wasn't sure what he'd need it for, but if ever he did, he'd have it on hand. It was, after all, the end of the world. No one would ever make those items again. Once the gasoline was gone, he'd be confined to wherever he settled.

He had figured out where to go. It was where he'd gone hunting with his friends and camping with Christa. R.B. Winter State Park, a couple of hours northwest of him. There were numerous parks in Pennsylvania, any one of them a good choice. He was most familiar with Winter.

He'd hunted and fished there for the last thirty years or so. He and Christa had walked the trails and had enjoyed the wildness of it. Brian figured that location would be his best bet. There was plenty of space there, and cabins. Worst case, he'd take over an RV or find one and tow it behind his truck. He would not live in a tent; that wouldn't do for winter, and the child he'd assumed responsibility for required more than that. On that thought, he wrote down "chainsaw" on his list, with extra chains and oil. He'd have to cut down a lot of trees for winter firewood. He'd swing by the salvage yard and see about locating a mini potbelly stove along with flashing. The cabins didn't have fireplaces.

So much to think about and do before he had to leave. Once the gas was gone, he'd be stuck at Winter Park, so he needed to get this right. He was a handyman and tinkered quite a bit. He chuckled, remembering Christa complaining about all his projects in the garage, most unfinished. Brian loved keeping busy and there never seemed to be enough time in the day. Now he had all the time in the world. He'd put a lock on the cabin door. He didn't know how many people would be in the vicinity, if any, and he didn't want to leave supplies at the park without locking them up. He'd make a run this afternoon and drop off a truckload, get a lay of the land.

He went down in the basement to check his rifles. He had his Mossberg Patriot and his childhood rifle, the Timber Classic Marlin. It was the first weapon he'd used to hunt with at the state park, with his father. Brian hummed gratifyingly at the memory of his first deer when he was thirteen. He'd been so proud.

He would have to teach Cooper to hunt when he got older and teach the boy not to touch the firearms. Brian didn't want a tragedy.

First things first. He needed to load up supplies and get over to the state park to find a place to live, see what conditions were. Brian hoped that if others lived there, they were good and decent people. People lost their minds in horrendous conditions. He'd seen it in his work. Devastation brought out the best and the worst in people. He didn't know if others would head out there too, because there were so many choices. He also didn't know how many people were even left alive. He hadn't seen very many. Brian suspected that R.B. Winter Park might be a place where others would congregate to live. If they did, should he join up with others and make a micro community, help each other to survive? Though it was late spring, winter would eventually arrive, regardless of how ready he was or wasn't. There wouldn't be anyone coming in to save the day. Whatever he found, hunted, or scavenged, was all they would have. It was an overwhelming and daunting prospect.

He needed more clothing for Cooper, long term clothing in ever increasing sizes. He'd stock up, along with a few things for himself. So many things to think about and plan for.

Brian extracted his case and placed the Mossberg in. He pulled out boxes of shells and stacked them on his work bench. He located the cleaning kit and set that aside. He'd need to get more oil, brushes, and bores.

Weapons were his first priority, right along with shelter and food.

He heard light squeaks on the wooden stairs. Cooper sat above, peering down with curiosity.

"Come on down, Cooper, I'll show you my hunting rifles. You must never touch these without permission, but when you get older, I'll teach you how to use them."

Cooper came down and stood beside Brian, his eyes large. "Wow!" he said in his childish voice.

Brian agreed. "Wow, indeed. We're going to be leaving soon. We're going on a long camping trip. How do you like that?"

"Oh, I like that, Daddy, I like that a lot!" Cooper beamed up at Brian. Brian ruffled his blond hair.

TWO

Flynn was starving. His fear was so great he was unable to bring himself to leave his apartment after his first venture out. Now he had no choice. He dug in his closet and found a rucksack. He was going to have to leave and find food and water. He dug up several bandanas and tied them on his face to block out the awful stench. From his window, he'd seen the progressive decomposition of the bodies on the streets, and more animals. A herd of zebra had run past his building two days ago. It was such a shock and he'd started laughing, which morphed to crying.

He'd have to take the stairs, and would bring his flashlight this time. His apartment was like an oven and he'd gone through all the bottled water he found in the other apartments. He'd even gone so far as to take water from the toilet tanks.

Flynn wished he had a hazmat suit, but no such luck. He stepped out into the living room and gritted his teeth as he walked to the front door, clutching his car keys in hand. He had to get food or he'd die, simple as that. As he made his way down the stairs, the light from the flashlight bounced off the walls of the stairwell, his footfalls echoing. The scent of putrefaction diminished slightly behind the bandana, but it had little effect overall. He stepped out onto the street, squinting in the bright light.

Flynn quickly walked along Lancaster Avenue to where he'd last parked his car. Averting his eyes from the bodies that littered the street, he marched past unrecognizable lumps and piles of vile things. He smelled the reek of rot and ruin. It was like a coat, covering his body, his skin, his hair.

He looked up, to the windows in the buildings and apartments, searching for faces behind the windows, but there were none. His once vibrant city was now silent. No traffic horns, rumbling buses, no street repair machines, nor chatter from pedestrians. The streets were empty but for the lumps and trash that blew about unchecked. The drone of flies from the massive swarms hovering over the bodies was mind-numbing. Flynn kept his eyes averted. His flesh shivered, like the flanks on a horse, rippling from revulsion.

When he reached his Honda Civic, he climbed in and held his breath as he started the ignition. He wasn't convinced the battery was still good, it was an old one, given to him by his father when he got a new one. It was rusted out, but it was a reliable ride. Letting out a sigh when the engine turned over, Flynn pulled out and headed east, figuring Whole Foods was his best bet. He'd grab a cart and fill it to the brim so he wouldn't have to venture out again for a while. Being outside gave him the creeps. Between the stench and the apocalyptic scenery, he'd just as soon avoid it all, not to mention the friggen *tiger* that was roaming somewhere. He seriously needed a weapon. Once he got what he needed, he'd hunker down for a while.

He'd lost track of time. Had it been over a couple of months since this all started? Or just a few weeks? In the first reports of the virus, only one news alert mentioned South Korea having patient zero. Did North

Korea start this mess? Then China had victims popping up and that was when the media went wild with accusations from China. Then the United States started hurling counterclaims. Within mere hours, cases of the Vermilion Strain were popping up all over the world at the same time. Was it a strategic attack? Flynn speculated whether it was China who started it. Or was it North Korea? Or was it the United States? He wouldn't put it past his government.

In short order, he arrived at Whole Foods. There were a few cars in the parking lot, but not many. He noticed an Andean condor land on a body. It must have come from the zoo. Holy shit. Flynn combed his vicinity, fearing a lion or tiger would jump him. Nothing twitched. He didn't see anyone or anything other than the condor. Sitting in his car, he scanned the surrounding area for movement. Bodies, or what was left of them, were scattered like trash on the ground. If he hid long enough, most of it would be gone on his next venture out. Hopefully.

He thought about swinging by Cramer's place, but didn't want to know the indisputable truth his best friend was dead. He wanted to remember Cramer as the laughing and lively man he was. Cramer was a jokester and a prankster. Flynn had been the victim more than once of one of Cramer's pranks, as had Roger.

Maybe he should go by Xandra's apartment? Had she already left the city? Might she already be dead? He hoped not.

Cutting off the engine, Flynn sighed heavily. His hands were clammy, and his stomach growled in anticipation of eating. He'd gone through the unoccupied apartments and taken all the food. The apartments with dead bodies he'd left alone. Perhaps he just wanted to get out of the apartment and see if there was food out there. He knew he was being foolish, but he needed to get out and see what was left of his world.

Exiting the car, Flynn scanned, searching for signs of life. Nothing. He didn't even see dogs. Would the tigers eat the dogs before people? He'd seen a lot of dogs lately. Here, there were none.

He stopped to get a shopping cart, went to the front of the store, and pushed through the glass front doors. The light was filtered, and the store was darker toward the rear. The reek from rotting produce and meat assaulted Flynn. He advanced cautiously, his head on a swivel. He wanted to kick himself at that moment for leaving his flashlight in the car.

"Stop!" someone shouted from the darkness.

Flynn's heart slammed into his throat and his legs nearly gave out. He clung to the cart, trying to discern the figure in the dark.

"Get out of here, this is the property of Casper," the disembodied voice claimed.

"What? Casper who? The freaking ghost?" Flynn barked with hysterical laughter, his heart still beating wildly. Sweat ran down his body and off his face. He tried to blink it away. He searched wildly but was unable to locate the person speaking to him.

"Casper runs this area, man. Get out or I got orders to shoot."

"What? Hey, there's plenty of food and I'm starving. At least let me get some."

"No way. Casper will have my ass. Get outta here."

"Damnit! I'm hungry. And I'm gonna—"

A gunshot erupted and Flynn jerked, shocked. His arm burned and he gaped at the wound. He'd been grazed by the bullet.

"Are you fucking crazy?" he screamed, clutching his arm.

"I told you! Casper owns this place. Get out of here," the guard bellowed.

Flynn ran out of the store clutching his arm. He tripped on a pile of gooey bones and went sprawling. The condor, ten feet away, took flight, the breeze from the massive flapping wings washing over him with the stench of death. Screaming in fear and rage, Flynn scrambled to his feet and staggered to his car. He pulled out and peeled away from the store. His hands shook badly on the steering wheel. He took the left on Hampstead Circle and headed to Sang Kee Bistro, hoping there would be food there. He parked, exited the car, and went to the front and peered in.

There was a man with a gun glaring at him. "This place is Casper's property. Get the hell out of here!" the man shouted, aiming the gun.

Flynn stared in frustration and disbelief. Had this Casper bastard taken over the whole city? Getting into his car, Flynn peeled away. He'd go to another store. Shit! He didn't think it would be so hard simply to get food. There weren't many people left, but apparently there were at least two assholes and a Casper.

Flynn exited onto King Road, heading east, and drove until he arrived at another Whole Foods supermarket. His arm was throbbing with each heartbeat. He got out, more cautious now. He gritted his teeth; each motion of his arm shot fire to his brain. He strode toward the storefront, visually probing the interior. He didn't see anyone standing near the doors. Cautiously, he opened the front door. He listened intently but heard nothing.

"Hello? Anyone here? I'm coming in, just to get a few things," he called loudly. His arm throbbed, his head pounded, and his gut hurt.

"Stop. This store is Casper's property!" a man called from inside the store.

Flynn cursed. Who was this Casper? How could one person take over everything? How in the hell was he supposed to eat?

"Has Casper got every store? How am I supposed to survive?" Flynn yelled.

"Not my problem. If you want to join Casper's crew, you'll need to go see him. If he lets you join, you can eat. Otherwise, he'll shoot you."

"That's crazy, man."

"Hey, that's the world we live in now. If I were you, I'd get out of town. Casper is going through every building in this city one at a time and taking what he wants. He's got a good-sized army now. Mister, if you're smart, you'll get outta here or you'll join him."

"Where am I supposed to go? Hell, there's plenty of food for everyone. There aren't even many people left," Flynn snarled.

35

"You stick around and he'll kill you. I'm tellin' you, man, he's a bad dude. And he's got assholes that work for him, that guard him. He ain't no one to screw with."

"Fine, then at least let me get some food to last me until I can get out of this place."

"Can't, man. The store has already been inventoried. If anything comes up missing they'll kill me, and not in a fast way with a bullet. Casper skins people who don't do what he tells' em. Like I said, get out of this place if you want to live. Otherwise, you take your chances with Casper."

Flynn shook his head. When had this Casper asshole taken over Philadelphia? How could one man do that? Had he been shut away so long that some scumbag took over?

Flynn walked out to his car and got in. His head was hurting, and his arm burned. Unquestionably, the air wasn't good for the open wound. He pulled away and drove toward home. He stopped at a gas station and went in. The shelves were empty of all food, though he found a few things on the floor. He scooped up a box of antibiotic cream. The box had part of a shoe print on it.

He picked up bits and pieces littering the trashed confines of the station. He got down on his knees when he spotted a candy bar under the shelf. He extended and stretched his fingers and snagged the treat. Peeling the paper, he bit into it. He groaned, eating the candy slowly. He sat on the floor of the station and stared at the ransacked space. How was he going to survive? His lips trembled and he tried not to cry. His life had twisted into some crazy-ass nightmare. He wiped angrily at the tears seeping out. He noticed a road atlas on the floor. He flipped open the book and studied it. He'd never been good at reading maps. He had a GPS for that. He wasn't convinced his GPS still worked. He flipped the pages and thought. Where should he go?

The image of Lancaster, where the Amish lived, popped into his head. Would the Amish take him in? He'd be willing to work for his food. At least there wouldn't be an asshole like Casper there. Well, he hoped there wouldn't be.

Finishing the candy bar, Flynn stood. He would go to his apartment and pack up his things. He'd have to scrounge the other apartments and collect food. Shit, that meant he'd have to see those dead, stinking bodies. He'd have to breathe that horrible air. He prayed he'd find enough to last him a while, in case the Amish weren't as hospitable as he hoped. It was only about an hour and a half drive to Lancaster. He sighed once more, his arm hurting badly, and his stomach too. That bastard who shot him damned near killed him. First the Vermilion virus, now this. In a world that had gone to hell, where was the compassion?

Ж

Emma finished cramming everything into the truck cab. Buddy waited for her in the passenger's seat, his tongue hanging out to the side. It had taken her three hours to locate the keys to the blue truck. She'd gone from one apartment to another hunting for truck keys. As it happened, the keys were located a block away, in the second-floor apartment of a colonial. The apartment stunk and she knew the occupants were dead in their beds. She'd gathered up supplies from the cupboards and had left the place behind. Luckily, the gas tank was full. It was a six-hour drive to Lancaster.

If she needed gas, she had two gas cans and a hose for siphoning. She hoped she wouldn't have to use it. The supplies she'd collected were shoved into big black plastic bags and taped up boxes. They were tied together to keep them from flying out of the truck. Emma didn't need a map. She'd driven home many times over the past three years.

She stood on the running board on the driver's side and surveyed the landscape. Columns of smoke spread in different directions. Perhaps someone was burning the bodies. If so, that was good. It would help keep down disease.

There was increased gunfire over the last couple of days, moving closer to her area. Emma ducked down into the truck and started it. She drove onto the street and navigated her way out of Jamaica Plain. She'd always taken a rental car home; she didn't need a car in Boston, nor had she wanted one. Boston had great public transportation, and besides, driving here was a nightmare. She was heading home in a big, badass pickup. At least she didn't have to worry about traffic. She hadn't seen any vehicles driving on her street for days.

Navigating easily, within twenty minutes, she was on the Massachusetts Turnpike headed westward. She scanned ahead. There were a few abandoned vehicles, though not many. It was eerie seeing no movement on the road. She spotted more columns of smoke in the distance and regarded the abandoned sections of neighborhoods below as she passed. She headed to I-90; the housing developments thinned. The tension between her shoulder blades eased, her panic abating. She'd lived in a constant state of fear and anxiety since the first cases rolled into Mass Gen.

She rolled her head and flexed her neck. Glancing at Buddy, she saw the dog was gazing at the passing scenery, his eyes half closed in contentment. She was going too fast to roll down the window. It would be better when they came to a place where she was a lot farther away. For now, she just wanted out of this area. When she got to New Haven, she planned on cutting west. There was no way she was going anywhere near New York or Philadelphia. Escaping one large city for another wasn't her idea of smart. There was no telling what kinds of hells were in those cities. Once she got near Allentown, she'd drop down toward the southwest.

She slowed her speed, searching for a place to park. Emma wanted to take a short break, do a little target practice, and let Buddy out to sniff, run around, and go potty. She'd give him water and a bit of kibble. She pulled to the emergency lane. A car was ahead of her, abandoned on the side of the road.

Rifling in her rucksack, Emma found a black sharpie and stuck it in her pocket. Stepping to the driver's side, she checked for any bodies decomposing inside. There were none.

She looked around. There were fields and stands of trees in the distance. It was peaceful, nothing but the wind and the songs of birds that flitted through the high grass running along the turnpike. Invisible insects droned in low conversations. Emma opened the driver's side door and popped the trunk. She checked the visor, but there were no keys in the car. Her gas cans were full, and she'd only used a quarter tank, so she didn't need any gas from this car. Opening the trunk, she found it was empty. The previous owner had simply abandoned the car.

Buddy wandered, sniffing and marking clumps of grass.

"Make sure you pee on every single one. Yeesh, dogs," she muttered to herself.

Closing the trunk, she took out the sharpie and drew several bullseyes on it, then went back to her truck. She didn't know if the gunshots would startle Buddy or not.

"Come on, Buddy, get in the truck. I don't want you running off." She lifted the dish of water and placed it in the footwell on the passenger's side. The dog jumped up and she shut the door. Going to her side, she withdrew the Sig Sauer. Emma scanned, bringing her hand up to shade her eyes, the heat of the sun beating down on her. She took a deep breath, her nostrils flaring. She didn't detect the rotting stench of the city. That was good. In the distance, she heard the strident call of a blue jay. It was almost otherworldly here. Turning in a circle, she checked out her new world. Would this be her life now? Living alone?

Tears suddenly prickled. She wiped them away angrily.

"Don't be a baby," Emma hissed at herself.

Clearing her throat, she went in front of the truck. Taking a standard shooting stance, the one her ex-husband taught her, she brought her weapon up. Aiming carefully, she shot a single round. Missed. She glanced at Buddy, who was observing her intently, but he didn't appear frightened. She refocused and aimed, trying to relax her body. She fired, this time closer to the target. The third shot was well within the circles she drew, and she smirked.

Stepping back ten feet, she aimed again, sighted the target, and fired. Her round landed just near her target's center. Emma aimed and hit within the target's bullseye. It wasn't dead center, but she'd at least hit what she aimed at. Center mass. She didn't have the ammo to waste target practicing, however. Once she got to Lancaster, she'd go and see what her father had in his basement. Hopefully, she'd find something for the Sig.

Emma put the weapon in her homemade holster, which was up by her chest. Easy access for when she drove. She didn't want to have to search for the weapon if a threat suddenly appeared. Before getting into the truck, she stepped up on the running board. She laid her arm across the top of the truck and felt the heat of it. It was so damned quiet and so empty. Emma tried not to think about that. Tried not to think about the loneliness of never seeing another human. People were out there, but more probable than not, they were a threat she'd need to be wary of.

Ж

Brian pulled away from the house, he'd shut the generator off. No need wasting fuel, nor did he want to draw attention to his home. It was cool out. The early morning air was fresh and he kept the windows down. Cooper had his blanket hugged up against his face. The child was still sleepy and stared vacantly, his thumb rubbing his lower lip. Cooper had stopped sucking his thumb last year. Since his parents' deaths, Brian had seen Cooper sucking his thumb from time to time. It was a comforting mechanism. He'd remembered the car seat in Coop's father's vehicle and retrieved it. He didn't know what was out there, but he didn't need the four-year-old unsecure in the truck. The child was light, bitty, and fine boned, and would go through the window, even with a seatbelt across him. He had the child securely seated and belted in.

The air was cool, and he distinguished the stench of decomposition from other odors in the air. It wasn't as prevalent as it once was, yet it was a reminder that his world wasn't the same. Time was taking care of that. Brian just hoped he didn't see piles of dead bodies.

He wove the RAM through the subdivision, studying the houses. Morning birds sang their hearts out. Lawns were now overgrown. There was no stirring, no other sound.

"Guess mowing isn't high on anyone's list these days," he said absently to Cooper, who didn't answer. Ahead Brian sighted something which provoked a lift to his lips. Parked on the side of a driveway was a U-

Haul trailer. With his truck bed and rear seat crammed full, this would be perfect to hook up to his truck. He'd fill it with his list of items from Lowes and the other hardware stores along the way. And the trailer would be handy for storage when all was said and done. He stopped close to the trailer.

"Coop, stay put, I'm going to check out that trailer."

"Okay," the boy said sleepily, his eyelids half closed.

Brian switched off the engine and got out of the truck. He walked over and opened the trailer. There were a few boxes, but it was virtually empty. He walked up to the house and knocked on the door. While he waited, he surveyed the area. His Glock was in the holster at his back, covered by his shirttail. He didn't think anyone was home, or if they were, they were dead. He knocked once more.

"Hello, inside. I'm going to take that trailer. I'll empty the boxes and leave them on the driveway. If you don't want me to take it, please let me know. Otherwise, I hope you don't mind. Thanks."

He waited a few moments, listening intently. Hearing nothing, he walked to the trailer. He pulled the cartons out and set them on the driveway. He didn't bother searching them. Once the trailer was empty, Brian secured the doors. Getting in his truck, he pulled up and around, then aimed the truck to the hitch. Within ten minutes, he was on the road. He glanced over at Cooper, who grinned, his blue eyes crinkling.

Forty minutes later, Brian arrived at Lowe's and parked near the entrance. The glass doors were standing wide open. Getting out of the truck, he went to help Cooper out.

"Stay close to me, Coop. If you see anything, let me know, okay?"

"Okay, Daddy," Coop piped up, his wee hand clutching Brian's.

Brian winked at him and they went inside. Brian found a large, wide cart and set Cooper up on it for a ride. First, he went to plumbing for various PVC pipes and joints. Then he went over to the tool department, carefully choosing what he might need in the future. There was so much he figured it would take a few trips of stuffing the trailer. He planned to build a couple of storage buildings. That way, he'd house the propane tanks and other building material inside. They would be on hand if and when he needed them.

He wheeled the cart outside and neatly packed the trailer. Then he and Cooper headed back in. He stopped by one of the mini refrigerators and retrieved a bottle of water. He got a package of chips and handed both to Cooper, who ate the snack while Brian pushed the cart to the lumber section. When he passed the wood stoves, he stopped. He perused the selection of stoves and decided to get a micro unit. It would heat up to sixteen hundred square feet. That was overkill for the tiny cabins, but at least they'd be warm. He would cook on it too.

It took a bit of maneuvering. Though the stove was miniature, it was quite heavy. He got flashing and double insulated stovepipe. Not knowing how much the project called for, he gathered extra. Heading out, he loaded the trailer with the stove.

He peered at Cooper. "Maybe I should get one of the smaller stoves, just in case you decide to move out when you get grown. Set up your own place. Two is better than one."

Two hours later, the trailer was jammed with building items.

"Guess we better find us a place to live with all this stuff. Good thing I grabbed that length of chain, I'm gonna have to chain the cabin closed until we relocate permanently."

Cooper nodded in agreement and Brian chuckled. Behind the driver's seat, he found the bag he'd packed with snacks and lunch. He handed Cooper a peanut butter and jelly sandwich and a juice box. He'd have to stock up on those. Brian headed for the highway. He'd seen no one. It was a peculiar feeling. Besides Cooper, he had not spoken to another person in weeks. Cooper didn't appear to mind and stared out the window. Ahead, Brian noted a sign—Gary's Guns and Ammo—and pulled off the highway. He figured he'd have a need for more ammo and something a bit more substantial than his Mossberg.

When he got out, he realized the shop was closed. No surprise. What did surprise him was that the windows were still intact. He'd figured this would definitely be one place to get plundered, but so far, he hadn't seen a lot of looting. Perhaps people were still hunkered down for fear of getting the Vermilion virus. Beneath his seat, he located a tire iron and went to the door, leaving Cooper in the truck. He gently tapped and the door's glass spider webbed, with micro fractures. It didn't take much for the door to shatter.

He returned to the truck and retrieved Cooper. He helped the child enter the store, careful of the broken shards of glass. He was impressed with the stock. There was even a camping and fishing section. His eyes were immediately drawn to an AR-15. He'd never considered getting that type of weapon before, but figured he'd do well to have it in his arsenal. He went behind the counter and pulled it from the case. He was surprised by the light weight. Boxes of shells were neatly stacked on the shelf behind it. Brian chose boxes of his preferred ammo, gathering ammo for his Glock, Marlin, and Mossberg.

"You can never have enough ammo. Remember that," he said solemnly to Cooper. Brian's eyes crinkled up at the sides and he gently patted the boy's blond head. He loaded the weapon and ammo into the truck. After a moment's consideration, he went back inside and chose a Glock 19, along with a handful of mags. He next went over to the fishing and camping area of the store. There were tents, sleeping bags, and other items. He spotted a shiny canister and walked over.

"It's a travel Berkey water filtration system, something we might need, Coop." He examined the box and was impressed. The twin filters strained out damned near anything, and it cleaned up to three thousand gallons of water with the filters. He selected two boxes of the system, then added all of the filters in the store. It would hopefully last them a lifetime. If not his lifetime, then Coop's. Taking those items to the truck, he loaded up Cooper and they were off again.

A little over an hour later, Brian pulled into the R.B. Winter State Park. Exiting Sand Mountain Road, he pulled onto Keystone Road. Finding the side road, he followed it. He stopped at the entrance and rolled down his window, listening. He heard nothing but the wind. Sniffing the air, he caught no scent of putrefaction. It was a wilderness unto its own. Surrounded by Bald Eagle State Forest, there were numerous parks in the area. Brian calculated in time, many people would come to the parks to hunt and settle, and if not there, then the abandoned farms that peppered the area.

Brian continued on and stopped in the parking lot across from Halfway Lake. There was a large building facing the lake, the Beach House. He parked the truck, helped Cooper out, and let the boy run to the lake, following behind him. It was peaceful here. The last time he'd been here, the place was packed with swimmers, tourists, and campers. Now, only he and Coop stood at the water's edge. He spied a family of wood ducks swimming in the water weeds. Farther away, he recognized the tufted duck and some waterfowl he didn't know.

Unquestioningly, if people were at the lake, the ducks and other waterfowl would not be. Or at least he would not see as many. There were sandpipers farther up the shore, likely stopping over on their flight to the coasts. Perhaps at some point, they'd add duck to their menu. For now, he'd let the creatures be and enjoy studying them.

In the trees, he heard chickadees fussing and he spotted the bright cardinals. Since it was spring, the brightly colored males were everywhere. He tracked several goldfinches; they were easy to see as they flew among the branches of the conifers. Brian scanned the grounds and building.

He'd been set to take a cabin, build onto it, and fix it up for the two of them. But seeing this location, by the water, he might need to rethink the original plan. Here, the water was at their doorstep if he chose to take over the large building. There was cleared ground, just perfect for planting a large garden. He wouldn't need to clear forested land. That in itself would have taken a lot of time and sweat, and he needed to get a garden in ASAP. Confident he'd be able to gather enough food for the coming year, Brian wanted fresh vegetables nonetheless. He needed to learn how to farm and raise crops for them to survive the coming years. Their supplies would only last so long.

A tranquil, tired smile rippled across his face as he watched Cooper scampering up and down the beach. The sandpipers ran frantically away but didn't take flight. He'd have fresh water for toilets, drinking, bathing, and cooking. It would be easy enough to use plywood to block and compartmentalize a section of the large building and set up his wood stove to heat that area.

"Come on, Coop, let's unload the truck. We'll need to make another run to a hardware store before we head home."

"Okay, Daddy."

THREE

Flynn geared up with a double bandana on his face and smeared deodorant under his nose. He hadn't shaved, so the deodorant clumped on his mustache. He donned rubber gloves. Standing outside the first apartment, he detected the stench already. He gagged and swallowed hard. He had to go in and get whatever food was inside. If he was to escape this place, he needed food. He tried the door, it was unlocked. He'd brought a hammer and screwdriver as breaking-in tools.

Gradually opening the door, he braced himself for the stench and was not disappointed when a wave of flies and putrid odor hit him. His mouth filled with saliva and he swallowed over and over, commanding himself not to puke. His eyes teared up and his hands knotted into fists. For several moments, the urge to vomit was strong, until he regained control over himself. Stepping into the apartment, he peeked quickly, ready to avert his eyes from any gruesome images. He saw nothing. It was a two-bedroom apartment, by the layout. He'd go nowhere near the bedrooms.

Flynn went directly to the tiny kitchen. It was neat, but the appliances were old. He opened cabinets and skipped over the dishes. Flynn came upon a cabinet with canned foods and loaded his knapsack. His tightness eased. He would not starve. That bastard, Casper, hadn't beaten him yet.

He'd have to gather whatever he laid hands on and get the hell out of Philadelphia. He'd head to Amish country and see about working there. If he learned from them, he'd survive on his own. It had to be better than staying in the city.

Leaving the apartment with a full knapsack, he returned to his place. After he dumped the contents, he'd snag a few shopping bags and fill those at the next apartment. He hit another apartment, getting in and out quickly.

When he returned to his apartment, he was drawn to a noise outside. He'd left the windows open since the apartment was unbearably hot. He leaned out the window and his jaw dropped. A troupe of black headed spider monkeys were running and jumping over vehicles and off utility poles, screeching loudly. There appeared to be twenty of them. He viewed the incongruous scene below and then saw why the monkeys were screaming and running. A lynx was chasing them, hot on their trail. Flynn doubted the cat would catch the swift creatures. More from the zoo, no doubt.

He retrieved his empty pack and plastic shopping bags, opened a bottle of water, and drained it. Sighing in satisfaction, he tossed the empty bottle on the kitchen counter. He had a dozen bottles of water now, and hoped he found more. Leaving his apartment, he went to the next. This one was locked. He knocked on the door, a perfunctory knock. Putrid stench from within leaked from beneath the door. He placed the screwdriver on the lock and hammered away. The noise made him wince as it bounced off the walls of the hallway. Finally, the door gave in and opened.

He stepped in cautiously, quickly scanning the apartment. On the floor lay a dog, a small, yappy one. It had died of starvation or dehydration. Flynn hadn't thought about pets. It saddened him that the poor thing had suffered so. He went to the kitchen and rifled through the cupboards, then opened a pantry and exhaled happily. Bottles of water and packs of instant noodles, along with cans of fruits and vegetables. He didn't dare open the refrigerator; he wanted to keep whatever he had in his stomach.

With the water, the food stuff was weighty, and he was sweating in the hotbox of an apartment building. He'd make another run and then he'd call it a day. It was getting late. He'd start his trip in the morning. At least tonight he would feast and eat well. The food would be cold, but as hot as it was in his apartment, he was fine with that.

Ж

In the distance ahead, Emma spotted a solitary figure walking along the highway. She laid the Sig Sauer on her lap. As she drew near, she noted the person had a large haversack, stuffed with odds and ends hanging off. It was one of those kinds professional and serious hikers used. She dropped her speed, steering the blue Silverado, and the figure halted.

It was a round face, brown, with round glasses. Black eyebrows raised in question as Emma pulled up and stopped. She stared down at the diminutive woman dressed in jeans and a light blue jacket.

"Hi," she said smiling down. "Where ya heading?"

"Hey! No clue. Where are you heading?" said the short woman with a thick Boston accent.

Her smile was infectious, and Emma returned it. She loved hearing the Boston accent, it never ceased to crack her up.

"I'm heading to Pennsylvania," Emma replied. "To a nice little state park to start a new life."

"How would you like some company?" The woman laughed. "It sounds as good a place to go as any."

"Hell yeah, I'd love some company. I was afraid I was the only person left on Earth. Hop on in. Buddy, get in the backseat, boy," Emma said to the dog, who seemed to understand and hopped into the packed back seat. The woman opened the passenger's side, took off her large haversack, and groaned in pleasure.

"Oh, holy Christmas, that's damned wicked heavy, I'll tell you." The woman shoved the pack into the rear of the cab, pushing Buddy over toward the driver's side. When she climbed up into the truck, Emma noticed the woman's waist holster. It appeared tactical, not like her own. The woman noticed her gaze.

"I'm a cop. Or I was. Boston P.D. Name's Paadini Sullivan. My friends call me Paadi," she said, her dark eyebrows bouncing up and down with good humor.

Emma knew she'd found a friend and kindred spirit.

"I'm Emma Prichard, and I was a nurse. Now I'm a post-apocalyptic survivor." She rolled her eyes wildly.

Paadi laughed. Settling in, she buckled her seatbelt. "Nice police dog you got there. Did you find him or did he find you?" Paadi asked.

"What? I just thought he was a mutt. We found each other. How do you know he's a police dog?"

"He's a Belgian Malinois, and when I get a chance I'll check his ears for a tattoo. Sometimes the trainer has them tattooed. Lucky, he's bonded with you and he'll protect you with his life."

"Wow, I really just figured he was a mutt of some kind," Emma said, stunned. She recalled a tidbit of trivia about those dogs and knew them to be very intelligent and expensive. They were used for bomb sniffing and drug detection.

"Sounds like he found a good mom. What made you decide on Pennsylvania?"

"I'm from Lancaster and my family and I used to go to R.B. Winter State Park a few times a year. I'm hoping with all the forested land and other parks I'll have a good chance of surviving. I got some books on survival and Winter has great fishing and hunting. I'll be honest, I've no clue how to garden or hunt. I can fish, though."

"So do I! My husband taught me. Poor bastard died in the first week of the damned virus." Paadi's large brown eyes shimmered with sudden tears.

Emma squeezed her hand. "I'm sorry."

Paadi wiped her eyes and shook her head. "We've all lost a lot of loved ones, friends, family, and co-workers. None of my police family survived. I'd have hooked up with them and headed out. Same with family. Do you know if any of your family have survived in Lancaster?"

"I don't think so. My mom called to say my father had fallen ill. A couple days after that, I was unable to contact either one of them. I didn't try calling my ex-husband, but I bet he is gone. Honestly, you're the first person I've seen in weeks. I've seen cars and such, but no people. There was an increase in gunshots, so I figured it was best to get out of the city. I figure someone was taking over territory in Boston."

"Yah huh, you said it, sister. The bad'uns will start popping up like zits on a teenager. That's why I figured I'd get out. Just didn't know where I'd go, so I started driving. I figured anywhere was better than the middle of the city. Besides, I figured that the virus wasn't the only thing I should worry about."

"Absolutely. I thought the same. Typhoid and cholera are a real threat now with all those rotting bodies. I did see smoke, and I wondered if someone was burning them." Emma scanned the road ahead. She spotted several deer about fifty feet from the road. She didn't want to hit them, so she decelerated a bit.

"I'm glad you stopped and invited me to tag along, Emma. A couple of hours ago, some chowderhead stopped me. I smelled beer on him and didn't like the looks of 'im. Had to pull my weapon to encourage him to be on his way." Her mouth twisted and her Boston accent became heavier.

"I had the same notion. Got my Sig Sauer handy. And Buddy, of course. I guess together we should be able to guard each other," Emma said.

Paadi laughed. "I'd say you're right about that."

"Why didn't you drive?"

"I did. Started out that way anyway. The bastard car died thirty miles out so I just started walking. Figured I'd find a vehicle at some point. It was nice to just walk and not inhale the stench."

Over the next hour, both women were quiet, each in their own thoughts. Emma kept a constant speed, wanting to get to Lancaster by early afternoon. She wasn't looking forward to going into her parents' home. Then it would all be real. She heard Paadi's delicate snores and eyed her, so happy she'd come across her. She liked the woman. Paadi was down to earth and quite capable. It was good to have someone with her who knew how to shoot a gun. She had an upbeat personality, and that was essential in a post-apocalyptic world. Having a cool head was important and an added bonus.

Coming over a hill she tapered her speed. Ahead, roughly a half mile away, a vehicle was spanning both lanes. That was not good.

"Paadi, I think you need to see this."

Ж

Brian pulled up to the hardware store. It was only fifteen miles from the state park, and he figured it was just as good a place to source as Lowe's and closer at hand. Coop was sound asleep. He didn't have the heart to wake the boy so he pulled the truck and trailer close to the structure. The sun cast a long shadow over the front of the building and the truck would be in the shade. It wasn't a large hardware store, so he kept the truck in view from the inside. Rolling the windows halfway down, Brian got out and locked the doors.

Striding past the truck, he opened the doors to the hardware store. It had not been locked up. A brass bell sounded and he peered inside.

"Hello?" he called. Nothing. He walked farther in, then glanced behind at the truck. The top of Cooper's bright blond head was visible. Considering for a moment, he shoved the door to the hardware store open, blocking it with a sack of grass seed. He'd be able to hear if Cooper woke and called out for him.

He strolled along the aisles and selected items from the shelves. He chose several metal buckets, figuring he'd use them to heat water for baths. He gathered quite a few five-gallon buckets with lids and metal trashcans. Those would make great storage for food; mice couldn't chew through them. He found fifty-pound bags of chicken feed along with scratch grain. He'd driven by several farms and figured that perhaps there might be chickens. Likely, the bigger farm animals were dead, but chickens scavenged and scratched for their food. He'd build a coop and they'd have chickens and eggs to eat.

He went to the truck, peeking in on Coop, who was still sound asleep, a string of drool hanging from his lower lip to his striped blue shirt. Brian opened the trailer and loaded it with what he'd found. Reentering the store, he chose bales of chicken wire, stakes, and lumber to build the coop. He found a few miniature wooden crates and figured he'd make them nesting boxes. He added a few bundles of nesting material. Brian didn't know much about chickens, but the videos he'd viewed were straightforward.

He discovered several large dog kennels and loaded them for the trailer, thinking he could use them to transport the chickens he found. He wandered by another aisle displaying camping gear. Not much there, but he did find several hurricane lanterns and lamp oil. He added an ash bucket and fireplace implements, along with several pairs of leather work gloves.

He took these out to the truck, then located a couple of hoes, shovels, axes, and found a rasp to sharpen the axes. The lists in his head were endless. That frightened him. If he got this wrong, he wouldn't be the only one to suffer for it, now Cooper would as well. His heart twisted at the notion of the child suffering. He couldn't afford to screw this up. He checked Cooper once more and returned inside. At the front of the store was a refrigerator packed with bottles of water, juices, and soft drinks. He emptied the refrigerator. He enjoyed the occasional soda pop and once they were gone, they were gone. Coop would like the juices.

Their new lives would have few extravagances, and that reminded him to hit the grocery stores for coffee, which made him hunt for a camp coffee pot or two. Acquiring more than one of an item was essential. One was good, two was better, three, what the hell, why not? These items would need to last a lifetime.

He expanded his mental list for books, games, and other educational items. He'd swing by the local Walmart on the way to the park and pick up paper, pens, pencils, and whatever else. He confiscated all the toilet paper and paper towels he was able to stuff into the trailer. His heart raced and his mouth dried. It was too much. So much to get and do before he lost the ability to leave the park. His legs trembled with weakness and Brian knew it was a panic attack. He'd pushed all the fear and sorrow down, having to deal with everyday living. Now it was catching up to him. He sat down hard on the inside of the trailer.

Holding his hands in front of his face, he realized they were trembling wildly. He took a deep breath and held it. Then, measuredly, he blew it out. Tears stung his eyes and he wiped them.

"Don't lose your shit, buddy, not now," he whispered to himself.

"Daddy?" Cooper called, his voice sleepy. Brian got up and went to the truck, his legs a little wobbly.

"I'm here, tiger. You ready to get out?"

"I gotta go potty."

"Okay, let me get you out of there. I'll see if this place has a bathroom." He lifted Cooper out of the truck and guided him in, tugging a small LED flashlight from his pocket. He found the bathroom and lifted the lid to the tank. There was water in it, so a flush was possible.

"Do you need my help, Cooper?"

"I just gotta pee pee."

"Okay, I'll be out in the store, come find me when you're finished. I'll leave the door open so it isn't dark. I'll put the flashlight on the floor for you. Bring it with you, alright?"

"Okay, Daddy," he chirped sleepily.

Brian wedged the door open. The store's large windows ensured the place received plenty of light in the store, but the late day shadows made the store dim. A few minutes later Cooper came out and found Brian. Spotting a box of pocket bottles of hand sanitizer at the counter, Brian grabbed a bottle. He washed Cooper's hands, then tucked the bottle in the boy's front pocket and ruffled his blond hair. He stuck a few bottles in his pockets.

"We're going to get some chickens. How does that sound?"

"Really?" Cooper squeaked happily.

"Heck yeah. In fact, we can head out in a few minutes. I'll build something to hold them and we'll return tomorrow and make them a proper coop," he said, smiling at Cooper.

After selecting a few more things, Brian finished loading the trailer. He was closing it up when the tiny hairs on his neck stood. He sensed a presence behind him. He swiveled, his hand drifting to the base of his back, where his Glock rested. An older woman stood ten feet away, eyeing him, her head cocked to the side.

"Coop, come here," he called. Cooper walked out of the store, a bottle of juice in his hand. The boy noticed the woman and hurried to Brian, standing behind him, his tiny hand seeking Brian's larger one.

"Can I help you?" Brian said politely.

"You robbing this place?"

"No ma'am, I'm getting things that I need. Are you the owner?"

"No, I ain't. Bobby died. Everyone died. What you doin' with that boy?"

"Daddy?" Cooper said nervously.

"It's okay, Coop." Brian gathered up the child, holding him close. Cooper's arms linked tightly on Brian's neck, his little body trembling.

"You need to leave that boy here, with his own kind," the old woman croaked.

Something about her made the hair on Brian's arms rise. She was crazy, insane perhaps by all the deaths surrounding her. She was thin and wiry, and her clothing was dirtier than what Brian thought was normal. His eyes went to her hands, which were knotted with arthritis. They were roped with thick blue veins and her nails were chipped and dirty.

"What do you mean *his own kind?*" Brian asked, though he knew what she meant.

"That boy ain't yours. He's white and you ain't. You need to leave him with me. He don't need to learn your dirty ways," she said in a nasty voice.

Yeah, batshit crazy.

Brian didn't say a word but put Cooper in his car seat, keeping the old woman in his peripheral. His hands shook but he managed to get Cooper buckled in then hurried to the driver's side as the woman walked closer. Hopping up into the truck, he locked the doors and then started the engine.

"You need to leave that boy here, he don't belong to you!" she yelled at him. "He ain't your kind!"

Brian hit the button to close all the windows and then flicked on the MP3 plugged in the console. Music filled the cab and drowned out the old woman's rants. He pulled away and a loud thump vibrated the truck. She'd thrown something at the vehicle and it had bounced off. Brian pulled out onto the road and sped away as fast as it was safe to do. He checked the side mirrors and she was running after him, her hands waving wildly in the air. The encounter rattled him more than he liked to admit.

He'd never met batshit crazy before, but he damned well had met one now. He figured she was crazy long before the virus. Her appearance indicated a long-term lack of sanity. Perhaps she was let go from those who'd cared for her, or perhaps they'd died? He'd never know. He would not return, not wanting to run into her again.

Brian eyed the clock; it was just after three. He'd hit the farm that was a few miles away and see if he had any luck in wrangling some chickens, then head to the park and fix up a temporary coop for them. Tomorrow he'd swing by Lowe's and hunt down a gas-powered tiller and begin getting his new home ready for living.

Brian left the road and drove onto a long, winding drive. It led up to a faded two-story farmhouse. He beeped his horn, announcing his arrival. Being shot as a trespasser was not on his list of things to do today.

"Coop, stay in the truck." Brian said, thinking about the crazy old woman. He got out and locked the truck. The windows were slightly opened to let a breeze in. He went up the steps to the house and knocked heavily on the door. The faint scent of decay seeped from the home.

"Hello? Anyone here? I'm going to go get some of your chickens. If you're there, please let me know and I'll leave you. I don't want to take anything if you're still here and alive. I won't hurt you, I'm just hoping to find some chickens!" he yelled.

He felt foolish, but if someone were alive, he would not want to take their food from them. He waited, keeping his ears attuned to any noise. Nothing from within.

The pleasant clucking of chickens came from the far side of the house. He went to the trailer and opened it. Flicking his knife, he cut open the bag of scratch grain and put several handfuls inside one of the metal buckets. Then he took one of the large kennels out of the trailer and walked to the rear of the house. Unsurprisingly, inside a large enclosure were chickens, scratching in the dirt. He scented the reek of decay and searched. There were several dead chickens. Maggots wiggled on the dead and the live chickens pecked at them. Gruesome. There was a low trough that had less than an inch of water in it. It was possible the rain kept the other chickens alive.

He opened the door to the enclosure and set up the kennel. He started calling the chickens and throwing the scratch grain inside the kennel. At the sound of the grain hitting the kennel, the chickens came running like crazed fiends. Squawking and pecking, they surrounded Brian. It damned near sent him running. He threw more grain into the large kennel and seven hens and a rooster rushed in. There were six outside the kennel, but he figured seven hens and a rooster was a good start. The option of returning to collect the rest was on the table. He closed the kennel and trapped the chickens inside, then scattered more grain for the other hens.

He hauled the kennel out of the enclosure and walked to the RAM. Placing the kennel in the bed, he then retrieved several bottles of water and returned to the chicken yard. He dumped the water into the trough, then at the chicken house, he peered inside. He noticed two bantam hens sitting on nests. He lifted each hen, receiving severe pecks for his efforts. Both hens sat on half a dozen eggs each. Great! He figured they'd hatch these babies.

He retrieved the other kennel from the trailer, along with a wooden crate. He spotted a hand towel and snatched it up, carrying the items to the pen and into the coop. With care and caution, Brian laid the towel over the unhappy brooding hen. He carefully lifted the hen, along with the nesting material, keeping the eggs cupped in his hands, and set it all in the wooden crate. He then set the crate, hen, and eggs into the larger kennel. He left the towel on her. He was afraid she'd freak out inside the kennel and burst the eggs.

He was planning to build her a separate brooder coop, away from the main flock. He'd return and recover the other chickens and the other brooding hen. Once he had a big enough coop and yard he'd return for more. He just wanted to ensure he did it right. For now, he needed to get back to the park and get the chickens settled and then head back to his home.

Leaving the chicken lot, Brian was elated. He'd accomplished quite a bit today. It would be evening by the time he arrived home, but it was a good, productive day after all. Climbing in the RAM, he glanced at Coop, who looked up expectantly.

"We got us some chickens!" Brian hooted with glee and the rooster crowed at that moment. A wide smile split the boy's face.

"Woohoo!" Cooper crowed.

Ж

Casper sat by the fountain at the Board Game Art Park, surveying his province. The city was deadly quiet but for the wind whipping between the buildings. Bird songs punctuated the silence. It was now all *his* domain. He and a few others had survived the Vermilion Strain. He'd contracted the sickness within the first week of the deadly EV-01-H virus. His girlfriend had shown the first symptoms and within hours, he'd begun to feel the insidious infection creep along his body. Deathly ill, he'd been unable to leave the bed and had lived in his own filth and Rachael's decaying body. It was a hellish time, and yet he'd survived.

Day after day, he'd watched the maggots squirm across her once beautiful face. The putrid gore and stench were unbearable, until he became nose deaf. But for the numerous bottles of water by the bed, he too would have succumbed to death. For a long time, while he lay beside Rachael, he'd wished for death. When he realized he would not die, his eyesight began to dim and fade. Though he retained his vision, the world was cocooned in a semitransparent shroud.

His once brown hair was now whitish gray, from the extensive trauma his body had endured. He'd stumbled out of his apartment and wandered the streets. Surviving people feared him, running from him. No one would help him. He hadn't understood why until he'd glimpsed himself in a department store mirror. His skin was a deep vermilion hue, his hair grayish white and matted with blood. His eyes were milky white. Though he didn't smell himself, he irrefutably stunk badly.

After wandering the streets, Casper went to his apartment and took a shower. He collapsed on the bathroom floor, exhausted. He guesstimated that a full day had passed when he woke next. He was still weak, but his body was now hungry and thirsty. He supposed that was how he knew he'd live. Over the next couple of weeks, he watched the population of Philadelphia dwindle. He'd gone by Pennsylvania Hospital, Thomas Jefferson University Hospital, and Hospital of the University of Pennsylvania. All three were forsaken to the departed, bodies littering the emergency bays, hallways, and waiting rooms. Along the sidewalks and parking lots there were heaps of bones.

Corpses littered the sidewalks and streets and he stepped past them. The sight of it didn't bother him anymore and he'd gone nose deaf to the noxious stench. He rarely returned to the apartment, sleeping in various buildings. On one of his outings he'd gone to the zoo. As a child, he'd adored the zoo and he and Rachael had spent many hours there. With no one feeding them, the animals were dying. Something inside of him couldn't stand for that.

It took three days, but he'd busted open, broke, bent, and unlocked every cage. He wasn't sure if any of the animals would survive in the city, but they would definitely die in their cages. The big cats in the enclosures kept their distance from him. He apparently didn't smell very appetizing. The animals skirted him while making their escape, as did the bears. He was walking death, a ghost. Albeit, a benign and friendly ghost. He'd sneered at that thought. He'd named himself Casper, since his old life and old self was over, dead, and gone. Rotted and gone to corruption of the body, soul, and mind.

He'd wandered for days, not seeing another living soul, then he'd gone into Old City Hall and found two men, twin brothers. Like himself, they actually survived. He'd gone to a convenience store to get bottled water and sat for hours helping the two brothers. He'd cleaned them and cared for them. He understood their pain. They'd been large men once, but the virus had taken its toll. The brothers, Javier and Ramon Pena, were visiting from Orlando. They were caught in the city when the virus struck and like himself, were hit in the first week.

In the following weeks, it was apparent he and the brothers would have to fend for themselves. They'd been attacked by several men and nearly killed. Casper located a gun store and armed himself and the brothers. He inherently knew that his brain had changed, that he and the brothers had slight brain damage. Casper wasn't too far gone to realize that he'd have to go on the offensive. Javier and Ramon were loyal to him, and over a few days, Casper recruited people with brute efficiency.

If he and his new friends were to survive, they'd have to secure the city and all its resources. Casper understood showing compassion and humanity would be perceived as a weakness. Only to Javier and Ramon did he reveal his true self and compassion. He sent his growing band outward to secure food supplies. One person per store. They were to inventory and live at those locations. He figured this way, that person would have a very personal and good reason to guard the supply with his or her life. Then, should Casper need the resource, he'd have the ability to tap into that. He only had about thirty-five people, but day by day, that number grew.

He and the brothers had come across a man raping a woman who'd resembled his Rachael. Casper was so enraged he'd taken the rapist to Love Park and had skinned the man before horrified witnesses.

"Any who cross me, any who do not obey, I'll tear your skin from your body!" he'd raged, spittle flying from his mouth. He was drowned out by the screams of the rapist. He'd then slit the man's throat, leaving the bloody corpse as a reminder. Word quickly spread that Casper was not a man to cross. The brothers gradually regained their strength and bulk. They were his shadows, his confidants, his bodyguards. From a mild-mannered man, Casper had grown into some kind of deadly legend. Javier and Ramon killed all threats. There weren't many, and Casper guaranteed the few who'd survived the virus would survive a dead Philadelphia.

He was building something here, something greater than himself. He was building a new world. A small world perhaps, but he was building a vision. He would singularly choose the people to populate his new world, his hand-selected few. It was akin to being God. It was a heady feeling and Casper let the pleasure wash over him. He was in charge of his destiny, rebuilding himself and this broken city.

FOUR

Paadi didn't like what she saw. She scanned the tree line, but she didn't detect anyone hiding among the trees and bushes. She grasped her Sig Sauer P226, her service weapon. She was gratified to see Emma held her weapon as well. There was a low rumbling growl from the rear, Buddy adding his voice to their concerns.

"Slow to about ten meters, keep your weapon hidden. Let's see what he wants," Paadi said calmly.

"I don't see anyone else near the truck. You think it's an ambush?"

"Might be. I didn't see anyone in the tree line, but that doesn't mean much. I'd say ram the bastard, except the airbags would stun us. That wouldn't do," Paadi grouched and tugged at her long black braid.

Emma decelerated and both women rolled down their windows. Paadi leaned out of hers, keeping her weapon down and out of view. It was at the ready, however, and she would not hesitate to use it.

"Hey, what's this all about?" she called.

"This is a toll booth. You got to pay, give over some of your provisions," a man, roughly in his mid-thirties, said. The fellow was filthy and was missing several important teeth.

He stood before a beat down and rusted truck, leisurely cradling an AR-15. Paadi noted the idiot didn't see the women as a threat.

Good.

"That's just crazy. There aren't any more people in the world for Christ's sakes. If you hit up any number

70

of stores, you'll find all you need. Why bother us?" she said, her tone amiable, her features relaxed.

"You must be from Boston. You sound like it, though you don't look like it. Figure you'd have one of them red dots in the middle of your head. Just let me see what you got and I'll let you pass. 'Sides, ain't seen anyone for a long time now."

Paadi's brow raised. This guy was an idiot. Stopping someone with a weapon was asking to get his ass blown to hell.

"Listen, mister, I'm sorry you're lonely, but we gotta leave. It's dangerous and as women, we can't stay to chit chat. Let us pass. We got nothing you'd be interested in."

"Well, you ain't gettin' past me unless you let me search your vehicle," he said obstinately.

"What do we do now? We're only an hour away from my home," Emma asked, her voice tight.

"Drive up closer, I'm gonna wing him if he doesn't get out of our way. If he raises his weapon, I'll kill him."

"Paadi, is that necessary?" Emma asked nervously.

"I hate to do it, but I don't see we have a choice. He's an idiot and he's either drunk or high. We can't stop the truck and get out, that would leave us vulnerable, especially if he has friends. They shoot out our tires, we're not going anywhere, and I don't fancy getting raped today," Paadi said in a hard tone.

"Well shit. Okay, I'll leave the shooting to you and I'll see about getting us past the truck."

"Keep it slow and steady on approach. If I see anyone from the tree line, I'll take him out and then the others if I can. You just get us away from this."

Emma pulled the truck forward. Paadi drew herself up in the seat, pulling her legs under her, leveraging her body into a better firing position. When the truck was within ten feet, Paadi raised her weapon. The man's eyes went wide.

"Alright, mister, I'm a Boston police officer and I'm a damn wicked shot. Put your weapon on the ground and step away. You raise it and I'll put one between your eyes before you can blink."

The highwayman raised the AR-15, retreating. Paadi caught the fear but also the desperation and anger in his expression. She didn't want to kill this man.

"Drop the fucking weapon. Now!" she ordered, her gun trained on him. He continued to bring the AR-15 up and she double tapped, two rounds going into the man's chest. The weapon fell to the ground and the extortionist crumpled in a heap. Paadi searched quickly, expecting others to rush from the trees. Three heartbeats later, there was no sound. Nothing.

"You stupid bastard," she hissed, enraged that the dumbass had forced her hand. If he'd have just left it alone, had just let them pass. Yet he hadn't done that, and he'd paid with his life.

"Cover me, Emma. I'm gonna retrieve his weapon and move that truck. You see anyone, start shooting."

Emma's face was the color of day-old paste, her head bobbled, her mouth gaping in shock.

Paadi reached over and shook her, bringing her into focus. "Emma, I mean it, keep an eye out."

"Sorry, okay," Emma mumbled. She snapped to attention and stared at Paadi, then nodded again.

Paadi exited the Silverado and hurried over to the dead man. His face was frozen with a look of surprise. She shook her head. Fool. She confiscated his weapon and peered inside the old truck. The keys were in the ignition. She noticed odds and ends, several loaded magazines, and several boxes of shells. Paadi climbed into the truck and drove it to the side of the road. She spotted a plastic bag on the passenger floor-well and grabbed it. Dumping it on the seat, Paadi saw the man had collected bottles of prescription medicines. She used the bag to carry the ammunition.

Exiting the vehicle, she ran to the blue Silverado and jumped in. "Get us out of here. There's no telling if anyone heard me. The guy had a ton of scripts. He was either a junkie or an idiot. Either way, he's dead."

"Damn. I can't believe he was going to fire on us. You had him and he still raised his weapon."

"He might have been too high to have used his brain or his brain was just plain mush. Poor bastard paid with his life," Paadi growled.

"I'm going to drive a lot faster," said Emma. "I want to get to Lancaster. It's getting late, we can find a hotel and hunker down for the night after we leave my parents' house. I don't think we'll be able to stay there."

"I'm there with you, sister. Get this baby up to eighty. There are plenty of empty rooms, no doubt."

Emma was quiet, concentrating on driving. Paadi stared into space. In all her years on the force, she'd never killed anyone, or even ever needed to fire her weapon. She had always used her cunning, her mind, and her forceful personality. She'd walked the streets of Boston, chased down suspects, and helped victims. She'd arrested drunks, druggies, thieves, and gangbangers. She'd been kicked, bitten, spit on, puked on, and smacked, but she'd taken it all in stride as part of her job.

This, however... if the bastard had just let them pass. Paadi knew the idiot was more than likely high, and stupid to boot. He'd survived the virus only to be killed by his own stupidity. She blew out a breath, watching the landscape pass by in a blur. She didn't understand why she'd shed a tear over killing a dumbass. Perhaps it was because so few humans were left, each life was precious. Memories of her husband flooded her and tears slid down her cheeks.

Shane was a sweet man and kind beyond words. He'd gone so fast, just like the rest of her family. She'd held Shane in her arms as he bled out. The hospitals were full to overflowing and they'd told her to take him home and care for him. He'd either survive or he'd die. Her entire family died. Her mother, father, her two older brothers and their families—all gone. She'd remained in Boston as long as she dared, but the city only held the painful memories of lost loved ones. It was no place to stay. It was silent and lonely.

Emma seemed a good sort. Paadi had met plenty of nurses in her line of work, especially when dealing with victims of crimes. It was good to have a nurse handy in this uncertain world. It was also better to have a friend. She was certain friends would be few and far between. She only hoped that the two of them wouldn't run into any more trouble. Being a realist, however, Paadi knew it would only be a matter of time before trouble found them.

Emma took an exit off the highway and onto a town road. More alert, Paadi scanned the area. There were stores, gas stations, and restaurants. She didn't see a soul. No one walked the streets, no vehicles moved, nothing. Dogs were roaming the area and a few cats sat atop high perches. Those were the lucky animals. For sure there were dead pets in many of the homes.

Emma aimed the truck down a residential street and slowed. The lawns were all overgrown, some homes had broken windows and doors. It was odd, why break into a home when everything was available and free? There was no telling. Perhaps a desperate person? Or just an angry person?

The vehicle turned on several streets and Emma stopped in front of a one story, mid-century ranch. Paadi noted there was sadness etched on her new friend's face.

Ж

Flynn was sweating profusely; he was bringing down the last load of his life. He shoved all the food he'd foraged into the Honda. He had two cases of water, seven large bags full of various canned foods, eight bags of flour, sugar, coffee, oil, and every other box and bag of food he'd scrounged. He packed most of his clothes. He paused a moment and bent at the waist. Going up and down the stairs was the most exercise he'd done in well over a month. He'd gorged himself on cookies and canned fruit the previous night and was suffering from a sugar hangover.

He wiped the dripping sweat away with his forearm and surveyed his surroundings, remembering there were now four legged predators out there. It wouldn't do to forget, which he had. At night, he'd listened to the grunts and groans from strange things in the dark. It caused the hair on his body to lift in primordial fear. He now heard the occasional screech of some animal or other. Dogs barked furiously at things he was unable to see. His skin rippled with unease.

Flynn got into the car and pulled out his map. He'd always lived in Philadelphia and only left the city with his parents or as a passenger with one of his friends driving. Now he'd have to find his way to Lancaster. His GPS didn't work, and he missed that bit of technology very much right now. He hoped the Amish would take him in, otherwise he didn't know how he was going to survive. He was absolute in his belief that all the big cities contained more assholes like Casper running them. He was certain there was plenty of food in the city, and for one man to monopolize it was complete bullshit. He took a deep breath, trying to tamp down the impotent rage.

He flipped the map. If he got to I-95, he should be able to find it easily. He made a U-turn and drove along the empty streets. The bodies were now unrecognizable.

He eyed the lumps of black material and grisly remains. Each of those things had been people.

Flynn desperately attempted to come to grips with his new reality. His eyes stung with the prickling of tears and he blinked rapidly. He came to a stop at a stop sign and started laughing at himself. Why stop? No one was driving but him. Shaking his head, he pulled forward. He was driving along West Oregon Avenue when something from his peripheral caught his eye. He crawled along the street and glanced at Marconi Park. His jaw dropped. Several giraffes loped across the park. His eyes tracked the animals until they disappeared behind a stand of trees.

It was then that he noticed the elephants. He steered the car to the side and stopped. Flynn wished he had binoculars to see if there were any other animals in the park. He wondered if the polar bears were out, and if they would die in the heat. Even if the bears found the fountains, would that save them? There was no telling. He was glad he was leaving Philadelphia. It was no longer suited for human habitation.

He resumed driving, his head on a swivel. Just past a blind curve he slammed on his brakes to avoid hitting a roadblock. He wondered what was going on. All he wanted was to get out of the city and away from the growing nightmare. He pulled to within fifteen feet and leaned his head out.

"Hey, what's going on? I need to get out of this place!" he yelled, his face heating with anger, frustration, and fear.

"Casper has us blocking all major roadways into the city," a tall, skinny man told him. He held some kind of rifle in front of his chest. Flynn wasn't familiar with weapons, except what he played with in his virtual games.

"Well I'm not coming into the goddamned city, I'm leaving. Let me pass, I just want to get out of here!"

Another man—this one had a pitted face and a broken nose—walked toward him, a handgun in his grip and pointed at Flynn.

Damnit! Can't I just leave in peace?

Flynn was near panic. He shrank away when the guard bent down to peer into the window.

"What all you got in this piece of shit car?" Pitted Face asked, his voice gravelly.

"Dude, I only got a few things from my apartment. Please, just let me get on my way. I don't want any trouble," he pleaded, "I just want to get out of here."

"You'll need to see Casper first," Skinny said, shrugging with indifference.

"What if I don't want to?" Flynn asked defiantly.

"Then I shoot you here and we take your shit," Pitted Face said, smirking.

Skinny opened the passenger's side door and got in. He sneered at Flynn and Flynn's shoulders slumped. He truly did need to find a gun.

Ж

Brian was tired. He'd returned to the park and set up the temporary coop for the chickens. It had taken over an hour, ensuring water buckets were in place and there was plenty of food for the chickens. The sitting hen was still on her eggs, though the towel was on the bottom of the kennel beside her. She raised up threateningly when he placed the water dispenser inside her kennel. Brian dropped a handful of food in there for her and closed it.

He'd headed home after that. Exhausted, poor Cooper slept the whole way home. He'd hoped to make a stop or two on the way home but didn't have the heart to wake the child. After getting home, he switched on the generator and started dinner. He prepped for using the meat left in the freezer and made sandwiches for tomorrow's trip. He'd given Coop a bath and fed him dinner, and decided to leave the next morning. With so much of the supplies at the new camp, he figured it was better just to complete the relocation. There was nothing holding him here. Driving round trips to the park would be a waste of gas. He needed to work smarter, not harder. He was only putting off the inevitable, and dragging his feet didn't change things.

Brian never lied to himself. He was aware why he was reluctant to leave. He'd be leaving his old life, all that he knew. He'd be leaving the home and the life he and Christa had built. He'd be leaving Christa behind. That was difficult to even comprehend, leaving her, but for Coop's sake and his own, he'd have to leave the old life behind.

Once Cooper was in bed, Brian set about packing all of his clothing. He'd load up tonight. He'd swing by a mattress store tomorrow to select a couple of mattresses. His bed was bloody and in wretched shape. It reminded him of Christa. Until now, he hadn't thought of her and shame crawled over him like biting ants. His life was so consumed with moving out to Winter Park that thoughts of his wife were set aside for the survival of himself and Cooper.

Feeling the sting of tears, he let them fall, knowing he needed to grieve. He missed Christa's laughter and her touch. He missed having her near, puttering in the garden or cuddling up while they watched a movie. He leaned against the wall and held his face in his hands. His heart broke over and over, like ocean waves crashing over jagged rocks.

He wiped his face and packed clothing into several of the suitcases he pulled out from the closet. He went to the hall closet and pulled out his winter gear and packed that.

Tomorrow would be even busier. He needed to stop by not only the mattress store, but hardware stores again. Seeds were at the top of his list, along with fertilizer, the gas-powered tiller, and more lumber for his growing pile. Again, there was no telling what need might arise in the future, so he had to get while the getting was good. It was his new motto.

The large building should hold quite a bit, especially if he organized it right. He decided a sun oven might be useful. It used the sun and magnified the heat to cook or bake foods. It was that powerful.

The oven would have its uses during sunny days. Preparing and cooking their meals in the sun oven would save their precious resources, such as wood or propane, for when it was overcast, raining, or simply too cold to cook outside. The videos he'd sifted through mentioned having more than one option for cooking. One was good, two better, three the best. He was planning to swing by CVS and raid the pharmacy for medicines, antibiotics, bandages, and all other items he'd need in case of an injury or illness. He wanted children's vitamins and some for himself. Brian just hoped he was able to handle whatever came up. As a firefighter, he'd been trained in basic first aid, but he didn't know how to suture open wounds. He might be able to set a broken arm or leg, but if it were a compound fracture, he was helpless.

The possibility of Cooper getting hurt or seriously injured frightened him beyond measure. He'd do his best to keep the boy safe. How did parents deal with the threat of their child's illnesses or injuries? The notion left him a quivering mess. With these dreadful thoughts spinning in his brain, he finished packing. He went to his bookshelves and pulled the books he wanted. There were some excellent reference books he'd gotten years ago. Though basic for first aid, it was better than nothing. Brian hoped to find a bookstore to expand his collection, perhaps at one of the many strip malls.

It was near midnight when he finished up everything. He wasn't planning on coming back here, he was simply delaying the inevitable. There was no need. When they left in the morning, it would be forever. His heart twisted, leaving Christa here, without him. His mind shied away from the painful thoughts; he was too fragile emotionally.

With everything at the park, all his supplies, he needed to be there to protect them. It was only a matter of time before someone thought to travel to the park and try and survive there. If he left the food and supplies unprotected, someone would take over and claim the Beach House as their own. He'd worked too hard and done too much to let that happen. Besides, Cooper was depending on him.

Brian went outside and shut off the generator. The night was at once quiet. Not a sound. By now, any other generators had run out of fuel. There was no sound, nothing in the dark night but the crickets. He was about to go in when he caught headlights from a vehicle. They shone like a radiant beacon. The lights in the house were off, so Brian closed the door and sat in the rocking chair on the porch. The overhang of the eaves ensured he was deep in the shadows. There was a thin moon out, playing hide and seek with the clouds.

The vehicle wove deliberately three hundred yards up the road. Brian waited patiently, his heart racing with the implications. There were surely others out there, and reasonably, some were good people. Some, however, were crazy, like the old woman he'd run into earlier today. There were dangerous people too. Those he *did* have to worry about. Brian doubted the vehicle would stop at his place specifically, especially now that the generator was off. He was glad he'd left it off while he was gone.

There were enough houses out there filled with food and supplies to keep others busy and away from his home. He sat still as stone as the car, an SUV of some kind, drew closer. Someone waved a flashlight, skimming past the houses. Searching for what? Brian watched the pattern of light dance across the homes. Were they searching for a special home? A specific address? Was someone hunting for a loved one? It was after midnight and Brian wasn't a fool. They were looking for trouble. If they stopped at his house, they'd find trouble there.

He sat in the dark with his Glock in his lap, waiting for the SUV to draw near. As they passed, the flashlight played over him and the vehicle crept along his street. Brian waited, his mouth dry. He didn't raise his weapon yet. The SUV stopped, the flashlight played over his body. He lifted the weapon and aimed it at the SUV, which pulled away and resumed its course, though a little faster now.

A long breath seeped out and Brian slumped in the rocking chair. The red taillights blinked, vanishing when the SUV took a corner.

In the distance, from perhaps a couple of miles away, came a scattering of rapid gunshots. Animals hunted at night, especially predators. These human predators were no different. He remained on the porch, listening to the night. It was silent but for the distant gunshots.

Brian soon found himself drowsy. Two hours had ticked along since the SUV drove past the house. Standing, he peered up and down the street, but there were no lights, no headlights, nothing.

He went into the house, closed the door, and locked it, then laid down on the couch. He knew he should keep guard, but he needed sleep. He leaned his Mossberg against the couch and held the holster with his Glock against his chest. They'd have to make noise getting into his house, and he hoped it would be enough time for him to wake and use his weapons.

The repetitive, aggressive barking of a dog woke Brian suddenly, his heart racing. Weak sunlight filtered through the windows announced morning had arrived. He checked his watch: 5:30 am. He groaned. The dog's barking had woken him from a dead sleep. He rolled off the couch and stepped to the living room window to look outside. It was the Andersons' German shepherd, Daisy. He slid his holster in the waist of his pants and went outside, the Glock in his hand. Three houses away was the SUV from the night before and two men were trying to catch Daisy.

The dog was snarling and barking at the two men, who had a rope. They were trying to surround and corner her at the same time. Daisy wasn't having it. There were multiple dogs inside the SUV, barking and sticking their noses out of the cracked windows. Daisy was thin and Brian suspected she'd been on her own for a while now. Most pets were. If the dogs were let loose, they stood a better chance of survival. In the houses, they either starved to death or died the horrible death of dehydration.

Bringing his weapon up, he walked quickly toward the two men. They didn't hear him since Daisy was making so much noise. He was ten feet away when he shot a round into the ground. Both men jerked as though the bullet struck them and spun, gaping in shock at Brian. The two men appeared rough, their clothing dirty. Apparently they'd spent the night rounding up dogs, though for what, Brian didn't know.

"You two assholes leave that dog alone. She doesn't want to go with you."

"Is she your dog?" one man snarled. It was obvious Brian had frightened the dognapper.

"She is now. Get the fuck out of my neighborhood. Go find your dogs someplace else. Come, Daisy," he called in a low, commanding tone. She immediately ran to him. He caressed her muzzle with one hand, and she rammed it into his hand.

The thief looked like he wanted to say something and the other man, a short, stocky, bull of a man, nudged his arm and withdrew. Both men kept their eyes glued to Brian and his weapon, still pointed at them and tracking their actions. Both men got into the SUV, shoving the dogs inside. The dogs barked even louder. The first man scowled menacingly and drove away. The tension bled from Brian and he eyed the dog.

"I know a certain little boy who's going to be happy he has a new dog. Let's go get you fed. I think I have enough eggs left. We'll swing by and get some dog food on the way to our new home." Daisy wagged her tail.

Brian holstered his weapon and petted Daisy, who enjoyed the attention with lots of tail wagging.

He walked to the house, pleased Daisy followed him. He remembered when Pat and Terry Anderson had gotten her, and she was about two years old now. She'd been a rambunctious puppy and as happy to run as any dog he'd known. Cooper was two at the time. Pat and Terry were careful that their dog didn't jump on the toddler. Brian was certain Cooper would be tickled to have a playmate. Human friends would likely be few and far between. He experienced a pang of sorrow for the child. Losing his parents and perhaps never seeing another child had to be rough.

Heading to the rear of the house, Brian started the generator. He'd cook them some breakfast and take his very last shower. Bathing would be something on a reduced scale from now on. Though the Beach House in front of Halfway Lake had bathrooms, they did not have showers inside and the outdoor showers needed power to work. With the lake sitting in front, he imagined in the summer he'd manage baths. During the winter he'd be heating the water anyway. He might figure out a way to rig something and run a PVC pipe out to drain a tub. He made a mental note to nab a standalone bathtub. One more thing for the list. Add a lifetime supply of soap, shampoo, toothpaste, toothbrushes, floss, and anything else which made their lives better. Crap, more lists.

In the kitchen he grabbed the last of the eggs, a half dozen. He found sausages in the freezer and he had half a loaf of bread. He peeled the last two potatoes, cut them up, fried them, then put the sausages in the pan to heat. Within twenty minutes, he and Daisy enjoyed a hot breakfast.

After eating, Brian went to wake Cooper and the boy came out and sat at the table, hair standing on end. The boy's eyes widened upon noticing Daisy, who laid her head in his lap. Cooper giggled and gently petted the dog's large head. Brian made some pancakes and used the last of the butter.

Within an hour, he had the truck packed with the last of his belongings. He went to the backyard and switched off the generator, then stepped over to the roses and his wife's grave. He squatted down, tears pricking his eyes.

"I've got to go, honey. I won't return to our home again, but I've got a feeling you'll be with me always. I'm sorry I couldn't join you so soon, but Coop needs me, and I need him. I love you, babe, and I miss you so damned much," he choked out.

Coop's hand touched his neck. He turned, picked the boy up, and hugged him. Walking away one last time, he went to the truck and placed Cooper in the car seat.

"Daisy!" he called. She easily jumped into the truck cab.

"Okay, guys, we're going to the mini-mall. I'm gonna get some clothes for you, Coop, and a bed for both of us, and we'll get dog food for Daisy. How does that sound?" He beamed at the boy and the dog.

"Awesome!" Cooper shrieked.

Brian laughed. He backed the truck and U-Haul trailer out and left his neighborhood. He didn't look back at his home, and it was one of the hardest things he'd had to do in his life. There was only one course for him now, to forge ahead.

Ж

Emma awoke exhausted and confused. Upon opening her eyes, she spied a gossamer film above her. There was ornate molding on the ceiling. Then she remembered. She and Paadi stopped at a bed and breakfast to spend the night. She'd chosen the McLaren Vale suite at the Australian Walkabout Inn. Yesterday was a remarkably hard day. Her new friend Paadi shot and killed a man because he was too stupid or too high to realize the danger he presented by pointing a weapon at them.

Though they hadn't discussed it, she sensed the incident upset Paadi. When she arrived at her parents' house, she dreaded going in. Upon entering her childhood home, she scented the oppressive odor of decay. Emma's heart plunged into her stomach. It was real, her parents were dead and gone. The living room was the same but for the coating of dust. She'd walked into her once loved home, now empty except for the relics of a lost life. Her parents were there, but not how she remembered them.

At the rear of the house her parents' bedroom door was shut. On the door was an envelope with her name on it taped to the door. She took the note off the door but didn't open the bedroom door. She didn't want that gruesome scene to be her last memory of her parents.

That was yesterday and felt like a lifetime ago. Rubbing her eyes, Emma hung her head sadly. The envelope was on the nightstand and she fingered her mother's letter. She scooted up in the large bed and plumped the pillows. The sheets were crisp and clean and so wonderful against her skin. It was a lovely room and the windows were wide open, letting the morning breeze in. Mourning doves outside her window flitted across the ground, cooing. There were several other birds singing, it was spring after all. It was almost normal. It was so weird. At least it didn't stink as bad as Boston. There was a miasma of rot here in Lancaster, but not on the large scale of Boston.

Paadi chose the Victoria suite. It was smaller, but she wanted to keep an eye on the Silverado, which she could see from her room. She had cracked the sliding glass door to the outside, letting in a nice breeze and night air.

Emma's room was spacious, and the sheets clean. There was no one at the B&B, and the kitchen door was unlocked. Thankfully, there were no bodies at least. They'd searched each of the rooms.

Raking her long hair together with her fingers, Emma tied it with an elastic band. She reread the letter her mother had written to her.

Dear Em, if you're reading this, I'm afraid your father and I didn't fare as well as we'd hoped. Please don't open our door, I'd not have you remember us this way. If you're reading this, it means that you've survived this horrible virus. I hope you can find a way to live. Know that your father and I love you so very much. Please be safe, my love. I'll see you in heaven when it is your time. Don't grieve for your father and me, we've lived a wonderful life, having you as our daughter. Love Mom.

Emma sniffled and wiped away the tears. She'd loaded up the photographs of her family, removed them from the frames and placed them in plastic bags.

She took most of the photo albums. They were her only link to her past. She searched the home and then she and Paadi emptied the pantry of every scrap of food. They raided the linen closet for TP, towels, shampoos, and toothpaste. There was never enough TP. They'd have to raid a few stores for feminine hygiene products. They couldn't have enough of those either. A future without such necessities and luxuries elicited a mental cringe.

She'd used the bathrooms in other rooms, saving her bathroom for her final usage before they headed to the park. This morning, they'd empty out the hotel's kitchen before leaving, and take all the TP here. Her thought process had changed in the last weeks. Innocuous conveniences, such as a flushing toilet and toilet paper, meant a lot.

Emma sat up and shoved the covers away from her, exhaling unhappily. It would be the last convenience she'd have. The cabins at the park weren't this lavish. Still, they would be a shelter she didn't have to build. She didn't know if there were other people there. If there were, she hoped they'd be good people and not crazies or druggies like the idiot they ran into yesterday. At least she wasn't alone, she had Paadi and that woman sure was good with a weapon. She also had Buddy, who would protect them both. The dog was on the floor beside the bed, still asleep.

She scratched the dog's belly. "Get up, lazy bones. We have a long day ahead of us. We're going to find us a new home." He thumped his tail on the hardwood floors.

Emma got dressed and wandered into the kitchen. Paadi was there already, pouring steaming liquid into a mug from a pot. "Coffee, the old-fashioned way." She grinned.

"How did you manage that?" Emma giddily took a coffee cup from the counter.

"This is a gas stove, so I just added water and coffee grounds. Boiled them and carefully poured it into the cup. There's powdered creamer and sugar. Don't even bother with the Sub-Zero, I'm positive it's been long dead."

Emma carefully poured the coffee into the cup, mindful of the coffee grounds. She added sugar but left it black. Cautiously sipping the heady brew, she closed her eyes in appreciation. It had been a while since she'd had coffee. On the table were an assortment of prepackaged pastries. She snared one and tore it open.

"It seems almost normal," she breathed as she took a bite. "Coffee and pastries."

"Yeah, it does. Once we get to the park, I figure we find us a place, lay claim, and then empty out the truck. We can head to the nearest store and scavenge more items that we might need in the future. Once your gas is gone, we'll be stranded at the park."

"Good idea. It's a frightening thought, having whatever we have and never having more. We screw it up and we're dead. Let's look for more gas cans. I want to try to siphon more fuel. That should give us longer use of the truck. I can't remember if there are many stores within walking distance of the park, especially where we'll be settling. We do need to get this right the first time."

"Sounds great about gas cans," said Paadi. "Siphoning fuel is harder than you think. Let's get this place cleaned out and go to this wonderful place you've told me of and find our new home!"

Ж

Paadi was glad Emma had chosen this place. It was nice to sleep in a clean bed, and one she didn't have to make. Lancaster was a pretty city, despite the decaying bodies on the ground. Though there weren't as many as in Boston.

She'd had a fitful night, dreams of shooting that man plaguing her sleep. She missed her husband Shane, her family, and her friends.

She was happy to have found her new friend Emma. She liked the woman, and they were about the same age. Emma had a kind and generous heart. Finding the dog was awesome too. Police dogs were pretty loyal to and protective of their masters, and it appeared Emma earned Buddy's love.

Paadi contemplated what their life at this park would be like. She was confident of her ability to shoot an animal, not so much on butchering it, and she did know how to fish. Hopefully, they would raise crops, but they'd have to pick up a hell of a lot of food supplies to last them until they got the hang of growing things. She wasn't prepared for this kind of disaster, no one was. The Vermilion Strain was so virulent it took her breath away. Whoever had set this monster loose surely had no idea how relentless the contagion was. Would they have unleashed it on the world had they known? Probably so, only a madman would have done it in the first place.

Their lives were forever changed. So many losses, so much pain. Paadi shook the dark musings away. She refused to allow herself to become bogged down with negativity. That would make her careless. She needed to focus all her energies into surviving. If she didn't, it would dishonor Shane and her family. She'd try for them, because they'd *want* her to live, survive, and thrive. Just as she'd want that very thing for them.

FIVE

Flynn pressed his fingers to the flutter in his chest. He was desperately trying to think of a way to escape. He didn't want to meet this Casper character. The guy sounded like an overlord maniac. A smart maniac, but still, someone bad. The greedy lunatic had taken over Philadelphia with only a few people. What gave him the right to take over? Christ. He just wanted to go to Amish country and find a safe place and live. Philadelphia was a dead city and it now had wild animals roaming the streets. He didn't want to end up as tiger shit.

The person driving hadn't answered any of Flynn's questions, just drove in silence. The vehicle stopped at a massive building, the rear of the Philadelphia Museum of Art.

Why are we at a museum of all places?

They got out of the car and started walking past the structure.

"Casper lives all over the city," said Skinny. "He says he might as well enjoy it."

"What's he like?" Flynn asked.

"He's a good man. He's helped a lot of us. He keeps order. There would be a lot more bullshit going on if it weren't for him and his bodyguards."

Flynn shook his head. "How can he be a good man if he skins people and won't let others have food?"

"Hey, it's a whole new brutal world now. Only the strongest survive. We're all survivors. Casper just makes sure it's a level playing field. He's not that bad, just listen to him. I reckon you'll be surprised. He's started cleaning up the city, getting rid of the bodies and burning them. It's actually starting to get better. Not as nasty," Skinny said with half a shrug.

This guy is delusional, this place reeks, Flynn thought, but said nothing out loud.

They entered the large structure. It was surprisingly cool in the interior. There was a strange smell, either stale air or the empty building and its contents. Ahead was a man surrounded by several candelabras, and he was reading a book. A shock of shaggy pale gray hair fell across his forehead and when his head came up, his eyes were milky. Then shock jolted Flynn's body like a live wire.

"I don't believe it. Cramer? Is that you?" he croaked, his steps faltering.

The figure looked up, his head cocked oddly to the side, then swung to the other side. He stood up, stepping forward. "Flynn? You're alive?" A broad smile opened the man's face and he rushed forward.

"You're Casper?" Flynn asked in a weak voice.

"Yeah. I died, or damned near. Rachael's gone. She died and rotted beside me in the bed. I'm a ghost now. Not truly dead, but not actually alive either." Cramer leered oddly and shrugged. Flynn wasn't sure if he wanted to hug his old friend or run away. It was Cramer, but it wasn't. The specter before him had changed dramatically in form and the essence of him. Had Cramer gone insane?

"I'm glad you're alive, Cramer. I tried calling you, and Roger too. Then the cell service died and the power went out," he said in a lame voice, shrugging.

"Call me Casper, Flynn. Cramer is no longer here. You didn't try to come by? I swung by Roger's apartment. He's dead. Everyone is dead, except for us. How do you like my city now?" Casper grinned and it gave Flynn the willies.

"Well, I was leaving. I'm heading to someplace else, anyplace else. I'm going to try to find a place outside the city to live out there and survive as a farmer." Although Flynn was uncertain why he didn't tell Cramer about going to the Amish, something in his paranoid brain warned him not to. The less Cramer knew about his plans, the better.

"Leaving? No, you can't leave now Flynn, I need you. You have to stay here and help me keep Philadelphia. We got the food to last us for a long time. There ain't many left here. I've been killing all the bad apples," Casper said in a singsong voice.

Flynn felt the hair raise up on his arm. Yes, something had changed in Cramer, something in his brain had died. He would not and did not trust this person in front of him.

"I'd like to, Cram... Casper, but I'd really rather go. It makes me too sad, too depressed to live in this place. If I can just get some food, I'll be gone."

Casper's face hardened, his milky eyes narrowing. "Sorry, that's just not going to happen. You'll be staying here with us. We need good people to hold onto this place. I stay where I want, but you can choose a place and live here in the heart of things. I want you by my side. I need my friends near." There was a tone of deadly finality to the statement.

Behind Casper, two large men stepped from the shadows. The pair were hulking figures and walked to stand behind Casper. Those two must be Casper's bodyguards the other man spoke of. They too appeared as though they'd survived the virus. Their skin was mottled from old bruising, just as Casper's was.

"We think you should stay. Our friend Casper, has asked you nicely." One of the men beamed, a hand going to Casper's shoulder.

"Yeah, Casper is a good man, with a good dream. We're helping him and you should too," the other man said, his face pallid and blotched.

It must be the last vestiges of the busted capillaries. Flynn looked at his friend, who was now a stranger. He didn't want to stay here, he wanted out of this dead city. How did he get out of here without pissing this man off? He shivered a little. He'd have to figure something out. The food here would last only so long, perhaps a few years, then what? He'd be in the same situation but with no transportation out of this place except by foot. Not to mention, there were wild animals.

Should he go along with his old friend? Perhaps play along until he figured a way to get free of this city? He'd known no other home, no other way of life. If he were to remain here with his friend, he'd have food and live another day. But for what, and for how long?

"Can I think about it? Maybe you can come too? Me and you, we could go find a place out there where there aren't a lot of dead. We work hard and have a family one day? Find a life away from the ashes."

"You can think on it, friend, but you're not leaving here. I won't leave here either. This is my home, my city. Here, I rule. I can't rule elsewhere. Here is where I stay."

"I'll stay for a while then, but I will leave one day. I hope you'll come with me. This place can't last, the food can't last."

The leer oozing across Cramer's face provoked a chill.

Ж

Brian shone the flashlight across the stores within the mall. It was eerily quiet. He'd just come from an outlet store, where plenty of clothing was available for Cooper. The clothes were various larger sizes. He headed to another store to select more items. Cooper wore a rucksack filled with shirts and socks. Brian wore a larger rucksack filled with jeans, sweaters, and light jackets. He brought a large, rolling suitcase to fill. At the next store, they'd search for shoes, boots, and adult wear. The plan was to gather enough clothing to last this child and himself a lifetime. Daisy was happily sniffing everything. Thankfully, there were no bodies in the stores. It was one thing he worried about with Cooper tagging along.

He chose simple but well-made clothing. It was difficult, because most of the clothing offered was cheaply made with cheap material and wouldn't last the harsh life ahead. He was guessing on Coop's eventual size from his father, who was a modest five foot ten. He hoped he got it right, especially with Cooper's shoes and coats. Pennsylvania was damned cold in winter and in the woods, it would be *very* cold.

By the end of it all, they had accumulated quite an assortment of clothing, including hats, scarves, and mittens. Those were found in the stockrooms, since it was mostly summer clothing on the shelves in the main store.

Cooper was humming happily to himself. Apparently, he was very pleased. Brian opened the door and Daisy jumped in. In the bed of the truck were more metal garbage cans along with fifty-pound bags of dog food.

Brian headed next to the hardware store. He needed more lumber, the gas tiller, seed packets, and bags of fertilizer. It was his hope to set up fencing for the garden to keep rabbits and deer from their precious food.

He was eating through the gas cans, yet thankful he'd had the forethought to store the gas. At least he didn't have to drive home. That would save on gas. Tonight they'd spend their first night at the Beach House, their new home.

He angled the trailer to the entrance to the store then let Daisy out. She went to sniffing. Upon entering the store with Cooper, Brian stood for a moment to listen. He detected nothing. He didn't think many people would be here shopping. Food would more than likely be their top priority. Depending on the total surviving population in this area, Brian didn't believe the number of survivors was a lot. He got a large cart and Cooper climbed happily aboard. He pushed the cart toward the gardening center, his powerful flashlight shining down the dim aisles.

He found an empty box, set it on the cart, and started loading up seeds: tomatoes, green peppers, corn, zucchini, carrots, beans, string beans, and all other sorts of seeds he'd need to live. He was ignorant in regard to how to plant, but he'd seen enough videos to get him started. He was surprised to see canning equipment and stopped, eyeing the paraphernalia. Jars, two pressure canners, strainers, and other canning implements. He was profoundly thankful he made notes and then a happy smile spread across his face. There beside the lot were books on canning. He laughed out loud when he read one of the books, *Canning & Preserving for Dummies*.

He'd have to swing by and get materials for building racks; he'd need to store his food someplace. He walked out to the outdoor part of the gardening section and came close to fainting. There on the shelves were pots of tomatoes and green peppers, squash, and zucchini, already growing. Because the rain reached them, the plants hadn't died. There were six-foot fruit trees, peaches, apples, and pears, along with a few cherry trees. He'd have to plant those, to ensure they'd have fruit in a couple of years. He laughed, delighted.

"Hopefully we'll at least have some fresh tomatoes soon, even some zucchini." He beamed at Cooper. "And some fruit in a few years."

"I can help, Daddy. I can help!" Cooper squealed.

It took a bit of doing, but they loaded up the trees and plants. He found sets of lettuce and added that to the cart. On their way home, he'd swing by the farm and wrangle the rest of the chickens. It would be their last stop before they got to the park. He'd spend the next few days building inside the structure, making it habitable.

Two hours later Brian pulled away from the large store. His heart was lighter. He had the beginnings of a garden, he had a dog for protection and a companion for Cooper, and he had hope.

He headed for the farm. He hoped the eggs hadn't hatched yet. He had a smaller gauge wire for a brooder coop, to keep the babies safe from predators. The more chickens, the better for him and Cooper. It was a continuing source of protein. He wouldn't eat the chickens, at least not until they had a heck of a lot more than seven or eight hens.

Brian blew out a breath. He had so much to do and he was overwhelmed as to how he was going to accomplish it. Sometimes it was as though he was drowning, barely keeping his head above the flood of work. If he got a few things accomplished today, he'd feel better about it.

He spotted the mattress store and drove to the parking area near the entrance. He left Coop in the truck with Daisy and ran into the store. He hauled a twin mattress and situated it into the trailer, then returned to the store and retrieved the box spring. On the next trip he got the bedframes, to keep the beds off the floor. Then he chose a queen-size mattress set. He needed a bit more room than a twin provided. Brian was pleased there were sheet sets in the store. He was about to depart the store when he spotted a leather loveseat where customers sat and waited. He shrugged. He'd need someplace to sit in the evenings. Why not? Now was the time to gather items which would make their lives better. He reminded himself that when the fuel was gone, the ability to retrieve items was lost.

He dragged the loveseat out; it wasn't that heavy, and he easily put it into the trailer. Checkout was a lot easier these days. On one of his visits, he figured he should locate an industrial dolly. Satisfied, he pulled away from the mattress store. He noted the Walmart up the road, that would be for future plundering. He sped along the highway and chose the exit to the farm. Before he pulled into the long drive, he slowed down. There was a car parked in the yard. Someone was there. He emitted a hushed curse under his breath. He'd just have to make do with the chickens he had. Perhaps he'd swing by another farm and hunt for more chickens. He drove past the farm and drove on for another few miles. Off in the distance, he spied another farmhouse. He decelerated and took the turn into the drive. He beeped his horn several times, waiting silently. It was quiet. Brian beeped another time before exiting the truck.

"Stay in here, Coop. I'll be right back," Brian instructed.

Daisy sniffed the air, but her tail was not wagging.

He detected the distinct scent of putrefaction and corruption. He didn't go up to the house, but went to the rear of the home. He found the coop, but all the chickens were dead. It was grisly and he walked away. This place was a bust. He climbed in the truck and left the farm behind. He was wasting time here and decided another day would do for chicken hunting. He needed to head to the park. It was getting late in the day and there was so much to do while daylight burned. Brian wondered if he'd ever catch up on things. If there would come a day when he'd say "I'm done." Probably not.

Half an hour later, he entered R.B. Winter State Park. He drove up to the large structure and breathed a sigh of relief. There was no one here and no one had bothered the impromptu chicken coop. He let Daisy out. She sniffed at the coop and then ran off toward the water. Brian lifted Cooper out of the truck.

"Stay close, where I can see you. Don't leave the area, okay?"

"Okay, Daddy." Cooper went running after the dog.

Brian kept his eye on the boy all the same. Unloading and carrying the clothing bundles and suitcases into the structure, he was now home. It was large and would hold quite a bit. He'd have to section it off, but that was a task for later, once he got the garden in and trees cut down for future firewood, along with all the other things on his long lists.

Cooper played by the chickens and Brian was satisfied the boy had settled, at least for the moment. He stripped off his light jacket as the morning heated up. He unloaded the trailer and set the contents out on the ground. He took the beds into the house and set the fruit tree containers out. He fingered the soil in the containers, the dirt was damp, so he didn't need to water them.

With the truck and trailer finally unloaded, Brian assembled the lumber for the new chicken coop. He had a simple idea in mind. Tall enough to stand in, the floor raised off the ground, and chicken wire surrounding the whole of it, with dowel rods for the chickens to roost on. A raised coop allowed the chickens to scratch beneath the structure in winter. It would be large enough once the chickens produced more chicks. It might take a couple of years to get a big flock, but he was confident it was achievable.

It would take a few days to build the finished coop. For now, he gathered the supplies and built an enclosure for the temporary chicken coop. Cooper came and helped him, handing him galvanized screws. Brian had his drill, with extra batteries. They'd been charging while he had the generator on at home. He figured he'd be needing all the batteries before it was all over. There were solar panels at Lowe's, and the inverters and deep cell batteries. Perhaps once he got things squared away here, he'd do a little appropriating. He was sure there were books on how to assemble and wire. He'd viewed quite a few videos in the past. It would be nice to have the water pump running so he'd have flushing toilets, the outdoor showers, and lights at night. To his mental list he added light fixtures with the LED bulbs so as not to draw too much power, extra panels, and inverters, so if the others wore out or broke, he'd have extras. It didn't hurt to have spares. There was the option of portable solar generators for camping. The list grew.

If he did that, he'd hunt for a solar refrigerator. Brian knew there were such appliances, he just had to find one. That would be very nice in summer. In winter, he wouldn't need it. As he worked on the coop, his mind buzzed with ideas for their new home. His brain hadn't had so much activity in years. So much to do. He'd have to get it done before he ran out of gas. He kept that thought in the forefront of his mind.

He had the posts in the ground for the chicken coop and for the fence that would surround the coop. He opened the new heavy-duty stapler and unrolled the chicken wire. For now, he just wanted to get the chicken yard enclosed. He'd work on the main coop little by little. The coop was located far enough from the house so as not to smell, but close enough to keep in view.

Although Cooper tried to help, he was no help at all. The boy had so much energy it caused Brian to chortle. They worked their way around all the poles, then started on the second layer, above the first pass. Brian wanted the fence high, to keep foxes out. He'd eventually put some kind of netting on top, to keep owls and hawks out. For now, he'd be happy with keeping the chickens in. He'd have to construct a door for access to the chicken yard. For now, he secured it with a nail. By the time he got the second tier up and attached, he allowed the chickens out of the kennel. He opened the door to the kennel that held the brooding hen and she wasn't pleased.

Unable to reach the third level of the fence, Cooper went to play by the shore of the lake. Brian watched him, ensuring the boy didn't go into the water. He didn't think the child would venture into the water — it was still cold — but he wasn't sure the child understood *not* to venture in. He was inexperienced as a parent, and it was a great unknown of what he should or shouldn't do nor what Cooper was capable of, so he kept a constant eye on the child. He was honor bound to do his best with the boy.

The day had warmed up considerably and Brian was sweating profusely. He finished with the last row of the chicken wire and called it quits for the coop project for today. He figured if he worked on each project a little each day, he would make progress. There was just so much to get done.

They broke for lunch and Brian pulled out the sandwiches he'd made the night before. He'd kept the food in a sealed plastic bag and had put the bag along with drinks in the lake, inside a pillowcase, held by a rock. He drank a Coke and sighed in satisfaction. The cold water kept the drinks and sandwiches reasonably cool. He'd thought about bringing beer, then thought better of it. He needed to keep a clear head. Though it was quiet now, there was no certainty others were not coming. How could they not? It was a prime location. Hunting, fishing, and space.

Cooper appeared a little droopy eyed. It was nap time.

"Come on, Coop, I want you to lay down for a bit. I'll be right outside, tilling the garden."

"I can help." He yawned, his eyes going owlish and large.

"I know, buddy, but you can help after you take a nap, okay?"

His narrow shoulders slumping, Cooper got up. Brian walked him into their new home to where he'd set up the twin bed with LEGO sheets.

"Don't worry, son, there's lots for you to do when you wake up, alright?"

"Okay," Cooper said sleepily and yawned again, his mouth filling his whole face. The boy tugged his blue blanket close to him and closed his eyes.

Brian went outside and started the laborious efforts of breaking soil for the new garden and the fruit trees. He jerked up at the echo of a shot.

Ж

Benjamin Jacob Hamm, BJ, exhaled in gratification. He was desperate. He'd only been here two days and had not seen any deer. He'd feared that perhaps he'd chosen wrong. He'd driven all the way from Cincinnati, Ohio. He'd spent his time gathering supplies and avoiding people. He'd hit sporting goods stores, such as Dick's, and other stores all along the way. He'd thought the Vermilion Strain wiped out most of the population, but it would seem that it only left assholes in its wake. Time and again on his travel across the country, he'd been robbed of all his possessions. He'd stopped again and again to gather up and scrounge and hoped he wouldn't be killed for them.

He was a carpenter and an assistant youth minister in his *before* life and was unable to cope with the rampant and unprovoked violence. He was thankful he hadn't been killed. The reasoning escaped him why those people took his supplies. There were plenty, all one had to do was walk into a store and take it. Yet, four times, he'd been stopped, a *toll*, he'd been told. A toll! It was a lazy man's way of stealing. He was not a violent man, but he was getting to the point where he could no longer turn the other cheek.

He was finally here, however, and had set up a camp. He'd claimed one of the cabins and unloaded his truck and fifth wheel trailer two days ago, then taken a full day just to rest and let his nerves settle. He'd visited and camped in this park over the years, with his wife Clair and their two boys, Brody and Timothy.

He'd finally wised up and stayed off the main highways coming to R.B. Winter State Park. It had taken him a long time and a lot of siphoning cars and trucks to get to the park.

He walked over to the animal; it was a clean shot. The buck he'd killed was a yearling. It was spring, and the animals weren't fattened up, but it would be fresh meat. The sorrow at losing his family wrapped him tightly. BJ was a good hunter, yet he was unable to save his family.

He tried not to blame God, but sometimes, in his darkest moments, he did. Why hadn't he died with them? Why had they suffered so horribly? Would he see them again one day, sitting with his Lord, Jesus Christ? He knew that evil men had done this thing. Man was capable of such cruelty. They were a brutal species. Well, whoever did this thing, let loose this horrible virus, had pretty much ended the human race. The people he'd seen were few and far between.

He unsheathed his knife and gutted the deer, planning to carry the animal to his camp. It was good to be off the road and the stress of hiding from marauders. The world had gone crazy. It was bad enough losing his family, but then losing the very supplies he'd needed to survive had driven him nearly over the edge. But he was here, he hadn't seen another human, and that was fine with him. Although he had not seen many people, he'd have to say the majority he did see were greedy and didn't want to do the work of locating supplies and learning the skills to survive. He was beginning to think that the human race was doomed.

BJ sighed. He'd skin and dress the deer when he returned to camp. For now, he needed to lighten the load. He cut off the animal's head, making it manageable to carry. BJ walked through the silent woods, the carcass slung over his shoulders.

The air was so fresh, and the forest was peaceful. The smell was negligible, compared to the stench of Cincinnati. It was an unbelievable nightmare there and after his family died, he'd wanted nothing more than to leave. The fog of flies was apocalyptic, like some science fiction scene from Hell, with body upon body stacked up and left in the streets.

The birds were singing and a slight breeze in the forest washed over him. It was as though he were the only person on Earth. He tilted his face to the breeze and it dried his tears. He needed to stop thinking of the past and concentrate on surviving.

He had water, but he would need to go to Halfway Lake to replenish his supply in a day or two. He'd have to boil a lot of it for drinking water. The rest would be used for bathing and washing clothing. The cabin had a toilet, and with the tanks filled with water, he could flush it. The toilet in the fifth wheel was useable too. He liked having options.

Walking into camp, he looked around appreciatively. So far so good. He wouldn't have the ability to guard everything, so he hoped no one would steal his supplies now that he was here. He decided to plan out areas to bury some of the supplies. Near enough to the camp for easy access, but not close enough to worry someone would stumble over it.

BJ missed his family and it was lonesome out in the woods, but there was a peace here and he needed it right now. He needed to heal.

Ж

Emma pulled off the road into R.B. Winter State Park. She hummed happily and glanced at Paadi. Her friend grinned widely, her dark eyebrows waggling up and down. She fairly vibrated with excitement. Emma took a curve, heading toward Halfway Lake. When she arrived, she was surprised to see a truck, U-Haul, and a big fellow digging what appeared to be a garden plot.

The big guy stopped what he was doing and faced her. She decelerated, not wishing to get too close.

"Easy now," Paadi said in a hushed voice. "Let's see if he's a good guy or a bad guy."

Emma nodded, "If you want, you stay in the truck and guard me. You're a good shot, so if things get hinky, you're my best bet."

"Okay, just keep out of my line of fire," Paadi warned. "I seriously don't wish to have a bad day and be all angry at you for making me shoot you by accident."

Emma climbed out of the Silverado. Although her heart was beating fast, she didn't feel afraid. She left Buddy inside, he was whining, low and excited. She smiled as she marched toward the man. There was something very familiar about him, but she was unable to think what it might be. Then she spotted a diminutive blond boy, sitting by some kind of chicken coop, of all things. The big man was smiling at her and then it clicked.

"Oh my gosh, *Brian*? Is that you?" She laughed, running to him.

"My god, Emma! I can't believe it's you!" He grabbed her in his big arms and swung her around, laughing. Tears were blurring her eyes as she hung onto him. He set her down and held her at arm's length, beaming down at her upturned face.

"Is Christa here?" she asked, searching excitedly. It was then she caught the pain in his eyes.

"Oh no. Brian, I'm so sorry. Oh god, I'm so sorry." She felt horrible for it and hugged him again.

She'd worked at the hospital, where she met Christa, a fellow nurse. Then when Christa was diagnosed with breast cancer, it evolved into a difficult time for the couple. Christa had gone through chemo, and Emma had come to know Christa and Brian well. They'd become close friends. When Emma went to Boston, she'd kept in sporadic touch with them through social media.

She was so thrilled when Christa beat the cancer and went into remission. Apparently the Vermilion virus had taken her. Emma's eyes filled with tears.

"Yeah, it was hard at the end," said Brian. "I wasn't sure I'd be able to go on, but then Cooper, my next-door neighbor's son, came over and kinda saved me."

Cooper came running up and grabbed onto Brian's leg, peering at Emma. She was enchanted immediately. His large blue eyes stared up at her with curiosity.

"Hi, Cooper, I'm Emma. That is my friend Paadi, and we came to live here in the woods."

"Hi, Emma." Cooper's gaze swung to Paadi, who stepped toward them. Buddy trotted to meet the German shepherd, both animals' tails wagging enthusiastically. Then the shepherd went down on her back in a submissive posture.

"That's Daisy," Brian said, observing the two dogs, who were sniffing, tails swishing.

"That's Buddy. We found each other in Boston. I met Paadini Sullivan, a former Boston police officer, on the road. Paadi, this is Brian Philips. I guess now a former firefighter from Lancaster. I knew him and his wife, Christa."

With an engaging smile, Paadi shook Brian's hand. Then she ruffled the child's blond head.

"Good to meet you, Brian. You too, Coop!" Paadi said in her thick Boston accent.

Emma suspected Paadi overdid the accent a bit. It elicited a wide grin to Brian's face and Emma stifled a snigger. Her eyes lit up with humor.

"So, you settling here, Brian? Great minds think alike. You didn't want to set up in one of the cabins?" Emma noted the stack of supplies, the garden, and the odds and ends.

"The best and most open place is here, for planting a large garden. I'd have to travel a lot just to retrieve heavy jugs of water and it just seemed the best idea to make the Beach House our home. It's a big building and I'm planning to put up walls inside. You two are more than welcome to live there," Brian graciously offered. It will be easier to defend if we're all together. Plus, I'm going to be getting some solar panels and see if I can't get a little power going."

Emma gaped at Paadi in an *aha* moment. A slow smile spread and a speculative glint blossomed in Paadi's dark brown eyes. It never occurred to Emma to use the Beach House.

"Emma, he's right. With all those seeds you found, it would be easier to grow here in this wide-open space. And we wouldn't have to carry water, like he said. I don't know about you, but that's a helluva lot of hard work we don't need to do."

"There aren't any beds there. At least the last time I was here there weren't. But I guess it's a solid idea."

Emma's brain was gaining momentum with ideas crashing in.

"Hey, I picked up mattresses and box springs for Coop and me. Later today we can head to the mattress store and get beds for you two," Brian offered. "We'll locate some furniture while I still have gas."

"Well, heck. I do believe that's a damned fine idea. Let me and Paadi unload the truck and get things inside the house. Then we'll help you with this garden. I see you already have plants. Just so you know, I've got canning stuff," said Emma. "Figured that would be the only way to preserve food for the long term. By next year, we'll have gone through all our provisions."

"Great minds *do* think alike. You'll see a bunch of stuff in there from me," Brian laughed.

Emma and Paadi unloaded the truck with Brian's help. It took less time to complete the task than it had to load. The Beach House was a large structure but was now filled with the combined belongings. With his U-Haul, Brian quadrupled the amount of food stores. That was smart, and Emma wanted to kick herself for not thinking of it. She noticed numerous metal trash cans and peeked inside one. It held a fifty-pound bag of rice. Smart. Perhaps while they were out getting a mattress later, she'd have him swing by one of the big box stores for more rice, flour, sugar, beans, and whatever else was left behind, scavenging everything they came across.

"Wow, this guy isn't playing," Paadi whistled, peering in the can.

"Yeah, no kidding. I should have thought to get a trailer. It would have been handy to pack away a lot of stuff," Emma grumbled.

"Hells bells, we'll pick some up today on our way. There was that SAM's we passed on the way here, I remember about where it was. If there is stuff there, we can load it up along with the mattresses." Paadi was thinking along the same lines as Emma. Why not? It was perfect here. There was no stench of the rotting or the toxic fires. The area was pristine.

Emma grinned. "I was thinking the very same thing. Let's get out there and help get that garden started. I can taste the fresh veggies now."

While Brian angled the tiller across the ground, the women tugged out clumps of grass and shook the dirt free, tossing them into a five-gallon bucket. There weren't many weeds and Emma hoped the park didn't use herbicides to kill them. She wouldn't want it getting into their food. She carried one of the buckets with her, putting the grass into it. She'd dump it later.

She watched Brian work, wrestling with the tiller, and her heart broke. She'd known him and Christa for years. She and Christa worked together, and she'd been there to celebrate her triumph over breast cancer. Now Christa was gone, taken by that horrible virus. Brian was clearly grieving, it was etched into his face. She was glad he'd taken the boy, and she was glad the orphaned boy had him. She didn't want to imagine how many children were out there, and by now many would have died without help from an adult. She only hoped others stepped in to take the children in. She hadn't seen any children, and only a few adults in the past few weeks.

Most of the world's population had been wiped out. Humans would be lucky to recover. It would never be the same again, at least not in her lifetime, and perhaps not even in Cooper's. There would be no more new technologies and the old technology would die away with no one to maintain or recover it. Solar panels were a viable option, but in a generation or so, those would be gone too. Fuel would be gone in a year or less, degraded beyond use. Diesel would work, if it was obtainable, but again, that would only last so long.

Any illnesses that came along would take their toll, with no hospitals, no more antibiotics, and people would die younger now. Any major accidents would likely result in death, and infection would be their enemy. Emma was glad she had the book on medicinal plants. She'd have to start learning how to use that knowledge to treat and heal others. They had a chance here, but should something happen that she was unable to mend or heal, death wouldn't be far off. If any of them developed cancer, their life span would be shortened. Coop might end up alone in twenty or thirty years. It was a dark thought and Emma shook her mind free of it. It did no good to ponder on the doom and gloom of the future. She needed to concentrate on the here and now.

She glanced up as Cooper sped across the lawn, screaming with laughter. Buddy and Daisy were galloping with the child, all of them having the best time.

"I swear, if I had a tenth of that energy, I'd rule the world," Paadi laughed, shaking her head.

Brian snorted. "If only we had the ability to harness it. My god, what we might accomplish!"

"At least the dogs are getting along," said Emma.

"Wait 'til Daisy comes into heat." Brian smirked, "They'll definitely be getting along then."

"She's intact?" Emma asked, her eyes growing wide.

"Yeah, my neighbors, Pat and Terry, were going to breed her next year. And if I'm not mistaken, Buddy wasn't neutered. So I guess we'll have a good supply of guard dogs handy." Brian wiped his sweaty forehead.

"Well, I guess that's a good thing, an early warning system!" Paadi said.

"I'd say you're right. Guess we'd best be getting plenty of meat set aside," Emma said, thinking about the dog food she'd gotten. She had several hundred pounds of it, but that wouldn't last that long.

"Don't worry, I got a nice smoker at Lowe's. I'll be going hunting in a few weeks, let the deer put on a bit more weight. I'll be hunting bear too. The more meat we can put away, the better. There's also fishing to be done," said Brian.

"I've never hunted, but hell, I'd definitely like to try." Paadi said, her dark brows moving up and down. Her face was so expressive it made Emma titter.

"I'd be happy to show you the ropes, Paadi," Brian offered, "It just takes patience. Perhaps we can build a tree stand near a natural deer trail. That helps too."

Brian got the fuel can and refilled the tiller. He'd cleared an area fifty feet long by twenty feet wide.

"How big are you going to make this thing?" Emma asked.

"As big as I can. No clue how much we can grow, but I'd like to give it a try. When we return to Lowe's, I'm going to snag a few more fruit trees that were in the garden section of Lowe's. I've planted some over there. It wouldn't hurt to have a few more pear and apple trees. That way in the fall, we have fruits. No idea if they have any nut trees, but we can check. I do know that this park has walnut trees, but I can't remember where I saw them. When I'm out hunting, I'll keep my eyes peeled for them," Brian said.

"Having walnuts would be great, and that's a good idea about more fruit trees. Hopefully in a couple years we'll have a good batch of apples and I can try my hand at applesauce and apple butter. Let's see if they have grapevines too. We can always use those to make raisins." Emma's mind was already thinking ahead.

Brian resumed tilling, while she and Paadi continued their attack on the clumps of grass and clearing the tilled ground. There were so many things to do and get before the gas ran out. She only hoped they got it all accomplished.

Ж

They were making great progress. Brian had undoubtedly done a hell of a lot in the very short time he'd been there. Paadi liked the chickens a lot. She'd never been near farm animals and she watched them while she worked. Something about the scratching in the dirt and the peaceful clucking was soothing to her. It reminded her of her family, talking all at once.

She scanned the lake. There were ducks, though she didn't know what kind they were. The ducklings trailed behind their mothers.

The place was pristine and peaceful, and she now understood why Emma wanted to come here. With the supplies they had, combined with Brian's, they should do very well here, bar anyone taking their things. That would be something they'd need to be ready for. At least there were the two dogs. She expected Buddy would guard the place, and Daisy just might. Buddy might teach her to be a great police dog.

From just the little she'd gleaned from Brian, he seemed like good people, taking the child in and caring for him, planning for their long-term survival. Apparently he'd lost a lot, as had they all.

Here in this tranquil place, Paadi hoped their souls would heal. It was peaceful and beautiful. She'd never been the outdoorsy type, being a city dweller all her life, but she appreciated this place and what it meant for their survival. She was lucky she met Emma and that Emma had taken her with her. She'd been so upset about her vehicle breaking down, yet if it hadn't, she'd never have met Emma. Life was funny. She'd have never envisioned herself here. She was a cop and that was all she'd ever wanted to be. This was a whole new world to her. A whole new life. She vowed to jump in with both feet.

SIX

Flynn walked along the streets. The stench permeated every breath. The noxious air was now mixed with the smoke and the foulness of burned hair and skin, rubber, and plastic. The whole of it was undoubtedly toxic. Casper—because Flynn no longer viewed that man as his friend Cramer—ordered pyres built and bodies thrown on. There were more people showing up, pledging their loyalty to Casper. Flynn thought their loyalty was overrated. They were hungry and desperate. A few were brought in at gunpoint, like himself, and they were not given much of a choice. He'd found himself a place to stay, though it was nothing like a home. It was hot as hell and finding a place for a toilet was difficult. It was only a matter of time before the bottled water was gone. Then what?

Not only that, but the bodies of some of the animals were popping up. There was a dead hippo over on the corner of Filbert Street and North Juniper Street. When it died, Casper had his people build a fire to cook the meat. It had stunk badly since no one knew how to butcher the animal. Several of them had gotten sick from eating it, and the remains of the carcass were rotting. It was as if Flynn was caught in some kind of bizarre apocalyptic nightmare. And Casper was at the eye of a shit storm that would not end well.

Flynn considered himself an average joe. He'd been fine with that and knew he'd never amount to anything more than a middle-class working man. He'd hoped one day for a wife, a couple if kids, and a mortgage. He never had any ambitions to be rich, make a ton of money, or climb a corporate ladder. His needs and wants in this life were very simple. A few beers, a game on TV, and a girl. Now he was trapped with a madman he'd once called a friend.

Flynn knew he had to leave, and soon. He'd paid enough attention in high school during science and biology classes to know disease would run rampant in the midst of this incredibly large-scale decay and corruption, fires notwithstanding. The trip would be daunting. He'd be alone.

He should search for Xandra. If she was alive, they might escape this hellhole together. She was a sweet girl and he'd hoped something would bloom before EV-01-H. He was only sorry that he'd been too much of a coward to not have checked on her.

Casper was sitting at the LOVE Park fountain and Flynn walked over.

"Hey, Casper, I'm planning to head out and do a bit of scrounging. I'm going to search for more survivors. I'm just sorry I haven't done it before," he confided honestly, though it was not the complete truth.

He'd been busting his ass to gain Casper's trust and confidence. He'd done everything he'd been told with enthusiasm and no complaining. It damned near killed his soul.

"That's good, Flynn. Yeah, go ahead. The more we can gather, the better. We can start our own rebuilding of civilization here." Casper granted a rare lift to his lips. It sent a shiver down Flynn's spine.

Rebuild here? Hell no. What woman would want to willingly bring a child up in this place?

Flynn was horrified at the very idea. Would they force women to become pregnant? Rape them to accomplish it? *Hell no.* His mind recoiled at the whole concept.

"Okay. If I have to go a little out there, is that okay? I don't want your people blowing my brains out." Flynn laughed nervously.

"They're your people too. Just give them the password. If you have new people with you, don't let them hear it. The password is King Casper."

"Good to know. Are there any specific foods you're looking for right now? Or just everything I can gather?"

"Everything you can gather. You can check with the occupied stores and verify our people are still there, guarding our supplies."

Flynn dipped his head, pivoting to leave. He just wanted to get the hell away from Casper. The dude gave him the creeps. The two brothers, Javier and Ramon, were almost as bad. Yesterday, a man tried to argue with Casper and the two brothers stepped in and beat the man to death while Casper sat calmly, observing. Flynn shuddered. His friend Cramer had indeed died.

He hoped Xandra was alive. She lived in a third-floor apartment over on Clay Street and Mt. Vernon. He'd only been there once.

It took him twenty minutes to walk to his Honda. It was parked well away from the city center and it made him nervous. He listened to the intermittent roars and grunts of the lions. The hair rose on his arms and neck. He was now the prey. He hadn't been given a weapon yet. He had to *earn* that, and he had not one clue how to do it. He did know that once he left this place, he'd find a few weapons and kill anyone who tried to stop him. At the moment he was defenseless with wild animals roaming around. Why on Earth did Casper let them out of their cages? He'd found out in one of their long chats that Casper had indeed let the animals out of the zoo. Who the hell would set predators loose?

Casper was a madman and Flynn had to leave. Not, however, before he tried to find Xandra Abran. Once more, he was filled with shame over his cowardice. His selfishness. He hadn't checked on Roger or Cramer. If he'd have found Cramer and helped his friend, would he have lost his mind? Flynn didn't know. He only knew that the dude was batshit crazy and he needed to get out of this place before the henchmen, disease, or a lion killed him.

He got to his car and breathed a huff of relief. He started it up and drove, weaving in and out of streets, going farther away from Casper's grasp and feeling all the better for it. Tears of self-pity slid down his face. He wasn't equipped for this kind of thing. Nothing in his short life prepared him for this. He bit down on his trembling lip. He hated himself for the coward he was. No more.

To date, his biggest challenge was avoiding bullies in high school. Then getting a job, and finally, finding his own place. His father died last year, heart attack. His dad smoked like a chimney. He'd mourned his father, but being young, Flynn went on with life. He was glad his father hadn't lived to face the Vermilion Strain. Shit, he wasn't sure if he'd survived his father's agonizing death.

Flynn took his foot off the gas when he spotted zebras running, a tiger close on their heels. He held his breath as the zebras skittered and slipped on the asphalt and stumbled. The tiger was virtually on them and they disappeared behind a building. His heart was racing with the near miss of the tiger. He pulled up and peered down the side street, but there was no sign of either the tiger or the zebras. He hoped they got away. Flynn wiped his face, attempting to get a grip on his emotions. He was exhausted.

He had not slept well since all this had begun. Even less now that Casper was trying to keep him here in the city. He'd stopped talking about wishing to leave and played along with scavenging and locating items to better the community. Flynn knew the more he spoke of wishes to leave, the more Casper would keep a tighter grip, so he'd gone on small scrounging trips, always returning faithfully. The brothers scrutinized him closely. This was the first time in days that he'd been allowed to leave by himself, and was given the password. No one ever shared it before and he hadn't asked.

He pulled up Clay Street and tapped the brake. It was like all other parts of the city, covered by lumps of decaying bodies. He just hoped some of the predators hadn't made it out this far, seeing how there was plenty of food closer to the zoo. The stench was just as prevalent here since there were no pyres.

He parked by Xandra's apartment building. It was silent outside. The wind was blowing but there were no other sounds. No birds, no dogs, nothing.

This place was truly dead. Trash blew across the streets and sidewalks, grass grew between the cracks. It had only been weeks, but it seemed like the nightmarish event had been longer, and the devastation was complete.

He got out of the car. Because he hadn't been given a weapon, Flynn lived in constant fear. There were very few people near Casper who carried weapons. Casper held a stash of them, but Flynn was not privy to them and he felt naked and vulnerable out here.

He'd heard that one man was killed by the lions, unable to defend himself. Casper hadn't seemed bothered by the event. His long-ago drinking buddy was crazy as a loon.

If Xandra wasn't still alive, he'd still leave. He had to get the hell out of there.

Ж

Javier watched Flynn leave, then looked at Casper. Flynn was Casper's weak spot because of their long friendship.

"You believe he's okay to go off by himself?" Javier asked, scratching his beard. The heat of the day made it itchy. Shaving was a waste of precious water.

"Yeah, he's a standup guy. We've been friends for years and years. I know he's a little quirky, but he's come through for us," said Casper.

"If you say so." Javier shrugged, unconvinced.

"I've been keeping track of him, and I've had others reporting in on him. He's getting along and busting his ass. He's settled into his place and he's been talking to a few of the women. I suspect he's just trying to find his own place here. Hopefully once he finds a woman, then you'll see."

"That's right, a woman can truly help," Javier said, thinking of a certain woman he'd met a few days ago. They were dancing around each other, the beginnings of courtship. It was very enjoyable.

"Yes, they can and don't think I haven't noticed your own interests," Casper said, giving a rare smile.

Javier grinned. Perhaps Casper would one day find a woman for himself. He hoped so, life was too short and too lonely without a woman to warm your bed and your heart.

Ж

Brian sat outside by the fire just after sunrise, thinking about the gunshot from the other day. Someone else was here in the park. Hunting no doubt. He was drinking coffee and letting the sun warm his body. The days were getting hotter and the mornings were warming up. A week had passed since Emma and Paadi arrived. He looked around the garden and noted the tips of green popping up. In another few days, the garden would be greener. He was excited. They'd have food for the future. If they successfully grew a garden, that would go a long way in their survival. It was hard work and a gamble.

Both women worked just as hard and they'd managed to get the house separated into rooms so they each had their own spaces. Brian had used some of the lumber and built walls in the concession area, away from the bathrooms. He'd taken a cubbyhole office space for his room. They chose doors at the hardware store, to afford privacy. The women helped him tear out the counters, and after a day of demolition, they built the walls. It wasn't perfect, but each had their own bedroom. Brian hauled the rubble and garbage away.

They'd returned to town and selected bed sets, along with more building supplies. They swung by various stores retrieving bulk foods, and more canning jars and lids. Emma thought there was no such thing as having too much. She possessed boundless energy, just as Brian remembered, and Cooper was becoming more animated with her and Paadi. The boy now had two mothers. Daisy and Buddy were by the water, sniffing up and down the beach together. The ducks edged out farther from the shore, not wishing to fly and leave their young. He'd seen more ducks on the lake and suspected that now that there weren't a lot of people splashing and making noise, the increasing number and variety of wildlife was coming into the area.

Emma emerged from the house. Brian no longer thought of it as the Beach House, but their home. Cooper was still asleep. It was becoming custom to come out and have coffee in the early morning, gearing up for the day ahead. Today, he was going to start on a large storage shed, to put all their bulk items. He'd finished up the chicken coop and built a brooder coop for the bantam hen. Her eggs hatched the day before and they had six chicks, nestled beneath her. Cooper was enthralled and visited them constantly.

"Morning. How'd you sleep?" he asked.

Emma strolled over to sit in a camp chair, patting his head on her way past him. They'd built a large firepit, which was used to cook food, and set a camp coffee pot to perk its magic. There was a stack of wood beside it. He'd taken the chainsaw and cut down quite a few hardwood trees near the edge of their forest. He planned to cut them into manageable portions while he had the chainsaw working. It would supply them with firewood for years to come. They wouldn't need much to heat the space in the house. For now, they had deadfall, the other wood would have to season.

"Working this hard, I just about die every night now." Emma laughed feebly, her hands going to her tangle of long brown hair. Her green eyes held a spark of humor in them.

"I hear you. I thought being a firefighter was a tough job. Apparently post-apocalyptic survivor is harder." He snorted and handed her a cup of coffee. He chuffed amusement when Emma wrapped herself over the cup and rocked back and forth.

She groaned exaggeratedly when she took a sip and he laughed. "Don't laugh, I need this brew. I'm so glad we got all those cans. I doubt I can live in this world without coffee," she whined in fake wretchedness. She petted her coffee cup and hissed, "My preciousssssssss."

"You're just too sad," Brian laughed and spotted Paadi emerging from the house. She wore a blanket wrapped across her, her long black hair loose. She made her way to the fire and sat in another camp chair.

"Morning, pilgrims." Her voice was rough with sleep. She fairly hummed when Brian handed her a cup of coffee. She took hers black.

"What's the plan for today?" Paadi asked, carefully sipping from her cup.

"I plan on building a storage shed. I'd like to get a lot of those supplies out of the house, give us a bit more moving around room."

"That sounds good. I was thinking about going into town for more shopping. I want to locate a couple of those yellow industrial mop buckets, the kind with squeegees, some clothesline and clothespins. I reckon it's time we started doing some laundry and a couple of buckets with squeegees should do the trick. If you can build a couple of T frames we can hang the lines on by the lake, that would help," Emma suggested.

"That's a damned good idea. I've been wearing the same clothes for a few days. Guess it's time to wash them. I do have liquid laundry detergent, but you might want to get more detergent. Extra strength," Brian chuckled and held his nose.

Emma laughed. "Goof. I definitely will."

"Yeah, we got to do it the old-fashioned way. Man, my poor hands. We can set up a dish washing station by the lake. We can find a couple of large plastic tubs for washing and rinsing, and a drying rack," Paadi piped in, smirking at Brian.

"Got it, couple of T frames and a washing station. Then can I start on the storage shed, ladies?" He eyed both women pointedly and they laughed. "My honey-do list is getting longer by the day," he grumbled good naturedly.

"At least you'll have Coop and the dogs here to help you." Emma smirked,

Brian shook his head and both women laughed. They all looked up when both dogs barked in low growls. Brian pointed. There was a man roughly three hundred yards up the beach. The interloper stood still, he had containers with him and was clearly gathering water. Brian wondered if he was the one who'd fired the weapon the other day.

Brian waved a greeting but didn't get out of his chair. The stranger lifted a hand, though cautiously, and waved. They observed the fellow for a few minutes and Brian figured the guy was trying to decide whether to come and introduce himself.

"Should we go meet him?" Emma asked.

"Naw. If he wants to be sociable he can come here. We don't want to make him nervous," Brian said quietly, his gaze not leaving the stranger.

"Buddy, come," Emma called and the dog trotted over. She placed her hand on his head and Daisy came over and sat beside Brian.

"He's coming this way. Should I go get my weapon?" Paadi questioned.

"No, I've got mine on me. I suggest you start carrying your weapon at all times from now on though. This guy might be nice, but the next one who shows up might not be and you might not have the time to go and get it," Brian said in a low tenor, observing as the fellow approached.

The man was of medium height and had brown hair and fair skin. It appeared he wasn't an outdoorsman. He had a rifle slung across his chest. Brian didn't spot a sidearm. The man had left the containers and carried nothing in his hands. He wore a solemn, if not worried expression. Brian guessed that the gentleman had run into trouble before and was cautious. Well, he should be. These days, you never knew who you were meeting.

"Hello, friend. Welcome," Brian called in a friendly voice.

"Hello. Wow, you've done a lot to this place. Nice work." The man eyed the structure and area.

"We've been hard at it," Emma said, an easy lift to her lips.

"I'm BJ and I got here a week and a half ago. I'm over at the cabins. Trying to get settled in. I have a fifth wheel, so it is pretty nice."

"Oh, great. I heard those RVs are pretty spacious and nice inside. I'm Paadi, by the way, and this is Brian and Emma. We have a boy, Cooper, he's still sleeping."

The newcomer's brows went up at her Boston accent. Brian hid a grin in his coffee cup.

"The fifth wheels are nice. My family and I used to come here camping during the summer breaks," BJ said, sadness etched into his face at the mention of his family.

"I take it you lost them?" Emma asked gently.

"Yeah, my two boys, Brody, nine, and Timothy, eight. My wife, Clair too." BJ cleared his throat several times, swallowing the grief. "I was a carpenter and assistant youth pastor and, well, I lost all our parishioners and their families. Pretty much everyone I knew, families and friends. I figured I'd make my way here, see if I survived. Cincinnati was horrible, just a nightmare." BJ shuddered, shutting his eyes briefly.

"Sounds bad. Boston was the same," Paadi said, shaking her head.

"I lived in Boston as well," said Emma. "There was a lot of gun play starting up when I left. I ran into Paadi on the road, on my way here."

"On my trip here, I was robbed four times, or rather, my supplies were confiscated. I just don't understand it. There are so few people, why would you take away someone's chance to survive?" BJ pondered, confusion on his face.

"Some crazy people out there. We ran into a man that was charging a toll just to go past him. Sadly, he was either stupid or high, but I ended up shooting him." Paadi shrugged. Brian caught the pain in Paadi's voice and suspected the incident bothered her a lot.

A spark of fear entered BJ's eyes at the news.

"She was a Boston police officer, Emma was a nurse, and I was a firefighter," Brian explained and BJ's face relaxed.

132

"I know this is presumptuous of me, but do you think I might bring my RV here? Park it over there? It would be easier getting water and I'd help you guys. You don't have to answer now. Think about it?" BJ asked, his eyes wide with hope.

Brian eyed the women and he noted their slight nods. He looked up at BJ. "We'd love to have you. You help us and we'll share what we have with you. I hope if we can defend this place, we'll be able to hold on to it. I don't know if others will come, but if they do, hopefully they'll be like us, good and hard-working people."

"Are you sure? Thank you so much! Bless you and thank you. I'll head to my camp and hook up the RV and I'll come back. It'll take me a bit, I have to load up all my supplies."

"I'm building a storage shed for a lot of our supplies," Brian said.

"Might I suggest that with some of your things, bury them? If someone comes and they take the supplies, you'll at least have some hidden," BJ suggested.

Brian stared at the women, startled. "That's a good idea, BJ. With all we have, storing them in one place would be easy pickings for bad guys. Thank you for suggesting that. Can you women get a bunch of fifty-gallon containers and more duct tape? We can dig holes, put the containers in the holes, seal them against moisture and then cover them," Brian said, rubbing his face. Why hadn't he thought of that?

"Sounds good, we'll take the trailer. I'll go get Cooper up and fix us some breakfast. Would you like to stay for some eggs and oatmeal, BJ? And a cup of coffee?" Emma asked, getting up.

"Oh, absolutely, thank you," BJ said happily, the tightness in his face vanishing.

Ж

Emma found the Walmart and pulled in, while Paadi looked around for others. Emma carried her weapon, but she depended on Paadi to guard her. She was safe with Paadi at her side. She'd be terrified alone and by herself. She thought about BJ. He had practically wept at seeing the large breakfast and coffee.

After breakfast, she and Paadi left Cooper with Brian, who'd started on the clothesline poles. The women had a long list of items to obtain. Each trip out, they tried to fill the trailer to capacity. Getting out of the truck, the women each grabbed a cart. Emma had parked the truck in front of the doors. They each had a flashlight and a headlamp, since the lights from the windows didn't penetrate very far into the store.

"I hate coming into these places. It is sooo damned quiet and it's spooky," Emma grumbled.

"Yeah, it's wicked spooky. I'm not a chicken, but I'll admit, these places make me nervous. If we hear screechy violin music, run!" Paadi chuckled, eliciting a laugh from Emma.

"It still stinks in here from all the produce rotting. What a waste of food," Emma bemoaned.

"You got that right. While we're here, I want to snag egg cartons. The eggs in them are more than likely bad, but we can use the cartons for our own eggs," Paadi suggested.

"Let's do that first. Here, I brought some Vicks VapoRub just in case we needed it. Put some under your nose. I don't think it will stink horribly, but you don't want to take a chance." Emma rubbed ointment under her nose then handed the bottle to Paadi, who did the same.

They went to the dairy cases and found the eggs. Milk cartons were bloated, some had exploded. It did stink, but not as bad as Boston had. Carefully taking the eggs out, they lined them up on the floor. They took a dozen empty egg cartons with them.

Both went to where the laundry items were located and grab packs of clothespins, clotheslines, and liquid laundry detergent. They pushed the carts to the truck and unloaded.

"This is a hell of a workout," Paadi huffed, lining the large bottles of detergent in a row. Heading in, they selected all the large plastic containers available. This would be their storage system.

"We can store our winter clothing in these and stack them up to save space. These are pretty rugged totes," Emma said, gathering the lids to the containers and stacking them inside the large containers.

"When Brian builds the storage shed, it will be nice to store a lot of the supplies in there. Storing stuff in these will keep the bugs and other yucky things out."

They confiscated more metal trash cans, and two mop buckets with wringers, then filled the totes with rolls of duct tape, taking the load to the trailer. Emma found it very satisfying to build up their reserves.

The women made their way to the baking section. Emma wanted to try and bake a cake with Brian's sun oven. Doing a box cake mix would be the least waste of materials if the project failed. They had a lot of eggs from the chickens. She was glad they'd added the egg cartons, storing them in cartons was much better and more efficient than in a bowl. She chose several glass baking pans, along with a few nonstick pans. They were strolling down the aisle, gathering packaged nuts, baking powder, baking soda, bread flour, yeast, and anything that wasn't nailed down. Out of the corner of her eye, Emma caught movement and almost screamed, slapping her hand across her mouth.

"What on Earth is the matter with you?" Paadi asked, pulling her weapon, searching. Her headlamp flashed across Emma's face and down the aisle.

"I think someone ran past us," Emma whispered, fear tight in her voice. Paadi's eyes grew large and she got in front of Emma, crouched over, her weapon pointing in different directions hunting for the threat.

"Which way?" Paadi whispered. Emma pointed and followed after Paadi, her own weapon in hand. Her finger was carefully outside the trigger guard, she didn't want to shoot Paadi. Her heart flip-flopped at the image. Paadi stepped swiftly, Emma right on her heels.

Ж

Flynn climbed the stairs, glad he had his flashlight. He'd hate to try to navigate this place without a light. The stench was so unbearable he half expected to find bodies in the stairwell. He stepped into the dark hall and searched the apartment door numbers. He found Xandra's, 312. His heart hammered hard. Was he too late? Did he wait too long? He knocked loudly, wincing at the loud sound reverberating in the hall.

"Xandra? Xandra, it's Flynn. Are you there? Are you alive?" he called, waiting, and listening.

Was that a noise? Is she there?

He banged again.

"Xandra, it's me. Please open up. Xandra, are you okay? I know I'm late in checking on you and I'm sorry. It's a long story, but please open up." Desperation laced his voice. Flynn's body quivered with fear and anticipation.

At the grating click of the deadbolt turning, he held his breath as the door cracked open. Xandra stared blankly at him. She was incredibly thin and she stank. He smelled her from three feet away. His heart broke at the pathetic human before him.

"Flynn?" Her voice croaked and she opened the door wider. Her lips were cracked from dehydration, her eyes hollow and dull.

"Xandra, are you okay? Christ, what happened?"

"I...I was afraid to leave. Is it safe to come out?" she asked. Xandra nervously peered up and down the hall. She opened wider and he stepped in, closing the door behind him.

"Kind of. If you've lived this long, I don't think you'll get the virus. I suspect we're immune. Here, I've got some food and water." He took his pack off and dug out a bottle of water. She snatched it and gulped it frantically.

He pried the bottle from her hands. "Easy, Xandra, you'll throw it up. Sip it, honey. I'm so sorry it's taken me so long to come. I've got no good excuse." He led her to her couch and sat her down.

It stank in the apartment and he gagged. The apartment smelled like an open sewer. He had to get her out of this place, and he had to get her out of Philly. He didn't think she had more than another day or two before she died of starvation and dehydration. Xandra's once dark, glossy hair was now greasy and lank. The bones of her shoulders and neck protruded. He berated himself for his cowardice. His selfishness. Flynn's eyes stung with his failures.

"Listen, Xandra, I'm leaving Philadelphia today. Now. I want you to come with me. There is a crazy guy who is running the city, but we can get out. Will you come with me? Please? We'll die here if we don't leave." He handed her a protein power bar. She tore at the paper and tried to shove it in her mouth. Flynn helped her and ensured she took small bites. His mouth trembled. She was like a starving animal and his heart broke all over again.

I've been such a damned coward.

He waited for her to eat and drink a bit more, knowing she wouldn't hear him or listen to him while she was concentrating on the food and water.

When she finished the bar, tears sheened her eyes. "I don't care where we go. Just get me out of here. I'll give you anything you want. I'll do anything you want," she croaked.

"You don't have to give me anything. I'm so sorry I didn't come sooner. You owe me nothing. Let's just leave. I'll help you pack your clothes and we'll head out." Tears were now falling down his face. She was so desperate she'd do anything. He didn't want Casper getting his hands on her. Shame filled him again and again. He burrowed in his pack and handed her another water bottle, and this time she sipped it. He pulled out a granola bar and handed it to her.

"Okay. I got a suitcase in the bedroom closet," she said weakly.

"You stay here, I'll go pack super quick. Just eat and drink." Getting up, he headed to her room. He gagged again when he went past the bathroom. The door was shut, but the stench wafted through. Going into her room, he pulled out the suitcase and then went to her dresser. Grabbing everything he laid his hands on, he stuffed all of it into the suitcase, shoving and packing more on top. They'd stop and find more clothing. He wasn't even planning on retrieving his own belongings. He'd gather food and any other supplies they needed when they escaped Philly. He just wanted her out of here.

He found her shoes and shoved them into the suitcase. He'd find toiletries and he'd find a place to bathe her. She stunk of starvation and filth. He walked into the living room; self-loathing punched him again for his cowardly actions.

"Do you have photos, pictures and such that you want to take?" he asked.

"Over there, there's an album." She pointed at a bookshelf. He nabbed the album and placed it in his haversack. Her suitcase was full.

"Okay, Xandra, we'll leave now. I'm going to warn you, there are bad people we're going to meet and I'm going to tell them I'm going to search for food and supplies and I'm coming back. But I'm not. Try not to say anything to them, don't answer any questions, okay? I can't let them know we are leaving for good, otherwise, they'll stop us," Flynn warned, wishing to prepare her.

"I'm afraid," she whimpered.

"I know, but please trust me. I'll get you to safety and I'll guarantee you have plenty of food and water."

"Okay." She latched onto his arm, her nails digging in as he led the way out of the apartment. He stalked down the dark hall, dragging the suitcase. He held the flashlight and they headed to the stairs. Her thin body vibrated violently. He didn't know if it was fear or anticipation of escaping this hellhole.

They stepped out on the street. The stairs had been painstaking. Xandra was very weak and he thought he might end up having to carry her down. He was sweating profusely, both from nerves and the heat that was trapped in the apartment building. He walked her to his car. He put her suitcase into the trunk.

"Lie down in the back seat, Xandra. Pretend you're passed out. I'll tell the roadblock that I found you and I'm hunting for more people and supplies," he told her as he helped her in.

Her eyes were dark and she appeared exhausted from their trek down to his car. He was convinced she'd be asleep within minutes.

Flynn got in and searched his surroundings. It was quiet out there. He wiped the sweat from his face. He wanted to kick himself a thousand times over. He had let her down. He'd left her to fend for herself. He would not make that mistake again. He'd guard Xandra and protect her. He'd make it up to her if it was the last thing he did.

He pulled out and drove toward the freeway. As expected, he came up to the roadblock. The two assholes who'd been there before were still there. It must be their normal post. At least this time he had a password. He did work for Casper after all.

Reducing speed, he rolled down his window, leaned his head out, and waved at the two men. He noticed they'd built up a shelter to keep out of the sun. He realized they had water and a few boxes of supplies. That was no way to live.

"Hey, guys. How's it going?" he asked in a friendly manner.

Both men eyed him suspiciously.

"What are you doing out this way?" the sentry, with the pockmarked face, Danny, he believed the name was, asked him.

"Casper sent me out to recruit and to collect supplies. He said I should get what I wanted." Flynn shrugged.

"Really?" Danny asked, clearly not believing.

"Yeah, of course. I already found a woman. She's almost dead, but I hope with some food and water, she'll live." Flynn dipped his chin to the back seat. The two men inspected the interior and Flynn rolled down the rear window. The stench rolled off Xandra, hitting both men, and they jerked back, covering their noses.

"Holy Hell! She smells like death warmed over," Danny exclaimed, covering his face with his hand.

"Hey, she's just about dead, but Casper wants me to find people. I figure she'd be extremely grateful. Besides, this is what we're supposed to be doing isn't it?" He stared each man pointedly in the eye.

"Fine. Try to clean her up before you take her to Casper. He might have a shit fit if he smells her. Damn, she stinks. What's the password?"

Flynn leaned forward and whispered, "King Casper."

The two men tipped their heads approvingly and shoved the large bar blocking the way. Flynn nodded to the men and pulled forward, driving cautiously. He waited until he was a couple of miles away. Glancing at the mirror, he pressed the accelerator, hauling ass. He drove as fast as safely possible. When his gas got low, he'd find a car and take the gas or the car. His hands shook badly, the adrenaline leaving his body. Spots danced before his eyes. He'd done it! He wasn't safe yet, but he'd gotten out of the city and he'd get far away from that madman Casper.

SEVEN

Emma's breath was coming in harsh pants. She was terrified, but they needed to find out who was in the store with them and if they were a threat. Why would they just not announce themselves? She'd only seen the motion of someone going by. Paadi's flashlight beam bounced across the aisles, skimming past products. Emma ran into Paadi when she stopped abruptly. Peeking past Paadi, she regarded two little girls, cowering in a corner.

"Oh my gosh, it's two children," Emma breathed.

"Girls, where are your parents?" Paadi asked tentatively, squatting down in front of them.

Both girls were thin and filthy. The older one appeared to be ten years old, the other about six. The older held the younger one protectively. The older girl had light brown coloring with a smattering of freckles on her cheeks. Her hair was a wild, tangled mass. The younger girl was sickly pale, translucent skin with dark hair in wild knots. Their eyes were large and fearful.

"Girls, I'm Emma and I'm a nurse. This is Paadi, she's a police officer. We won't hurt you; we want to help you," Emma said tenderly.

The older girl stared at her, then at Paadi. The girl was thinking hard and Emma held her breath hoping the girl would trust them.

"I'm Amanda. This is Lisa," the older girl answered cautiously.

"Hi, Amanda, I'm glad to meet you. You too, Lisa. Are your parents still alive, honey?" Emma asked gently.

"No, they're dead. My mom, my dad, and my brother," Amanda said. Her voice broke and tears slid down her thin cheeks.

"I'm so sorry, Amanda. Are Lisa's parents alive? Does she have any family?"

"No, but she doesn't talk either. I think something bad happened to her. I found her. I don't know her real name, I just gave her the name Lisa."

Emma's heart broke for the girls. They'd found each other and Amanda had taken the younger child into her care.

"Amanda, Paadi and I live over at Winter Park. We have a nice home, a lot of food, and we have water. We have two nice dogs that help keep us safe. We have another kid, Cooper, he's four. We have plenty of room there, and we can build you a nice room. Would you like to come live with us? We'd take good care of you and keep you safe."

Amanda seemed to think about it and Emma held her breath. She would not leave these children here to fend for themselves. They would take the children regardless of what Amanda said, it would just be easier if the two girls agreed.

"That'd be a good idea. There are some scary men and we've been hiding a long time. I got Lisa from them," Amanda whispered in confidence.

Emma's blood boiled with rage but she tamped it down. She needed to stay calm. Paadi glanced over at

Emma, her dark brown eyes seared with an inner blue flame.

A low growl emanated from the woman. "You'll be safe with us. We'll make sure no one hurts you ever again. If you help us, we're going to get cake mix and I'm going to try to make a cake. If you want, you two can choose what you like. How does that sound?" Paadi asked, a stiff smile plastered on her lips. She was trying hard not to show the rage that bubbled below the surface. Emma well understood Paadi's fury.

Both frightened girls agreed tentatively. Paadi took Lisa's fragile, dirty hand and Emma took Amanda's hand tight in her own. They didn't want the girls to change their minds and bolt.

They made their way to the cake aisle and the girls chose a chocolate cake and a strawberry cake. Emma figured they'd pick up more supplies later. For now, she wanted to get the girls home.

All four left the store and Emma helped the girls up into the truck. "How about we stop and find you two a bed to sleep in? Do you guys like chickens? We have chickens."

Lisa's eyes grew wide, and a timid smile creased her dirty face.

"I'd like a bed to sleep on," Amanda said, hopeful, holding the younger girl's hand.

"Okay. We'll head over and get you each a bed and then we'll head home. We'll introduce you to Cooper, Daisy, and Buddy. Daisy and Buddy are nice dogs. They protect us," Emma said, starting up the truck. She drove away from the store and headed to the mattress store, her mind reeling from what Amanda had told her and Paadi. She'd tell Brian about the men. It was disturbing. Paadi would undoubtedly shoot them on sight. Emma's face pulsed with rage. She wanted to kill those men herself. How could they do that to a child? Her eyes prickled with tears, and she tamped down on the sorrow. The girls needed a strong woman, not a weeping one.

She pulled into the mattress store and she and Paadi got out.

"Did you girls want to come in to choose?" Paadi asked. At their nods, Paadi opened the door and helped the girls out. They'd need to get clothing for the girls, a lot of clothing. A task for another day. She or Paadi would head out and find some. Her biggest priority was to get these girls home and safe.

Half an hour later, the girls were *helping* with the mattresses, box springs, and bed frames. They put the new beds into the trailer. It was a tight fit and they had to rearrange some of the supplies. They swung the doors and shut them tight.

"Well, well, what we got here?" a man said, his voice mocking. Emma and Paadi whirled. Paadi's weapon was out and pointed at the stranger.

"Whoa, whoa! We mean no harm, ladies." He was dressed in a torn T-shirt, filthy jeans, and unlaced boots. He had dirty blond hair and a large gap in his front teeth. His face was covered with freckles. The other man was thin, with dark brown hair and rat-like eyes that were beady and constantly moving. He stood behind the blond man.

Emma drew her weapon and glanced down when Lisa whimpered. She noticed the little girl wet herself. Paadi saw it and her eyes blazed.

"Are these the men who hurt you?" Emma asked Lisa gently.

"They are," Amanda said in a dead voice.

Before Emma could respond four shots rang out. Her gaze flew to the men and then to Paadi, who'd just shot both men. Emma gaped in shock and stared at Paadi, who walked over to the downed men. She stood over them and Emma pulled both girls to her, holding them tight.

"You fuckers are done," Paadi hissed in a low voice and spat on each man. Both men still jerked and twitched, but that was just the brain dying. After a minute, neither man stirred.

Paadi turned to the girls. "Those bastards won't ever hurt you again. You never have to worry that they'll find you. You understand, Lisa? You never have to worry again. Auntie Paadi took 'em out. You're safe now, honey," Paadi said lovingly, caressing the child's tangled hair.

"My name's Hailey, not Lisa," Hailey said in a tiny voice.

Paadi lifted the little girl and hugged her tightly to her. Her brown eyes filled with tears and she rocked the girl in her arms. Emma searched Amanda's face and realized the girl was crying, but smiling.

"Let's go home, girls." Emma hugged Amanda and helped her into the truck. It had happened so fast, but she was glad that Paadi had killed those bastards. She didn't know if it was good that the children witnessed the killing, but the girls knew at least that they'd never have to worry about those men again. Hailey's speaking proved that it was maybe a good thing.

Ж

Brian stood to admire his work, wiping the sweat from his face. He planted the two poles two feet in depth. After applying braces, he'd used a bag of Quikrete and filled the holes. The concrete should set up quickly.

Not bad if I do say so myself, and I do.

He glanced up at the growl of a truck engine and figured it was BJ moving his RV. The dogs and Cooper were by the chicken coop and Cooper ran over to stand with Brian.

Brian was impressed. BJ handled the massive fifth wheel expertly and backed it over to where he'd indicated earlier that morning. It was a nice-looking camper. They would have to set up some kind of miniature wood stove in the thing. That would be tricky to do and not burn the thing down. He'd have to talk to BJ about that, but they'd figure it out later.

When he'd first arrived, Brian doubted how he'd get everything done that needed getting done by himself. It wouldn't have been that big of a problem, but he had Cooper to care for and think about. There was no screwing this up, the child's very life depended on him. Then, Emma and Paadi came. Two more helping hands and two more defenders of their home. It was nice having other adults. He no longer felt the overwhelming panicked sensation which clung to him daily.

Now they had BJ, who seemed to be a good guy. Brian considered himself a pretty good judge of character, and so were Emma and Paadi. They'd each agreed, and Brian suspected that if Paadi didn't agree, they'd know about it pretty quickly. He chuckled. Paadi's accent cracked him up. It was a pleasure listening to her talk.

He walked over to the large RV, Cooper in his arms.

BJ jumped out of the truck. "Check this." He pushed a button. The RV extended arms from below and the camper righted itself.

"Self-leveling," BJ explained. "The RV has three bump outs." He pushed another button and the sides of the RV expanded outward.

"Wow. Nice, man, awfully nice. You mind if I come in and take a gander?" Brian put Cooper down and the boy jumped up and down in excitement, his mouth open in awe.

"Oh cool!" Cooper cried excitedly, hopping up and down beside Brian like a flea.

"You betcha. Let me give you the nickel tour." BJ laughed and ruffled Cooper's thatch of blond hair.

Brian lifted Cooper up and stepped into the RV. He was surprised at how spacious it was. Though the space was packed with supplies, Brian realized it was a very nice space indeed. At one end, there was a leather couch, bags and boxes stacked neatly on the three leather cushions. Beside the couch were two reclining chairs. Across from the chairs was a mounted flat screen

TV and below, an electric fireplace. Beside the reclining chairs was a kitchen table with two chairs. They were wooden and well made. There was a center island with a double sink. The countertop was Corian, a speckled cream color.

The kitchen was condensed but neat, with plenty of cabinets and a pantry. Opening them up, he saw they were well stocked and neat. The kitchen had a gas stovetop, and microwave but no oven.

"Wow, I've never been inside one of these. This is nice, BJ," Brian said. He was impressed.

"It's only about three years old, so it's still shiny. I have solar panels so I can still watch TV, use the fireplace. I've got quite a few propane tanks for the hot water heater and stove. The propane tanks were taken at my last toll booth, so I had to scavenge more. I have some in the storage under the RV and in the bed of the truck. I've got enough for now, but I'm thinking I should get more."

"I've got a few propane tanks. I was considering a plan to build a shed away from the house, in the woods, to store them. I don't like having the propane too near," Brian said.

"That's a good idea. No need for something to explode. Hell, that would set off a chain reaction. I can help build the shed. I'm pretty good with a hammer."

"That's great, BJ. I just put poles for a clothesline, and the women are grabbing buckets to do the wash."

"Let me show you something." BJ walked to the other end of the RV. Sliding open a door, he stepped aside, allowing Brian to check it out.

"Wow, nice bathroom." Brian took in the large shower, which held supplies stacked inside, a toilet, and vanity. It looked like a normal bathroom. Then BJ opened another door and inside were two sets of bunkbeds. They were crammed with more supplies, boxed food, toilet paper, and canned foods.

"This is where the boys slept. Past this is the master bedroom," BJ said.

Brian hadn't missed the sadness in BJ's voice at the mention of his sons. He was impressed with the spacious bedroom. The room boasted a queen-sized bed with nightstands on each side. There was a closet with sliding mirror doors and a highboy chest of drawers. BJ went over to the closet and slid the door open. Inside was a diminutive washing machine.

"Holy crap, does that washing machine work?" Brian asked, amazed.

"Oh yeah, it does. I can only use it on sunny days, but I imagine this will handle our laundry problem. If not all of it, perhaps most of it. Now that I have access to all that water in the lake, I can use the RV's pump. I have a couple of hoses that I can run to the lake. It will be a hell of a lot easier now. If you want, you all can use the shower if you'd like. Especially if I can get more propane tanks. I scavenged spare parts and filters for my systems over at Keystone RV in Greencastle on my way here. I should be good to go for years," said BJ.

"How will you dump the black water?" Brian asked.

"That's why I parked way over here. I was thinking about digging a deep trench. Perhaps I can get some

152

PVC pipes and run it out and down away from the RV. I can dig something like a leach field since it will only be me using the toilet. I'd keep it well away from the water source."

"That sounds like a good idea. I've got shovels, plenty of PVC piping, elbows, and Rectorseal. I was planning on setting up a bathtub in one of the toilet stalls in the house. We have four stalls with commodes, and I figured I'd rig something up with a bathtub. I found an acrylic slipper tub at Lowe's. We can go later today and carry it out of there. This place has a septic system in it."

The men left the RV. Brian set Cooper down and he ran off to play.

"That's great. Man, you're way ahead of the game," BJ said.

"I've been going crazy, trying to think of everything we might need. I knew plumbing and building was in my future here. So I hauled as much as I dared, every time I stopped at Lowe's or other hardware stores. I have a solar system too, I just need to figure out how to set it up," Brian said, leading BJ to the house, where much of the supplies were kept.

"I can help you with that. I hooked mine up. My wife Clair wanted power at all times," BJ said, though he choked a bit on his wife's name.

"I understand, BJ. I lost my wife Christa as well," he said, faltering.

BJ cleared his throat and wiped his eyes. "Thanks. It's still hard. All of it still so damned fresh. Anyway, if you want, after the sheds and the leach field, we can build a platform and see if we can't make it rotate, to catch the sun. Put the solar panels on it and build a housing shed for the equipment. Easy peasy."

BJ laughed and Brian started chuckling. The list just kept getting longer and longer, but he had someone here to help him with it, lightening his burden a little.

"We'll need to grab some insulation, to insulate the underneath of your RV. We want to ensure nothing freezes this winter. We can pick some up when we get the tub," Brian suggested.

"Good idea. Otherwise, it would kinda be useless, at least for the winter," BJ agreed.

The men walked to the house, Brian keeping an eye on the busy Cooper, who was now down by the water. The child tired him out. He hadn't dealt with many children. The boy had boundless energy and he was getting used to being *Daddy* to him. The notion elicited a long, happy exhalation.

"Coop, stay where I can see you. Don't go in that water," Brian called from the double doors at the house.

"Okay, Daddy," Cooper called out.

Daisy was running up and down the beach and Coop chased after her. Going into the house, Brian grabbed a couple of shovels.

"Let's get a trench dug," he said.

He and BJ took shovels over to the RV. Cooper came running.

"Can I help, Daddy?" Cooper chirped.

"You betcha you can, buddy. Go get a shovel in the house. Thanks, Tiger," Brian said, winking at BJ.

"You're lucky to have him," BJ said when Cooper was out of earshot. "I imagine he is very lucky to have you too."

"I have to say, he saved my life. He's a sweet child. I'm proud to call him my own. I hope I can protect him."

"I believe with all of us, we can raise this child to be a healthy and happy young man. My god, I am horrified to think about all those lost children out there. My heart breaks. I lost mine, but you found yours. I thought God hated me when he took away my family. But seeing Cooper, I suspect God took my family to His home in heaven, but blessed you with a child who needed you." BJ's voice was thick with emotion. He wiped his tears and cleared his throat as Cooper came up carrying a shovel twice as tall as him.

"I think we're all blessed to have found each other here, BJ," Brian said. He bent down and kissed the crown of Cooper's golden head. All three shoveled, Cooper simply moving the dirt in tiny piles. They made rapid progress as the sun rose higher.

Ж

Flynn pressed the accelerator and his eyes kept darting to the rearview mirror. His heart was racing and his mouth was dry. Tears of joy, fear, and triumph slid down his face. He'd need to get off the main roads and find his way on secondary roads. His old friend Cramer would surely be sad and disappointed at his departure, but he was certain the new Casper would be enraged. He didn't know what that madman would do and he'd be damned if he wished to find out.

After twenty minutes of going eighty, he sighted a billboard ahead. T.H. Smithwell's Gun Shop and Gun Club. Warily, Flynn took the exit. That was his first priority, getting weapons and killing anyone who got in his way. For too long, he'd been a coward, too passive. He'd hidden in his apartment in terror while the world burned. Xandra paid for his cowardice, damned near with her life. He was better than that. He hoped.

It took a bit of searching up and down streets, but he finally found the gun shop. He scanned the location cautiously, seeing no one. There were no vehicles parked at the store, nor along the shops that lined the street. There were a few stores, it was kind of like a strip mall. There was a Payless Shoes, Hobby Lobby, CVS, QuickClips, Clothes for Less, and a humble food court. He'd hit up the shoes, clothes, and CVS, sure he'd find what he needed in those stores.

He got out and peeked in the back seat. Xandra was sound asleep, low snores emitting from her slackened mouth. He ran up to the gun shop. The door was locked. He hurried back to the car. In the trunk, he found the jack and tire iron, using them to break the glass door of the gun shop. When he stepped in, his heart burst with joy. Guns and weapons of all kinds. Running up to the case, he found an AR-15. He and Roger had watched videos on how to safely operate and maintain the weapon. Roger threatened to get one, but he'd never done it. Flynn examined the weapon and then ejected the magazine. He located ammo and quickly loaded the rounds into the magazine. He found more mags and ran back to the car.

Xandra was still asleep, so he retrieved his pack. Running into the store, he loaded the knapsack with mags and boxes of ammo. He then chose a Ruger LC9S and several boxes of shells for it. He found a shoulder holster for the small gun, loaded it, and then secured it away. Last, he chose a Ruger mini-14 Ranch. He selected a couple of gun cleaning kits and several knives. His heart was racing. He didn't want anyone to stop him. He knew he needed to be armed but he didn't want to kill anyone. Not if he didn't have to. Wanting to protect himself was one thing, actually killing someone was something else.

Leaving the store, he put the weapons, except for the handgun, into the trunk, then walked over to Payless. That door was unlocked, and he opened it. He immediately smelled decay. Determined not to be deterred, he got a bag and kept his eyes solely on the shoes. He chose heavy wool socks and white athletic socks. He then went to his size section and grabbed a pair of boots, running shoes, and leather sandals. For now, those would have to suffice. He didn't want to stay long and ran out of the store.

He checked once more on Xandra. Getting into the car, he drove down to the next store. At the entrance, he grabbed several bags. The store might not have winter gear out, but he'd settle for a few pairs of jeans and some shirts. Making his way through the store, he found the men's department. He quickly grabbed five pairs of denim jeans, a few packs of underwear, more socks, T-shirts, and six button-down shirts. The clothing wasn't high quality, but right now, he wasn't choosy. The whole of his possessions were worthless if he remained in Philly with Casper. He was overjoyed to finally escape.

Arriving at the car, he realized Xandra was sitting up, confused. It wasn't a lot, but she appeared better.

"Hey, how do you feel?" he asked.

"Hungry and thirsty," she croaked, rubbing her eyes with grimy hands.

"Let's go to CVS. I have a feeling we can find plenty of water and some food there. We can get soap, toothpaste, toothbrushes, and shampoo. Oh, and some TP. Are you up to it?"

He drove to the CVS. He helped her out of the car and they walked to the store. It was locked.

"Hold on, let me get my tire iron."

"We won't get in trouble? I don't want to go to jail." Her brow was knotted in worry.

"There's no one. No police, no more anyone. We'll be okay and we can load up on supplies. I want to find us a place to lay low for a day or two so you can get your strength up. If I can find a place with a pool, you and me can get cleaned up. I haven't taken a bath in weeks."

Flynn tapped the glass and it shattered. He carefully guided Xandra into the store. It was dark inside and he took his flashlight from his pocket. He noticed tiny LED flashlights at the register. It was bright. He grabbed a plastic bag and threw a handful of flashlights into the bag. They'd be useful. He figured he'd get different sized batteries. He found bottled water and took his new knife out and cut the plastic. He handed Xandra a bottle and took one for himself. Both stood quietly, drinking the water. Xandra grabbed another and drank.

"I want to apologize again for not coming sooner. I'm really sorry, Xandra. I was so afraid, and I was such a coward," he said, shame-faced.

"Flynn, we'd just started dating. We didn't and don't know each other that well. I never expected it. I did expect the National Guard or the police to help though," she whispered, sounding coherent for the first time.

"They aren't around. I guess the Vermilion Strain got everyone. I reckon it was worse than anyone thought. Here, eat some of this dark chocolate. That might also help. There's some canned fruit over there. We can load up on crackers and canned meats. I'll get a couple of can openers. Oh, and some soups. If we can find a good place to hole up, I can make a fire and we can heat some of this stuff up."

Xandra tore at the candy wrapper and took a bite. Her gray eyes closed in bliss. Flynn found some cloth shopping bags and stuffed them. He went in and out of the store, shoving as much as would fit into the trunk and then the rear seat. He carried several bags out to the car. He might have to find a truck, something bigger to haul the supplies. The car was getting full. He hated to leave without taking everything, but he'd just have to find another store with a bigger vehicle. Hopefully, one full of gas.

He walked over to the drug and medical aisle. He filled a cloth bag with bandages, alcohol, hydrogen peroxide, aspirin, triple antibiotic ointments, and a couple bottles of Pedialyte. Xandra might wish to drink that since she lost so much fluids. He selected vitamins and supplements for them both. Stopping by the refrigerated section, he took juices and soft drinks. His hand hovered over the beer, but he stopped himself. He needed to be clear headed, especially if Casper followed him. No, he needed to be clear headed for Xandra. To keep her safe.

He handed her one of the bottles of Pedialyte.

"Drink this, it should help. I got some supplements to help you. Let's get out of here, I don't want to be out in the open," he said nervously.

"Why, what's the matter? I thought you said no one is alive." Fear now clouded her face.

"Remember I said we were getting out of Philly? Well, there might be a few people that might not like it. That was why I was leaving. We should be safe. I'm going to take the secondary roads to Amish country," he said, helping her into the front passenger seat.

Xandra stared at him in confusion. "We're going to Amish country?"

"Listen, there isn't any more food coming our way. No more deliveries. Whatever supplies we gather will eventually run out. I don't know how to farm, do you?"

"No, I've no clue."

"I'm hoping that if we go to the Amish that they will take us in. If they do, we can learn how to farm, grow things. We can survive. They've been living like that for hundreds of years. Other than the virus killing everyone, they probably won't notice the lack of people and electricity. Our best bet is the Amish. Unless you know of a place to go?" Flynn eyed her hopefully.

Shaking her head, Xandra scanned the area. "No, you're right. We need to find a place that can help us survive. I never even thought of that. I guess I was so afraid to leave my apartment, I didn't think about the aftermath. Do you think the Amish will take us in? They are a closed society."

"I honestly don't know, but I have to try. I don't know how to hunt, fish, or farm. I feel useless," Flynn said despondently.

Her hand covered his. "You came and you saved me. You're not useless. We'll figure this out together. Let's find a place, like you said, to lay low. Let me regain some of my strength and together, we can figure this out." She tilted her head and smiled at him.

Unable to speak, he drove away from the strip mall. He handed her a map and let her navigate.

"Just keep us off the highway and stick to secondary roads. Keep an eye out for a house with a truck. I'd like to trade up. Something with a crew cab. We can pile a lot of supplies into it," he said, checking each house as they passed. There was no activity. No movement. It was just after one, and his stomach growled.

"Hey, there's a couple of trucks in that driveway. Should we see if anyone is home?" Xandra pointed off to the left.

"Yeah, but you stay in the car. I don't know if it's safe or not." Flynn checked the windows. He detected no activity. He parked his car on the street. It was a residential area. The lots were huge, an acre or better. There were plenty of trees, a nice family kind of place. He saw a child's bike laying in the overgrown grass, the colorful fringed tassels on the handlebars rustling in the wind. It saddened him. The kid was more than likely dead.

He walked up the sidewalk that led to the front door and knocked loudly. He was trembling. It was scary, not knowing if someone was behind the door with a shotgun ready to blow his head off. He wiped his damp hands on his pants and knocked again.

"Hello? Anyone home? We want to stay here for a day. If someone is alive inside, let me know. I don't want to intrude on you. I don't want to disturb you. I'm going to open the door. Please don't shoot me. I don't want to rob you or anything!" he yelled. He glanced at Xandra and she shrugged.

Flynn gripped the doorknob and twisted. It was unlocked. The scent of decay was prevalent, but it was old.

"Hello?" He scanned the dim interior. He saw the kitchen, and it had large sliding glass doors which led out to the backyard.

"Hello? Anyone here? I'm not going to hurt you. I'll go away if you tell me to," he called a second time. He stepped further into the house. He went in and searched one of the bedrooms. There was a lump in a twin bed, and he leaned in and closed the door quietly.

It must be the child, the one who'd left the bike in the yard. He went to what he suspected was the master suite and peeked in. Two lumps were covered and he shut that door. He walked through the house opening windows, letting in fresh air. The house was hot.

He went back to the car, his head hanging. "They're dead, but the house doesn't smell too bad. I opened the windows. Let's take some food and stuff into the house. They have a backyard too. I'll check both of the trucks and see how full the tanks are. We can transfer the supplies to them if they have plenty of gas."

"Okay. I'm tired, so after we eat, I might bathe and then take a nap. Sorry I'm such a wimp." Xandra smiled wanly.

"Hey, you're a champ in my book. I'll get your suitcase so you can have some fresh clothes." Flynn went to the rear of the car, pulled her suitcase out, and retrieved one of the bags of new clothing for himself. A bath sounded great. Hopefully, the house had some bottled water so they wouldn't have to use their supply. They went into the house to the kitchen.

"Oh man, they have a pool out back," Xandra said. Flynn came up behind her. The water appeared relatively clean. It was just starting to get a bit of algae at the edges of the pool in the shady area.

"Why don't we use the pool as a bath?" Flynn suggested. "You can go first, and I'll see what I can fix us to eat. They have a gas stove, so I can at least heat us up some soup or something."

"Oh, that sounds like heaven. I'm going to their bathroom, see if they have towels. Thanks again, Flynn,

I mean that." She squeezed his arm and then disappeared into the rear of the house.

Xandra was trembling as she walked toward the bathroom. She was so weak but pushed past it. She was slightly nauseated from the chocolate. When she got to the bathroom, she vomited. She sipped from her Pedialyte bottle and it cooled the burning from her throat. She hoped it would help ease the nausea. She'd need to take it easy with food for a while, until her system regulated and adjusted to normal.

It all happened so fast; Flynn showing up, and then leaving the city and being away from her home. At first, she thought she was hallucinating when he knocked. Then he was there. It was all unfathomable and incomprehensible, but she was profoundly grateful he'd come to get her. She'd been so terrified. The world was so different, so empty and quiet. She grabbed a couple towels and went back to the kitchen.

Flynn was taking out pots and bowls from the kitchen cabinets. She stepped to a cupboard and retrieved a plastic cup, then went out to the pool.

Stripping down, she went to the shallow end of the pool. The water was cool, but not cold. Xandra noted Flynn had set out bottles of shampoo, conditioner, and a bar of soap. She submerged herself and let the water support her body. She was thin, too thin, and her ribs and hip bones were prominent. It was frightening to see herself like this, so god-awfully thin. The cloud which fogged her brain was beginning to clear. She now realized that she'd been near death. Had Flynn not arrived, she knew she'd have died.

Warm, salty tears slid down her face. She'd been so close to death. She cleared her throat. Her fear had damned near killed her. She'd been a fool. She should have left her apartment. There was no help for it, but she'd never be that foolish again. Flynn had given her a second chance at life. She was going to live it and survive. She promised herself she would not be that weak woman that Flynn found. She'd step out and beyond herself. She'd fight for every day. Live every day with purpose.

Xandra rubbed the shampoo through her matted hair, shivering in revulsion at her condition. She'd never been this dirty in her life. She was lucky and she knew it. She was safe now. She poured cups of the water and scented the chlorine. She didn't care, she just wanted to be clean.

EIGHT

Brian and BJ sat at the firepit. Brian had fixed a large pot of ramen, cracked a couple of eggs into it, cooking the eggs into the noodles. The chickens were one hell of an asset. They now had a surplus of eggs. He'd started dating and coating the eggs in a light film of food grade mineral oil. They remade one of the offices into a massive pantry, storing their foodstuffs there. The office was located on the north side of the building with the most shade, leaving the room constantly cool. The rest of the food was stacked in the building. He truly did need to get that storage shed build. The racks he'd picked up at the hardware store helped a great deal to keep their supplies sorted and neat, at least to some extent.

He and BJ drank soft drinks cooled in the pillowcase at the water's edge. Cooper had eaten earlier and was now taking a nap, though he hadn't been happy about it. The trench was dug and Brian and BJ connected thirty feet of PVC pipe, set at a downward slope, away from the RV. Later, they would get gravel and pea gravel, along with the bathtub and insulation.

"I figure if we get some rigid insulation to place over the pipe, it should keep it from freezing," Brian speculated.

The trench was a little over three feet deep and would be below the frost line. The rigid insulation would aid in preventing the sewage pipe freezing.

Brian spun when the growl of a truck engine drifted to him. He figured Emma and Paadi were home with a weighty load, since the vehicle was traveling controlled. He stood and walked to the truck. He quickened his pace when he noticed Emma's expression and then Paadi's face. The women were pale, their faces grim.

"BJ, get over here. Something's happened," Brian called.

Emma and Paadi jumped out of the truck and went to open the rear passenger doors. Paadi brought a little girl out, the child clinging to Paadi like a capuchin monkey. Emma held the hand of an older child, who appeared thin and frightened.

He smiled kindly at the children. "I see our family has increased. Where did you find these girls?" Brian said mildly, keeping his tone even.

"Over at the Walmart. I'll tell you about it later. We want to get these girls cleaned up and I want to check them out medically," Emma said, her eyes, going over to the little girl Paadi was holding.

A chill ran through Brian and his heart shattered for the little girl. Christ, what had this horrible world come to? Evil men definitely abounded.

"Okay. I have some noodle soup, would you like to have them eat after you clean them up? There's plenty of new clothing of different sizes, Cooper's clothes, but I suspect that you can find something for the girls," Brian offered.

"Thanks, Brian," said Emma. "This is Amanda and that is Hailey. Girls, this is Brian and that is BJ. Cooper napping, I'm guessing?"

"Hi, girls, welcome to our home. You'll be safe here. Coop is asleep, but he'll be excited to meet our two new friends," said Brian.

Amanda waved a little, shy and a little frightened. Brian knew it would take time for them to get used to all the new people, especially men, apparently.

"While you two do that, we'll unload the trailer and truck," Brian said. "Then BJ and I are going to head out and pick up more items at the hardware stores. How is the gas?"

"We used one of the cans and the tank is three-quarters full. You should be good to go." Paadi was swaying with the child still in her arms. The little girl was staring at Brian and BJ.

Brian smiled at the child then eyed BJ. "Let's get the stuff unloaded from the trailer and head out."

"Sounds good to me," BJ agreed. "Emma, Paadi, I'm glad you found these girls and I'm glad they're here. Two more babies safe. It never occurred to me about children left behind. I know I said it before, it just boggles my mind." BJ went to the trailer and opened it, sadness etched on his face.

"We'll take these beds inside and set them up for the girls. That way, if they need to take a nap, they can," BJ called from the trailer.

"Should I swing by while we're out and gather clothing for the girls?" Brian asked. "Some girly sheets?"

Emma squeezed his arm. "Yes, thank you so much, Brian. These girls have been through hell. I'd like to go slow and make their life a little easier."

Brian smiled. "No worries, Emma. I imagine these girls need a little TLC. BJ and I will take care of this."

Brian went to the trailer and helped BJ with the unloading. It didn't take long, and he and BJ transferred the contents to the house. With quick efficiency, they set up the beds. He'd have to pick up more lumber and build the girls a room. The house was beginning to become jam-packed. He laughed to himself. Three children and three adults. He didn't mind, helping these children was a privilege. To keep them safe, there was nothing better to do with his life, and Christa would be proud of him.

Twenty minutes later, BJ and Brian left the park and drove to Lowe's.

When they arrived, Brian grabbed a large cart. "Let's get the tub, more lumber, and the insulation. I've got to build those girls a room."

"Let's choose happy paint colors. They have samples we can use, and they're already mixed up. Coop will like it also," BJ suggested.

"That's a great idea. Thank God we don't have to pay for all of this. Then let's head to the insulation. I want to select LED lighting too, so once we get the solar panels set up we'll have light and a solar fridge. Might as well get everything we can."

"Cool beans. Things are coming together." BJ rubbed his hands together in anticipation.

They went about gathering supplies. Brian's mind kept going over and over all the lists. It was endless. Perhaps he and BJ should begin to tap abandoned cars' gas tanks. He only had a few full five-gallon cans left.

With the garden doing well, the fruit trees thriving, things were going well. The plastic containers would help secure their supplies, buried and safe, should bad guys come by. Bad guys were out there, and rage roiled over Brian at little Hailey's situation. He blew out a breath, he didn't need his blood pressure spiking. He'd protect these children from harm or die trying.

Ж

Emma carried the metal pail filled with hot water. They were using one of the fifty-gallon containers as a bathtub. It was set by the lake, where they'd add colder water. Amanda took the first bath and now Hailey was taking hers. They dumped the used water into the sand on the beach. Amanda was playing with Cooper and the two dogs. Emma had examined both girls. They both were malnourished, thin, and slightly dehydrated, which was an easy fix. Hailey had bruising, but as far as Emma's skill indicated, the girl only had the bruising, nothing more. She'd been thankful for it. It appeared Amanda rescued the child before irreversible grievous bodily harm was done. She didn't know what the men had done, but it might have been a hell of a lot worse.

Cooper graciously gave a couple of his toys to Hailey for bath time. Emma washed the child's hair and Paadi rinsed it. The mouth-watering scent of chocolate cake wafted over.

"I smell cake!" Hailey shrieked as she wiped water from her eyes.

"Yep, the cake should be done in about ten minutes. We'll let it cool and then I'll put icing on it," Emma said.

"YUMMM! I like chocolate cake!" Hailey cried happily. Emma looked over at Paadi and smirked.

"I believe she'll be okay, thank God," Paadi said solemnly.

"I hope so. Okay, young lady, let's get you rinsed off, dressed, and you can go play with Amanda and Cooper." Emma mixed hot water in with cold and then poured the warm water over the child. Hailey squealed and danced in the container. Paadi stepped forward with a large towel and engulfed the girl. Hailey clung to Paadi and twisted her arms about Paadi's neck. Paadi carried Hailey to the house and Emma dumped the water into the sand. It was a good substitute tub and she looked forward to the bathtub Brian was picking up. It would be nice to sit and soak from time to time.

Emma walked over to the sun oven. She had mittens to pull the glass pan out. Brian had made a table and had set up the sun oven. It was big enough to prepare meals. He was such a handyman. She and Paadi had strung up the clothes lines and hung the freshly washed clothes. The girls didn't have much and Emma wanted to try the yellow buckets. They worked perfectly. The girls' clothing was blowing in the breeze. Not bad at all.

She took the cake pan off the sun oven, using her fingertip to check the bounce of the top of the cake. It seemed cooked. She took a knife and slid it into the middle of the cake, then pulled it out. Clean. The cake was good to go. She shut down the sun oven carefully, the heat coming off of it was impressive. It amazed her. They had no power, but they possessed the ability to bake or cook on sunny days. She grunted. It was pretty damned cool.

Hailey ran past and joined the other children. They ran up and down the beach, the dogs chasing them and barking.

"You think I shouldn't have shot those assholes?" Paadi asked, stepping beside her to watch the children playing.

"You did just right. I'm guessing Hailey escaped worse by the grace of God. Amanda saved her, there is no doubt, but those men did *something* to her. Had they held onto her, they would have hurt her, with no equivocation. No, Paadi. They were animals and shouldn't live. You did the world a favor," Emma said darkly, brushing the hair from her face. "I'm only sorry you didn't make them die at an extremely leisurely pace. I expect Hailey will heal, but she'll never be who she was meant to be with all of this happening. None of the children will. Their young lives have been changed. All we can do is help them through this new world. Make them stronger and more resilient." Emma held a hand up across her eyes, checking the kids. She looked up at the sky and noted the gathering clouds. "It's gonna rain. Should we leave the clothes on the line?"

Paadi eyed the sky. "Might as well. At least we don't have to water the garden, and we got the cake baked. I'll take it in. We can make a nice dinner and then have an awesome dessert."

"Damn, it's been a long time since I've had cake. It might not be homemade, but it is a cake all the same," Emma said.

172

"It's been a long time since I've been with family. I reckon our family is pretty nice," Paadi said gently, her large brown eyes bright with tears.

Emma hugged her friend. Paadi might sound rough or gruff at times, but she had the biggest heart.

The first drop hit her face and she grabbed the cake. "Okay, kids, time to go in! Let's go!" Emma shouted.

"You sound like a mom," Paadi laughed, encircling Emma with her arm. The women headed to the house, the kids running to meet them. The dogs followed close behind. Emma hummed contentedly, glancing behind at her children, for they had become hers.

Ж

Flynn and Xandra made their bed by the large sliding glass door to the outside. The screen had been pulled shut to keep the bugs out. It was early evening and she was tired. She and Flynn had bathed in the pool, and it felt wonderful to be clean. Xandra was feeling almost human again. Unquestioningly, if Flynn hadn't come, she'd have been dead in two days. She had been on the verge. She'd been paralyzed with terror at the idea of going outside. From her apartment window, she saw the growing heaps of dead in the streets spread. Vans stopped from time to time and dumped the bodies like trash, then sped away.

She had seen no police to stop them. Then the dogs came, fighting and dragging the bodies. It was all so obscene to her. Her brain shut it out and she stopped going to the window. The stench in the building oozed its way into her apartment like a deadly and invisible fog. Thousands of flies droned, their buzzing unrelenting. She put cotton in her ears, but she still heard it, just outside her door and outside her windows.

Xandra sipped the Pedialyte. It was helping, she noticed. Flynn made chicken soup from a can and she'd nibbled on crackers. Her stomach was beginning to accept the food. She'd vomited her earlier meal. After drinking the Pedialyte, it seemed to help and she kept the soup down. She was stuffed, for the first time in weeks. She lost track of time. It all seemed like a distant nightmare now. The death count on TV; the videos of pyres built from the dead stacked up high as other countries tried to get a handle on the growing number of dead. When the banners came up and people stopped talking, it was the beginning of the end.

When she tried to call her family, no one answered, nor did any of her friends. Then the phone service went out, followed by the power. First her food ran out, then her water. She'd managed to get water from the rain, but it had let flies into her home. She'd spent hours chasing them and killing them, the sound of the buzzing driving her crazy.

"You okay, Xandra?" Flynn raised on his elbow, peering at her in the semi-darkness.

Xandra let out a long, shaky breath. She was hyperventilating. "Yeah, I was just thinking about being trapped in my apartment. It was a nightmare, a horrible nightmare."

"You're safe now. I'll do everything I can to keep you that way," he said, and gathered her in his arms.

She laid her head on his shoulder and stared into the night sky. It was weird to be in someone else's home while they lay rotting in their beds, but this was a new and different world. Nothing in her life had prepared her for this. Nothing. Even the movies she'd seen were nothing like this reality. She shuddered and Flynn held her tighter. He was a good man. She had been on the fence about dating him after the first couple of dates. He seemed slightly immature, though they were the same age. He was sweet and seemed to like her.

When he had come to her, she'd been so grateful she would have sold her soul to him. He was a valiant, stand-up guy and had not taken advantage of it. He helped her and took care of her and guarded her when she was unable to do it herself. He didn't have to come for her, after all, they hadn't known each other well. But he did come and she was grateful. She guessed they'd both grown up.

"Did either of the trucks work?" she asked after a long moment of silence.

"Yeah, they both did. The one truck had well over half a tank. I found two gas cans in the garage. A five-gallon can and a two-gallon one. Both are full, so we can take those with us. In a couple of days, I'll repack the truck and take some of the stuff from here. Pillows, blankets, towels and so on. A couple of pots and pans, along with cooking gear. That way, we don't have to eat our food cold. These people had a couple of cases of water in the garage too."

"It's sad, but I'm glad we stopped here. It is amazing how much better you feel when you're clean," she murmured.

"Hell yeah. Damn, it was like I had a coating of grease and dirt on me."

"I hope we can find a place to stay. I hope we can learn how to survive. I don't want to feel that helpless again." Xandra wiped the tear sliding down the side of her face.

"Me too, Xandra, me too. I promise I'll do my best to help us survive. No matter what."

Ж

Casper paced in front of Franklin Institute Science Museum. Tilting his head, he caught the distant howling of wolves. He'd seen them over in Logan Square some days ago. Flynn hadn't returned and it was nearing midnight. He stomped the sidewalk, agitated and angry. The brothers loomed in the shadows, watching him. They were his ever-faithful companions, unlike Flynn, who'd been his best friend in the *before*, and now was no longer by his side. The bastard had abandoned him and left the city. Casper thought Flynn had given up the desire to leave; he'd been wrong. He wanted to kill him now. Tear him apart for the betrayal. Yet Casper had no idea where his friend had gone. It was a wide-open world out there.

He wouldn't waste his energies searching for the little coward. He had to stay here, in the center of his universe, else it would spin out of control. If he ever found Flynn again, he'd kill the man. He spun and stomped inside. He'd waste no more energy on Flynn. The brothers followed behind as the wolves lamented the night.

Ж

BJ held the plywood in place while Brian tightened the galvanized screw in. Brian had let his batteries charge in BJ's trailer. They had plenty of juice, for now. The storage shed was nearly complete. He and Brian decided on house wrap, pine tongue-and-groove planks to side the sheds. That would give the structure longevity and blend into the camp's surroundings. They would work on the solar panels later today.

They put the bathtub into the fourth stall in the bathroom. It had taken some doing, but they removed the toilet and used several sizes of PVC pipe and lowered the slipper bathtub over the toilet hole. After several buckets of water, the bathtub was deemed useable. Emma had been the first to christen the tub.

"Though it's only a couple of inches of warm water, I'll take it," she'd laughed.

It would take many buckets of water to fill the thing, so all had agreed it would be a winter pleasure, where water was heated at all times on the wood stove. They'd use it to bathe the children, reusing the water for each child. Amanda would go first, then Hailey and last, Cooper.

Brian's grunt brought BJ from his musings.

"I suppose that will do it. We can now wrap this thing and get the shingles on the roof and she'll be watertight. The women will be in charge of putting the siding on."

They still had shelving from the hardware store and would set it up inside the large shed.

"I'm gonna build more shelving in there. I'm glad the door we chose has a deadbolt on it. It will at least hamper an intruder a bit." BJ inspected the shed. It was a foot off the ground, a ten by ten-foot structure, and six feet high. It wasn't tall, but wide and deep enough to store a lot of supplies. It was sturdy and structurally sound.

BJ smirked at Brian, waggling his eyebrows outrageously.

"What?" Brian asked.

"I think we should build another, after we build the one in the woods for the propane tanks."

"What? Why another?" Brian asked in surprise.

"Well, the next shed, we should insulate between the walls. We're going to need it to store the canned foods. That way, we won't have to worry about the glass jars freezing in winter and in the heat of summer, the thick walls will help keep the jars cool. It's either that or dig a root cellar. We can build the insulated shed in the tree line to keep it in the shade," BJ suggested.

"Dang, I don't want to dig a damned root cellar. That trench was bad enough, and all those holes for the plastic containers. My hands have so many blisters," Brian grumbled, flexing his hands.

"You ever gonna tell Emma and Paadi what happened at Walmart?" BJ asked, changing the subject to something that was eating at him. He gazed at the clearing, where the women were in the garden, the children by the chicken coop.

"No, it would only scare them. Besides, what's to tell? I killed a couple of maggots. Two less assholes in this world, two less child molesters," Brian said darkly. He walked over to pick up the house wrap.

When the two men had gone to Walmart to pick up girl clothing, and games and toys for the children, they were met on their third trip out to the trailer. Two grubby men had shown up just as they were loading the trailer with more food. Walmart's shelves were beginning to become bare of the foodstuffs.

"Hey! You assholes kill our friends?" a man screamed. The screamer's dull, red hair was laden with grease. He toted a shotgun and pointed it at Brian and BJ, who were startled into stillness.

"What? What in the hell are you talking about?" BJ asked, though he suspected he knew. Emma mentioned briefly about the men Paadi killed at the mattress place. It was only half a mile away from Walmart. BJ hadn't gotten the whole story before they'd left, only the barest of highlights. He and Brian figured they'd get the rest of the details once they finished their run and the children were out of earshot. Both men speculated Paadi had shot them on sight. It would appear that the dead men had friends.

"We just found our friends this morning. Did you kill them?" the other man snarled. With his missing front teeth, he was a real beauty, no doubt about it.

"Mister, we just got here a little while ago. We're only here to pick up supplies. We don't want trouble." Brian's voice was deadly calm.

He was an intimidating man; he was well over six feet and broad through the chest. He had to be strong, with upper body strength, to be a firefighter. BJ was on the slender side with narrow shoulders. Not intimidating at all.

"That don't answer our question, asshole," Toothless spat.

"No, we didn't kill your friends. Like my friend said, we only got here an hour ago," said BJ.

"You seen our kids, then?" the red headed man asked.

"Kids?" BJ repeated, surprised.

"Yeah, a little girl 'bout six and a little boy, about three," the stranger said.

BJ eyed Brian. The women said nothing about a little boy.

Oh hell, these animals have another little one. Where is he?

"We haven't seen any children here," Brian said, his voice now hard.

"I don't believe you," Toothless snarled.

"I don't care," said Brian.

What happened next was a blur. BJ was shoved to the ground, falling off the trailer. He didn't see Brian pull his Glock, but the two men dove to the ground. The bastard with the shotgun tried to raise it, but BJ saw the bloom of red spread across the stranger's chest, his eyes wide. Brian fired on Toothless, hitting him in the gut.

The man screamed in pain and clutched his stomach, blood gushing through his fingers.

BJ was stunned. Brian stalked over to the toothless man; the red-headed one was dead. Brian placed his foot on the man's gut, causing him to scream louder.

"Where is your place?" Brian snarled. "Where are you staying?"

"P...please, don't hurt me. Don't kill me!" the dying man shrieked.

Brian pressed his foot down and the fellow's shrill scream pierced BJ's ears.

"Where were you living? Tell me or I'll really make you hurt," Brian snarled.

"Over behind the mattress store, about a block and a half behind it. There's a liquor store. We were there!" gut shot cried, blood splattering out from his mouth.

Brian brought his leg high and stomped it down hard on the man's bloody gut. The villain's mouth flew open, but no sound came out, only blood rushing like a river out of his gaping mouth.

Brian stepped over to BJ and gave him a hand up.

"We need to search for that child. He can't be far from that store. I will not leave a baby out in this world if I can help it."

They'd closed up the trailer and went out and found the liquor store. From there they spent three hours hunting in every building and under every bush.

Lord, let me find this baby, BJ silently prayed.

Fear clawed its way in his brain. There was no telling how long the boy was without food and water. It was as though his very soul depended on him finding the child.

BJ finally found the child, asleep underneath a dumpster. BJ noticed a tiny bare foot sticking out from under the dumpster. The small foot was filthy. He gently extracted the boy. The youngster's eyes fluttered open as he woke. His eyes were dark blue, the color of an angry ocean. He was filthy and stank badly. His nose was crusted with green and his eyes swollen.

"Hey, buddy. I'm BJ. We won't hurt you. I believe I was supposed to find you. I suspect my prayers were answered. Our Father in heaven sent me to get you. I'm going to take you home. Alright?" His heart shattered into a million pieces.

He rejoined Brian and they headed to the park, another child in tow. BJ knew this would be *his* child. His son. Closing his eyes, the vision of his sons came to mind. He missed them so much. He didn't believe his family would begrudge him this child. He held tightly to the boy all the way to the park.

When they arrived, Emma had to pry the boy from him to clean him up, feed him, and check him out.

"He's fine, BJ, just malnourished and dehydrated. No abuse. He's had a cold and I'll keep an eye on that. Otherwise, he should be fine," Emma said, much to his relief.

They'd told the women that they found the boy under a dumpster. They hadn't told them about Brian killing the men, nor of the torture of Toothless, though it was well deserved. It had taken time, but they got the child's name. Dillan lived with BJ now.

He glanced at the child, who was holding a chick, a tiny grin on his thin features. Amanda was standing guard over the little ones. The children were starting to outnumber the adults. Dillan and Cooper had become fast friends.

"You okay, BJ? I lost you for a second," Brian asked, waving his hand in front of BJ's face.

BJ laughed, embarrassed. "Sorry, I was thinking about Dillan. He seems to be doing better."

Brian smacked him on the back. "He'll be fine. He has a dad now, a home, food, lots of love, and other siblings."

"Although I'm not a violent man, I'm really glad you stomped that bastard, Brian. I don't think we would have found Dillan if you hadn't."

"Yeah, I kinda figured the bastard wouldn't tell me otherwise," Brian grunted.

"Are the girls still having nightmares?" BJ asked.

"Yeah, but it isn't all night now, just once or twice a night. I guess it scares Cooper. He comes and gets in my bed. How about Dillan?"

"He didn't wet the bed last night. So that's a good thing. I hear him whimpering at times, but no more screaming," BJ said quietly.

No, he wasn't a violent man, but he wished Brian had just kept stomping that bastard. Something had awoken after the death of his own children. Upon finding Dillan, something dangerous had grown within him. Something protective, more protective than in his old life. He was becoming more deadly, with deadly intent. He was unable to save his boys, but he'd saved Dillan.

NINE

Flynn chose another road, and Xandra was navigating. They were in farming country, driving along Highway 23. The trees had started disappearing and the land was flattening out. Homes and suburbs were becoming fewer and farther between. It had taken them four days, driving, and stopping to gather more supplies. Because they'd both come close to starving to death, they each had a sense of urgency to continue hoarding food. When they came across a store, they stopped and gathered up all the food items. They had not seen anyone in four days. It was eerie, the lack of people.

"I imagine the virus killed almost everyone," Xandra whispered.

"Yeah. I thought there would be more people. Either that or they're hiding in their houses. Or, maybe they went someplace else, like us. It's hard to live in the city or suburbs."

Flynn gazed out over the vast expanse of the green and lush fields. They continued driving, agreeing not to stop until they found the Amish. They were getting closer to Lancaster, passing through New Holland, Pennsylvania. Flynn pulled the truck over to the side of the road and shut off the engine. Xandra eyed him questioningly.

"I just want to look around. Can you hand me the binoculars?"

"Absatively." Xandra handed him the pair of binos. "What are you looking for?"

"Signs of life. And I have to take a leak," he announced, causing her to chuckle.

They were getting to know each other better. Better than he would have in the old days. Their lives were so busy then and filled with texting, their phones, and social media, that they hadn't really even come close to actually communicating. Now all they did was talk, uninterrupted, without distractions.

They got out of the truck and Flynn let down the tailgate. He climbed up then helped Xandra up. He noticed she was gaining weight, beginning to fill her clothes out again. Her skin regained its healthy color and her face was fuller, not so hollowed out. He smiled at her and she smirked.

Bringing the binoculars up to his eyes he searched, spinning deliberately in a tight circle. Before him was a vastness of flat land. He picked out tiny horses in the far distance. Perhaps the Amish were there.

"Way over there, I see horses. We should head that way, see if someone is there." Flynn handed the binoculars to Xandra.

She searched in the direction he pointed and hummed in agreement. "It's as good a place and direction as any."

Flynn beamed. Hopping down from the bed, he helped her off the tailgate, relieved himself by the side of the road, then got back into the truck. He eased onto the road, keeping the vehicle headed in the direction he'd seen the horses. It was still startling, the silence. Even standing on the truck, all Flynn heard was the soft buzz of insects, a bird calling here or there, and nothing else. Adam and Eve came to mind, being the only two on Earth. He knew there were people out there; he'd certainly left a city full of fools. But not seeing anyone for days shook him badly.

"You alright, Flynn?"

"It's just freaky not to see another living soul. I mean, I'm scared to see someone, afraid they might hurt us, but again, afraid I won't see anyone else. At least it doesn't stink here."

"You're right about that. I keep thinking they're just hiding. You know, like me."

"Yeah. But away from the urban places, you would think you'd see *someone*. I'm hoping that whoever has those horses is still alive. I figure someone has to feed and water them." Flynn nibbled on his lip.

"I'm starting to get used to the quiet. It's nice. Especially if it doesn't involve flies buzzing. I don't mind insects, but living with millions of flies outside my window and outside the apartment really freaked me out." Xandra shuddered at the memory.

Flynn clasped her hand and winked at her. "Me too. I think we need to take this road, toward that direction."

He aimed the truck northward. Their windows were down, and Flynn kept the speed at about forty-five. They'd both agreed that they hated being closed in. The sun was beating down and it was hot, but the breeze had just the hint of rain in it. Perhaps tonight they'd get a thunderstorm.

Flynn slowed the vehicle when he spotted a house about half a mile down the road. There were several squat buildings and outbuildings. His heart beat faster when he noticed a man who appeared to be dressed in the Amish manner. He stared at Xandra, who held hope in her eyes, a calm expression on her face.

The farmer observed them and set off toward his house. Flynn slowed then stopped in front of the dwelling. The home was set away from the road and a fence surrounded the whole of the property. He spotted several goats in the yard, grazing away. The farmer stood on his porch and stared at Flynn and Xandra in the truck. Behind the older man on the porch was another man without the hat, just inside the house.

"Stay here. I'm going to see if they'll talk to me." Flynn climbed out, leaving his weapons in the truck. He didn't want these people to think he might be a threat.

His heart was slamming in his chest. It was kind of surreal, getting excited to see another person who wasn't pointing a gun at him. He approached the gate but didn't go up to it. The farmer on the porch stared at him closely.

"Good day, sir," Flynn called out in a clear, calm voice, though he didn't feel anywhere near calm.

The old man nodded but said nothing and remained on the porch, waiting. Flynn counted several other men in the darkened depths of the house. He didn't see any women. The man on the porch was older, he appeared to be in his sixties, with a salt and pepper beard. The flat brimmed hat shaded his eyes, but Flynn thought they were brown.

"Might I have a word with you, sir? I'm not sick. I don't carry the virus."

The Amish farmer scrutinized Flynn for a long moment, then glanced behind and tipped his head. The men inside the house faded into the interior. The gentleman farmer stepped off the porch and walked toward Flynn. Flynn's mouth was dry. This was so important, to find a place that would accept them, help them.

"What is it, young man?" The old man's face was heavily lined with fine webbing. It was the face of a man who had spent his life outdoors, working in the fields.

If Flynn was lucky, he'd spend the rest of his life doing the same.

"Sir, I'm sure you're aware of the nightmare that has affected our country, our world, in fact. I used to live in Philadelphia, which is now a dead city. Before we lost power, there were cities all over this country and the world that were devastated."

The farmer's eyes widened a bit and he paled beneath the tan.

"I did not know this. At least not the extent," he said in a deep voice.

"Yes, sir. My friend and I have been traveling and you're the first person we've seen for days. When I was in Philadelphia, out of over a million and a half people, there were forty or fifty left. These were people I actually counted. We have not seen another living soul, sir."

"We did not know it was this terrible," the farmer said gravely, shaking his head.

"Yes, sir. Our world has been cut down. Sir, my friend and I have no knowledge on how to survive. We were hoping if someone would take us in, teach us, we might become part of a community. We only know of the Amish, who live in a world with no electricity. My friend and I want to learn. We'd work hard if you'd let us join you," Flynn said earnestly.

The old man jerked as though stung, shaking his head vehemently.

"No, that isn't possible. No, I'm sorry. We cannot help you," he spluttered.

Flynn's mouth trembled; his eyes stung with unshed, defeated tears. His spirits fell along with his shoulders and he trudged back to the truck.

"Young man, go south, toward Paradise and past that to Belmont. There is a big farm there. My friend Cliff Richland owns that farm. It is a big farm and I believe they'd help you and your friend," the old gentleman said, his expression softening.

"Thank you, sir, thank you," Flynn said, ignoring the tears that were sliding down his face.

"Tell Cliff that Claus sent you." He climbed the stairs to the porch of his home.

Flynn climbed in the truck. "His name is Claus. He said for us to go see a Mr. Cliff Richland in Belmont. He said Mr. Richland is a farmer and might take us in."

"Oh my gosh, I hope so." Xandra squeezed his arm.

Flynn waved to Claus on the porch, and Claus returned the gesture of farewell.

Emma was standing shin-deep in the water. Amanda and Hailey were playing at the water's edge. Coop and Dillan were down for their naps. Brian and BJ were out hunting. They'd been eating quite a bit of fish and Emma and Paadi told the men they were about to revolt if they didn't get some kind of meat on the table tonight. She chuckled at the memory. The men had been happy to go out and hunt.

Paadi wanted to go but was reluctant to leave Hailey. She'd become very attached to the little girl. Every evening, Paadi read the children stories with Hailey planted square in her lap, her delicate fingers entwined in Paadi's long black hair. The child had started to mimic Paadi's Boston accent and it was hysterical. When Emma would snigger, Paadi would shoot her a dirty look. The children had changed their lives into something quite remarkable.

Some of the tomatoes had begun to ripen, along with a few green peppers. The zucchini and squash were ready to harvest. It was a good thing Brian found the grown plants. The seeds were coming along, but it would be weeks until the other plants began to produce. They would have fresh vegetables tonight with dinner, which Brian and BJ would provide. The bulk of the vegetables would be canned or dehydrated for long term use. Winter would be long, and though they had plenty of food stores, all had agreed that they should proceed as though they didn't.

Emma and Paadi spent hours going through all the store canned foods, and the boxed and dried foods, checking expiration dates. They wrote the dates on the front of the cans and boxes in marker so they were easily seen. Then they stacked and arranged their foods per expiration dates. Oldest first, so they wouldn't go out of date. Emma was sure it was safe to eat the out-of-date food, but they didn't want to waste anything. It allowed them to keep track of the volume of food and kept them conscious of their meals and daily menu.

They were surprised to see the apple trees Brian planted had apples on them. There weren't many, but each of the trees had a dozen or better. They were only about six feet tall, but Emma thought that next year they would hopefully double the number of fruits. This fall, she and Paadi would make apple butter. It wouldn't be a lot, but they might get half a dozen pint jars, maybe more. There were no peaches, but there had been. The tiny fruit had dried and fallen off the trees. That told her that next year they'd have peaches. Perhaps not a lot, but some.

The chicken poop would be kept and dried for fertilizer. They'd started a compost pile, turning it every so often. It was natural and organic. They were beginning to get into the rhythm of living in the park. It was quite a bit of work, but it was gratifying to see their efforts prove out and their camp becoming a real home. They had all run into horrible people, but Emma hoped those people would leave or die. She was certain within a year many people would die, because if they were unable to find a way to grow, preserve, and hunt food, they'd die. Supplies in stores had a finite shelf life.

If people remained in the cities, disease would surely be running rampant by now. Anyone who'd survived the Vermilion Strain would face probable death due to the abundance of biohazards. Here, it was wild and pristine, without the rotting bodies.

The building they lived in had become a home. Brian and BJ had transformed the interior into a cozy place to live. There were chairs, a couple of couches, and a bookshelf filled with books. The girls shared a room with two twin beds and brightly painted walls.

Cooper had his own room, smaller, but just as brightly painted. The bathroom had been fixed up with a tub. Although they used it from time to time, it was just easier to take a sponge bath. The men set up the solar panels on a rotating stand. There were lights in the evening, they had flushing toilets and running water. The men had rigged the toilet valve and used a long hose to hook to the faucet on the tub. It would at least fill the tub with cold water. This winter, they would have plenty of hot water heating on the wood stove. They worked hard each day and her body was telling her.

Brian and BJ had cut down hardwood trees throughout the nearby forest. Those would be for the following year's firewood. The deadfall in the forest was allocated for this year's winter. She, Paadi, and the children pulled wagons of branches and chunks of wood.

She and Paadi chopped wood for the wood stove that Brian would eventually put into the house. He and BJ were planning their strategy for the best location of the stove and the double insulated stovepipe. The men found a tiny wood stove for BJ's RV. It was cute as hell.

The work was hard and physically demanding. Amanda was a tremendous help, tending to the children when the adults were working, and she helped with laundry. She was still a child, but her eyes exposed a mature girl who'd lost too much and seen too much, as they all had.

Emma glanced up when Paadi came to stand beside her. She glanced at her friend and grinned.

"You lazy bitch," Paadi said, bumping Emma with her elbow.

Emma giggled. "Yeah, that's me alright."

"It's wicked hot today. I do figure summer is here. Man, this water feels perfect."

"You got that right. I'm glad we got those fans put in the house. That will make nights more bearable. It's too bad the place doesn't have more windows." Emma wiped her face.

"I was thinking…. Maybe the boys could pick up a honkin' big ass tent and when it's just too hot inside, we can sleep outside, in a tent. Run a long ass cord out to the tent and hook up a couple of fans."

"You know. Paadi, sometimes you're freaking brilliant!" Emma crowed.

"Yep, I'm modest though. Don't like to brag." Paadi grinned.

"Mommy!" Hailey called, and Paadi's head shot up.

"I'll be right there, honey." Paadi stared at Emma. "I never thought those words would ever be attached to me. I'll admit, though, they're music to my ears."

"You make a damned fine mom, hands down. Hopefully you can get the other kids to talk like you,

Hailey certainly is." Emma's eyes danced in teasing humor.

"Asshole." Which sounded like *aahhsole*, eliciting a laugh from Emma.

Paadi wandered over to the chicken coop. The children seemed fascinated by it. Emma eyed her watch. She'd be getting the boys up soon from their nap. Today might be a good day to teach them how to swim. Amanda was a great swimmer, but the other children didn't know how. They'd all agreed that the sooner the better for swimming lessons. They wanted no tragedies; life had already thrown them too many.

Ж

Brian and BJ trudged quietly through the woods. It was much cooler in the dense forest. It was still relatively early in the day, and they'd been walking through the forest for two hours. BJ had the compass, keeping them on a northwesterly trek. BJ was carrying his Weatherby Mark V and Brian carried his Marlin, along with his ever-present Glock. He'd given BJ the other Glock he'd picked up. Being well armed was essential.

The men paused when they caught the scent of decay. The wind had shifted and brought the odor to them.

"What do you think that is?" BJ whispered, his hand going up to his nose.

"Don't know, a dead animal? Take out your Glock, just in case. Let's proceed with caution." Brian had a feeling that something wasn't quite right.

He slung the Marlin over his shoulder and retrieved his Glock. He sniffed the air, proceeding carefully. Every ten feet he and BJ stopped, listening, and scenting the air. They started walking on a downslope, using the trees as stops. A hand landed on Brian's arm and he froze.

BJ stepped up close to him. "I think I hear voices. Let's slow down," he whispered close to Brian's ear.

Brian tilted his head, trying to catch the sound. He let BJ take the lead.

BJ crept vigilantly ahead, tipping his head this way and that. Then Brian caught the faint sound of human voices, along with the scent of wood smoke, and the reek of decay was becoming stronger.

Below them was dense forest. Brian watched his footing; he didn't want to slip on the soft ground beneath his feet. BJ stepped guardedly from tree to tree, using them as cover and a shield. Brian noted that BJ was also carefully placing his feet, avoiding branches and large twigs. No need to make their presence known with an ill placed step.

Now Brian clearly made out voices, though not the words. There were three distinct male voices. Someone laughed. His heart beat rapidly, as though a kettledrum was hammering away. This would be tricky and dangerous. Whoever was down there was roughly five or six miles from their camp. Brian wanted to know who was in the vicinity, and if they were good guys like themselves, or people they should be wary of. It was an uncertain world, one that brought out the best in people, as well as the absolute worst, as he'd seen with the two men he'd killed at the Walmart.

BJ stopped, raised a hand, and pointed down and over to their left. Brian came up beside him. At first, he saw nothing. Searching the dense forest, then between a heavy thicket, he saw three men sitting in camp chairs. They all wore camouflage hunting clothing. It appeared they were drinking. He and BJ crept toward them, slowly and carefully, keeping the larger trees between them and the men.

Their high vantage gave them a view of the camp below. Twenty feet from the men was a pile of rotting carcasses. It appeared they killed their prey, but only used parts of the animal, leaving the rest to rot.

Don't they know how to butcher? How can they stand the stench? Brian wondered.

Perhaps it was the mound of beer cans and empty liquor bottles? There were three tents, and beside the tents were boxes of liquor—whiskey, vodka, gin, and a couple of kegs.

Damn, these assholes were sitting around drunk. Brian was amazed.

Beside one man who had a large gut, from drinking beer no doubt, was an AR-15 laying in the dirt. All the men were bearded, filthy, and rough. The beards were no surprise, since shaving wasn't high on the list for most men during this time. He and BJ chose to shave and shower quite regularly, however. Another man of mixed race—black and Asian, Filipino—was stretched out in his camp chair, his booted feet propped up on a log. There was a low fire burning, nearly burned out.

There was a hunk of meat over a spit, the smoke spiraling up.

The third man, this one white, thin, and lanky, was smoking a pipe. It looked to Brian like a crack pipe, not a tobacco pipe. So, they were drinking and getting high in the woods. No problem unless they headed toward his group's home. There were three ATVs parked off to the side, with several five-gallon gas cans. There was a pile of empty food cans and various trash. Brian scrutinized each face, burning them into his memory. The fat one had rounded cheeks, with a patchy beard. He had a large mole in the middle of his eyebrows. Brian mentally named him Mole. The biracial man sported two gold earrings that stretched his earlobes. Brian named him Pirate. The third man had a unibrow and a hawkish nose. He was named Crackhead.

When they got home, he'd give the women their descriptions. He'd advised them to shoot the men on sight. While these men didn't present a problem now, when the booze, drugs, and food ran out, they would go hunting. He hoped at that point, they would depart in a different direction. Five miles was too close. The only alternative, however, was to kill them here and now, which was outright murder.

Brian observed the men for a long time. He vacillated; he didn't want to play God, but he didn't like knowing the men were that close to his home and children. If he let them live, would they be a threat to his new family? He'd need to talk to BJ and the women about this. It was easier to kill someone in the heat of rage. Brian wasn't sure he possessed the ability to kill someone in cold blood.

It had taken him and BJ well over two hours to walk this far in the woods. He doubted the men below possessed the ability or coordination to walk half a mile before collapsing. He eased away and BJ followed. They crept backward until the camp was completely indiscernible. The two made their way uphill and away from the threat. Neither man spoke as they headed southeast.

Half an hour later, BJ stopped. "What do you think?"

"I was seriously thinking of just shooting them all where they sat," Brian said, wiping the sweat off his face.

"Yeah, me too. Honestly, I don't think I could have done it. Somehow, I doubt they'd have noticed us."

"I doubt it too. They're a concern, but I have no idea if they're a threat. I want to speak to the women, see what they think. We give them those men's description, so they'll know should they ever show up. If they keep drinking like that, I'm certain one of them will accidentally shoot the others. Or leaving that food to rot, a bear will come by and take care of our problem for us," Brian snorted, shaking his head.

"I can't believe they just piled that mess up and let it rot. That's a serious biohazard. If we're lucky, they'll die by their own stupidity." BJ frowned. "Clearly, they have no idea how to preserve food."

"Let's head off and see if we can't get some meat. I don't know about you, but Paadi's starting to get a crazed look in her eyes. I don't think I'd wanna be on the wrong end of her temper." Brian's body shook with laughter.

"Don't I know it. *'Fish, fish, fish. Gwad daum it, I'm sick of gwad daum fish'* is what she told me before we left." BJ giggled, imitating Paadi's accent.

"Ohhh man, you're *so* in trouble! I'm gonna tell Paadi you're making fun of her accent," Brian said in singsong fashion, laughing harder now.

"You bedda not, I'll go wicked crazy on you, busta!" BJ howled in laughter. He was bent at the waist, laughing like a loon.

Tears ran from Brian's face at the stupidity of their joking. He was unable to help himself and the harder he tried to get it under control, the harder he laughed. That caused BJ to laugh. After several minutes of hilarity, both men gathered some semblance of dignity, with the occasional hiccup of giggles. By now they were leaning heavily on a tree, trying to remain standing. It was a near thing.

"Ah Christ, she'd kick both our asses, I'm damned sure," Brian snorted, wiping the residual tears from his eyes.

The diminutive Paadini Sullivan was a force to be reckoned with. She may not have been born Irish, but she had the temper of an Irishman.

She must have gotten that from her husband, by osmosis, Brian thought, a smile stretched across his face.

"I'll say. God, but I love when she talks. It's better than TV. Sometimes I piss her off just to listen to her throw a fit. I'm going to Hell, I just know it," BJ wheezed, his face burning bright pink.

"Dude, I could so blackmail you." Unslinging his Marlin, Brian stepped into the trees. It was time to get to serious hunting. He knew damned well they'd need to get something before returning home. He did not wish to evoke disappointment in either woman's eyes, and was positive he didn't want to get on the wrong side of Paadi's temper.

TEN

Flynn tapped the brakes when he saw a sign over a large gate. "Richland Farms" it read. Flynn took in the expanse of green farmland. In one field were acres and acres of corn. It was about four feet high or taller and it waved gently in the late morning breeze. In another field was some kind of grain growing, but Flynn knew nothing about farms, types of plants, or crops. He was completely clueless. That fact terrified him. He did, however, have a strong body and a desperate desire to live, no matter what it took. It would be hard and backbreaking work. No more free ride, no more easy jobs with long lunch breaks and weekends off. That life was dead and buried.

He got out and pushed the gate open. It wasn't locked, thankfully. He hopped back in the truck, drove through, then got out and closed the gate. When he climbed into the truck again he looked at Xandra. She smiled at him, her lips trembling.

He drew her hand to him and kissed it. "If they won't take me, I'll beg them to keep you," he said earnestly. Her eyes widened and she started to protest. "I mean it, Xandra. I care about you too much to drag you with me. It's dangerous out there and if I know you're here, eating and living, I'll be okay with that. I mean it. I will manage, you know I will. I just can't stand the idea of you out there with me and being in danger."

Her eyes filled with tears and she nodded silently. He'd let her down in the beginning. He would not let her down again.

He cleared his throat and drove up the winding driveway. It was a mile to the house and Flynn suspected the people in the house spotted the truck coming. There was a plume of dust behind his truck. He went neither too fast nor too slow. He wanted to guarantee the people here knew he wasn't a threat, nor was he sneaking up. He doubted anyone might sneak up, since visibility was clear for miles in practically every direction.

In the distance, he spotted several large windmills sprinkled about the property. They were picturesque, but he didn't know what they were for. His heart was beating wildly as he pondered what he would say. He had no pride. He'd lie on the ground and beg and cry if it took that.

Ahead four men came out to a wraparound porch on a large two-story farmhouse. At one time, the house had been blue, but the sun and wind had chipped and faded the paint. Large windows were opened and several had faded red gingham curtains waving like standards.

Though worn, the house was strong and solid. Flynn decelerated the truck. The men did not come off the large wraparound porch. All of them held weapons, though not pointed directly at them. The men stood with wary expressions, ready to raise their weapons in a split second if a threat came.

Flynn stopped the truck twenty feet away and shut the engine off. For a moment, he held Xandra's hand, his thumb stroking the top. Cautiously, the two exited the truck.

"State your business," an older man called.

"I'm looking for Cliff Richland. Claus from New Holland said that I should come to you. He said to speak with you," Flynn said, his voice shaking with fear and hope.

"I'm Cliff. What do you want?" Cliff said sternly, though not unkindly.

"Sir, my friend Xandra and I are searching for work, a place to live. We're both young, healthy, and strong. There is nothing out there, sir. Nothing. I know nothing about how to survive, I don't know anything about growing things. But I do know how to work hard. If you let us stay here, we'll bust our butts for you. We'll work hard and we'll learn. We only ask to be taught. To learn and have a chance at living. I know you don't know us, but we're good people, sir. We're honest and we have good hearts," Flynn finished, his voice cracking.

"How do I know you won't shoot me in my sleep?" Cliff called out and the other men shifted.

"Sir, I do have weapons in my truck. Honestly, I don't even know how to use them. I've never shot anyone. You're absolutely welcome to them. Sir, I don't want anything I don't earn and work hard for. We aren't here for a free meal. We want, no, we *need* to earn our way. There is nothing for us out there. There are bad people and I don't know how to keep Xandra safe by myself. If you won't take me, then please, sir, take her in. I can probably get by, but not with her while also trying to keep her safe."

"Give me and my boys a minute," Cliff Richland said. The other men gathered to speak quietly.

Flynn's mouth was dry, and he didn't dare look at Xandra for fear he'd break down and cry. He didn't feel very brave or confident, he was terrified these people would send them away. His nerves were raw, as raw as they'd ever been.

The man faced Flynn and walked down the steps. The farmhands behind him remained on the porch, observing silently.

"Where did you come from, young man?" Cliff asked, coming up to Flynn.

"From Philadelphia, sir. It's a terrible place. There's a gang running the city now. Honestly, though, they won't make it very long there. They have food, but it can only last for so long. I knew it was important to leave that place. It's only a matter of time before it implodes."

"Alright. So you know nothing on farming, right? What do you think you can do for me?" Cliff asked.

"Sir, I'll do anything you tell me. I'll shovel crap, haul water, dig holes, pick weeds, whatever you need, sir, we'll do. I don't know anything about farming, except that it is arduous work and I'll bust my ass for you." Flynn stared the older man in the eye.

Cliff scrutinized Flynn for a long moment and Flynn didn't flinch. Then he turned to Xandra and

Flynn noticed his eyes soften a bit. "She looks a little thin," he remarked.

"It's been a hard time for us, Mr. Richland. But like Flynn said, we'll work hard for you and you won't hear us complain. If you'd just give us a chance, we'll prove it to you," said Xandra. Her voice was strong and firm, her body straight.

Flynn was proud of her and his heart swelled.

"Alright then. We were lucky. When the virus first hit the country, all our farmhands stayed here. We've hunkered down and rode out the storm. We've only just started leaving the farm to see what is going on out in the rest of the world," said Cliff.

"Sir, it's dead out there. We haven't seen anyone. When I left Philadelphia there were less than a hundred people there. Out of over a million or better, less than a hundred," Flynn said softly.

Cliff paled beneath his sun beaten bronze skin. "You didn't see any military? Maybe the National Guard or FEMA?"

"No, sir. No one. I don't think anyone is left. I reckon that virus killed the world. I might be wrong, but there wasn't any looting that we noticed while we drove here. There are a few people out there, but there's no need to loot, you just walk in and get what you need. The stores were still full when I left. There might be random pockets of people who kept to themselves, like the Amish and those on your farm, but otherwise, I'm thinking there just aren't a whole lot of people left." Flynn's voice was weighty with sorrow.

"My God. So we're essentially on our own? All we have is all we'll ever have?" Cliff Richland breathed, shaking his head.

"Yes, sir. That's why Xandra and I need to learn how to farm, how to survive. In a few years, all that food in the stores and such will run out. People will die of disease and illness. We know people lived just fine hundreds of years ago, farmers and such. We thought if we learned how to farm, to grow food, we hoped we could learn how to survive."

Cliff cleared his throat. "Alright then, you'll come and stay with us. We have a few houses on the property. Our ranch hands live in the cottage style houses or the bunkhouse. We eat in the main house. My wife, Sarah, will help you get settled in. You can drive your truck to the side of the house and unload your belongings. Then drive the truck to the big red barn," Cliff instructed. "That's where we keep our vehicles. Once you get settled, come to the main house, lunch is in about an hour or so."

Flynn grasped Cliff's hand with both of his, shaking hard. "Thank you, sir. Thank you! We have a lot of food supplies in the truck. Where do you want me to put those?"

"Leave those in the truck. I'll have the boys fetch them and take them to our storage units. I'll get Sarah to meet you at the cottage," Cliff said, heading up to the porch. The men on the porch pivoted and went into the house.

Flynn eyed Xandra, his tears glistening. He drew her into his arms and hugged her hard.

"Oh, my god, I can't believe they'll let us stay," Xandra whimpered. Flynn nodded; his throat was too tight with emotion to say anything. He let go and climbed in the truck. He drove the vehicle carefully along the side of the farmhouse and noticed several cottages. There was a woman with a calico apron on, hands resting on her hips. Her hair was short and beginning to gray. She was sturdy in build, and tall. The gentle tilt to her lips bespoke of someone who loved to laugh.

Pulling the truck to a stop, Flynn got out.

"I'm Sarah. Cliff said you two were to stay here and work the farm with us. This will be your place. It has electricity, but not too much. Enough to flush the toilet and run the lights. Cliff and I always have everyone in for all the meals. We require everyone be well fed for a long day of work." The woman beamed and seemed genuinely happy to have them.

"Thank you, Sarah, we really appreciate your kindness, and Cliff's. Thank you for letting us come work for you," Xandra said.

"Yes, ma'am, we really do appreciate it," Flynn put in.

They stepped into the little cottage. It had a compact kitchen area, but only a sink and counter. There was no stove or refrigerator. There was a coffee pot on the counter, and a couple of jars with sugar and powdered creamer. It was simple but clean. There was a kitchen table with two chairs, a red gingham tablecloth spread across the table. The living room bled into the kitchen. There was a sofa and coffee table. There was a bookshelf with an assortment of paperbacks.

The wood floors were clean, unfinished pine. There was a braided rug on the floor, faded but in good repair. One room was a bedroom with an old-fashioned brass bed. There was a soft yellow handmade quilt on the bed, with crisp white pillows atop, a tall, narrow chest of drawers, and a closet. The other room was a bathroom that had a small window. White curtains with strawberries embroidered on the bottom edge hung from a rod. A toilet, a simple sink, and a shower stall. On the floor was a bathmat and a trash can under the sink. It was compact, but neat. To Flynn, it was wonderful.

"It's just perfect, Sarah, thank you."

"I'm glad you like it. The water comes from the house, so you'll have hot water. We only ask that you don't take long hot showers. We're conservative here.".

"Ma'am, a cold shower would be just fine for us. The ability to get clean and stay clean is something Xandra and I have come to cherish. In the truck, we've got a lot of supplies we brought with us. Quite a bit of that is soap and shampoo."

Flynn's face flamed a bit. He and Xandra had gone weeks without bathing. He'd never been a neat freak, but he had always been a clean man. When he'd lost electricity, he'd lost his ability to bathe. When he found Xandra, and she stunk so badly, he guessed he'd been the same. Bathing wasn't a high priority at that time.

"Alright then, you two get settled. We'll be eating in an hour. If you miss a meal, you don't get to eat later, so be on time. After lunch, Cliff will give you a tour of the farm and assign you both chores," Sarah said, smiling at both.

"Yes, ma'am," Xandra and Flynn said at once, and Sarah left them alone. Flynn faced Xandra and hugged her tightly to him.

"I can't believe we found a place to live. We have a bed, food, and water. And it's so nice here," Xandra said in amazement.

"I know. Let's get our stuff out of the truck and you can unpack. I'll take the truck over to the red barn and then return to help you."

It didn't take long to unload their possessions; they didn't have much. Flynn pulled several bottles of shampoo, a few bars of soap, and two cans of coffee out of the supplies. The rest he drove over to the barn. He left the weapons inside the truck. He figured if Cliff wanted to arm him, he would. He hoped Cliff would teach him how to use the weapons. He strode to the cottage, now his home. For the first time in months, *months*, he felt safe. He felt at peace. Whatever Cliff asked of him, he'd bust his ass like nobody's business.

Ж

Casper's gut cramped hard. He leaned over and vomited, his body jerking hard. He must have eaten something that didn't agree with him. His hand shook as he took a drink of water. He'd have to send someone out to get more bottled water. His community had grown to nearly one hundred and twenty people. Many were here in the center of the city with him. Javier and

Ramon kept the citizens in line. There were only a few trusted souls with weapons; he'd confiscated them early on.

"Casper, you okay?" Javier asked. Casper thought Javier was pale as death warmed over too.

"I suspect it was something I ate. You need to make sure those women are cooking the food right. Especially the fresh meat." He bent, clutching his gut with a fresh bout of vomiting.

"You're right. There are quite a few people sick. Hell, a stomach virus? I'll talk to them," Javier agreed.

"See about getting more bottled water. If we can't, make them boil the water from the fountains." Casper wiped foulness from his chin. He felt weak and a fever was brewing. Was this the virus coming to finish off its work? Or was it typhoid? Some other virus or disease?

"I'll get on it," Javier said, leaving Casper.

Casper questioned if it was the food that was being prepared. The women they'd found had taken over cooking for the group. Except for those in the outlying areas who kept the food stores guarded, everyone ate in the center of the city. There was a fire going all the time, with things brought from the homes to burn. Tables, chairs, books, and so on.

Some of the men had shot a gazelle. Casper had not been happy, but he welcomed the fresh meat. It had tasted a bit gamey, a little rare for his tastes. Perhaps that was it? Did the women wash their hands? They didn't bathe, but did they wash their hands? Had they butchered the meat properly? Then his heart skipped a beat, was this some kind of disease? Like cholera or E. coli?

Ж

Paadi and BJ were making a run. Since finding the three men in the woods, Brian had suggested that one man stay at the camp at all times. If he were to go hunting, Paadi or Emma would go with him. If they went out to scavenge, BJ and one of the women would go. It spooked them all, knowing the strangers were roughly five miles from their camp. Walking, it would only take a couple of hours, driving, a matter of minutes.

They'd all agreed that if any of the men showed up, they were to be shot immediately. They had children and supplies to protect. Paadi was sure the men wouldn't blink at hurting the children and stealing everything they'd worked so hard for. They were making fewer runs now, having gotten everything they calculated they'd need. They'd retrieved books, notebooks, paper, pens, pencils, crayons, and so on, for the children. In the fall, they'd start an abbreviated school for Hailey and Amanda. Coop and Dillan were a bit young, but they'd at least be exposed to learning.

Today, they were scavenging for movies and books. Because of the solar panels, they'd decided to get a couple of flat screen TVs, several DVD players, and movies. Come winter, there would be a lot of time on their hands. Reading and movies would keep them happy, along with boardgames. BJ had some DVDs in his RV that were for his boys. Paadi figured the adults might like their own movies. She was an avid reader and wanted books and child appropriate books. They were heading to a strip mall that had a bookstore along with JoAnn's Fabrics. Emma had asked for bolts of material, threads, needles, and anything Paadi could get her hands on. Even a sewing machine. Push came to shove, they'd sew clothing, recycle, and repair clothing.

Paadi glanced at BJ. His eyes were on the road, scanning constantly. She was glad. When she'd first met him, she'd thought he was something of a milquetoast, weak. She'd been wrong. He was a good man and a good father. They all understood Dillan wasn't a replacement for his boys, but BJ had emerged from the shell he'd been hiding in. He laughed more and joked more. Paadi was glad. She too was laughing more, as were Brian and Emma. They were healing from their losses. Their loved ones were never to be forgotten, but life went on, as did the struggle to survive.

She and Emma had spent the entire day yesterday canning green beans. They'd gotten a bumper crop of the beans. They'd replanted a few weeks after planting the first crop and in a couple of weeks, they'd have more beans to can. They'd put up thirty quarts. That was a hell of a lot. She was glad BJ and Brian were building the second storage shed, thankful it would be well insulated. She wouldn't want to lose all they'd canned because the jars froze. The building was taking longer because they were essentially building a building inside another. The walls were ten inches thick, along with the floor and ceiling.

The men brought spray insulation to cover the plywood on the interior walls and ceiling. It wasn't pretty, but it would keep the interior cool in the summer and warm enough in the winter so nothing froze. BJ built a thick door to go along with it. It had required special hinges, which they'd had to fabricate. It wasn't pretty, but it worked.

Emma had set up one of the utility rooms in the house as the medical storage. BJ made her shelves that lined each wall. He'd even made a hidden compartment in one of the high shelves for drugs. It was to keep the children out, but also anyone who broke into the place. Paadi didn't anticipate that, because if anyone got that close to the storage closet, then they had bigger problems than prescription drugs.

Little by little, things were getting sorted out. The large ten by ten storage shed helped get much of the bulky goods out of the house. The children's seasonal clothing, along with their future clothing, was stored there, stacked neatly along the walls. It was now easier to navigate inside the house, fewer tripping hazards.

BJ was working on a kitchen. There had been a utility closet with a sink, so he tore down part of the wall and was in the process of making them counters. They'd chosen countertops from the showroom. Brian and BJ had taken the sink and countertop off the floor model, and a few of the cabinets. He'd hung the cabinets, which now held their dishes. It was all a work in progress.

BJ was pulling into the strip mall. She had quite a few empty boxes with her and cloth shopping bags. She wasn't leaving here without entertainment. BJ carried the AR-15 and his Glock; she had a shotgun, along with her service weapon. They'd all set aside time each week for target practice and drills. The dogs had begun to patrol their camp on their own. It was funny to watch them. They took their job seriously. She'd found the tattoo on the inside of Buddy's ear. He was definitely a police dog.

They raided a veterinary clinic when they found out Daisy was pregnant by Buddy. They got ampoules of distemper and rabies serum, flea and tick prevention, and heartworm medicine. She hoped the serums would work and not harm the puppies. They found puppy wormer too. Paadi shivered at that thought. *Ewww*.

"What's the matter? Your face looks funny," BJ said, smirking at her.

"I was just thinking about worming the dogs. Geeze, the images of it in my head makes me want to puke." Paadi leaned over and made gagging noises.

BJ blazed bright red and began to snigger. She shot him a filthy glance. He swallowed the laughter down.

"I sure as hell don't see what's so *gowddamned* funny about that," she said, peering over her glasses. BJ's eyes crinkled but he didn't laugh again. She guessed he wanted to but knew better.

They took out their flashlights and walked into the bookstore. The door was unlocked.

"You head to the kid's section; you know what they like. If you can find any puzzle books and that kind of thing for them, get it. It will be kind of like a fun school activity for them. I'm going for *adult* content," Paadi snarked.

BJ walked through the aisle. The store smelled of stale air and paper, books, and old carpet. The lights from the window helped, and the store wasn't so deep that the light didn't filter to the rearmost.

An hour later, they loaded up the truck and drove the short distance to JoAnne's. Paadi ended up grabbing twenty bolts of cloth, two sewing machines, scissors, and spools of thread of all colors. She found crafts and projects, knitting, several how-to books, cross stitch, and everything she might even conceive. There was quite a lot she had not even considered, so she added it. They just might have to build another storage shed.

"I almost feel like a hoarder. All this stuff," Paadi laughed as they pushed two carts.

"I'd be afraid if we didn't get as much as we did. I keep telling myself once the gas goes, we'll essentially be alone and on our own. That is a frightening thought," said BJ.

Paadi raised one of her blocky eyebrows and smiled crookedly. "We're already on our own and *have been* on our own."

"Ah, yes, guess you're right."

"I know. It's just once the gasoline is gone, we can only travel on foot. And unless our three assholes turn into delightful neighbors, there is no need to leave our camp. I'm hoping at some point someone, or several someone's who are decent people, will head our way. It just seems like there are more assholes out there than decent people."

"You said it. I've nearly lost my hope for humanity. I still wonder whether Brian and I should have out-and-out killed those men." BJ eyed her sideways.

She reached up and patted him on the head. "You probably should have shot them, but it would have been at the cost of your soul. They show up, trust me, I'll blow their asses to Hell."

"Yeah. But if I do have to shoot them, I won't lose sleep over it."

On the way home, they took a different route, wanting to see what was going on elsewhere. There were homes few and far between, but most appeared abandoned. They found no one in their yards, no signs of gardens. Pulling over, BJ shut off the engine.

"What's the deal?" Paadi asked, leaning against her door. She'd been enjoying the ride and watching the houses they passed.

"Just wanted to stop and listen. We're a couple of miles from the back entrance. I wanted to see if I hear anything close to this entrance to the park."

Paadi opened her door and stood on the running board. There was the ubiquitous buzz of insects in the bushes at the side of the road. Birds flitted in and out of branches. In the distance, several woodpeckers hammered away at trees. A phoebe resting in an oak quarreled at them. More than likely a nest was nearby. In this moment in time, this snapshot, the world was peaceful, serene, and blissful.

"It smells… *green* here," BJ said, glancing over the roof, flexing his nostrils.

"What does green smell like? You're just pulling my leg." Paadi snickered.

"No, seriously. I don't know how to explain, but it just smells green. You know, plants, plant life." He shrugged.

"Chowderhead." Paadi laughed and climbed in the truck.

BJ pulled onto the road. Up ahead, they spotted two people on horseback and Paadi eyed BJ, drawing her Sig Sauer. So much for peaceful. Fundamentally, she knew not everyone was a threat, not everyone a bad guy. Her recent encounters, however, made her extremely cautious. She didn't want to kill, but she would, easily. The fellow at the roadblock was her first kill. Then the two at the mattress store. They wouldn't be her last. No, she didn't want to kill, but she damned sure would.

"Slow down and be ready. I don't think they're a threat, but let's meet our neighbors. That's what they seem like anyway," Paadi whispered.

ELEVEN

Xandra stood in the shower, letting the cool water wash over her tired body. She'd found out that Richland Farm made biodiesel from the corn they grew. Not only that, but they had a cattle ranch, with twenty head of cattle, six milk cows, goats, chickens, and pigs. Cliff's father, Cliff, Senior, was the patriarch and was still active. Cliff had taken over the reins and transitioned it into a money-making farm. With the price of oil and gas, Cliff transformed his farm into a gold mine with the biodiesel. They possessed several massive generators which ran the farm, and supplied their own fuel.

Their equipment ran off the biodiesel and the property had several enormous holding tanks for the fuel. Flynn had been amazed at the operation and had told her all about it. He seemed to be blossoming here. After a large breakfast, he'd leave, and she wouldn't see him until lunch. Then he'd leave again and she'd see him at dinner. There were a few chores after dinner, but then the evening was theirs.

Xandra was up at four and went to the house to start making biscuits and bread for the day. Sarah seemed to have boundless energy. She was upbeat and Xandra liked her very much. She was learning so much and she was feeling more and more at home here.

Along with the corn, they grew wheat, oats, and potatoes. The farm boasted an orchard of apples and peaches. Sarah tended her personal garden, that was where Xandra helped her. It was a three-acre garden with every kind of vegetable she'd ever seen.

Xandra was learning how to can the vegetables and how to kill and pluck chickens. She didn't enjoy the process but loved the end result. There was a large chicken lot with a long building that housed the chickens. There were hundreds of chickens, pullets, and chicks. The amount of eggs was staggering. No wonder they ate eggs for breakfast. She was getting good at making the biscuits and she was happy for that.

The farm had seven farmhands, three of them married. They lived in three other cottages. Those cottages were bigger, since they had children. Cliff had two sons, Jake and Randy, who were in their thirties, along with their wives, Beth and Mary, and their children. The large farmhouse was full of people and laughter. Xandra was learning how to cook and how to take care of the garden, pigs, goats, and chickens. Cliff's daughters-in-law helped Xandra. She liked both women. Though they were a little older than her, they'd taken her under their wings. They had pushed food on her, trying to fatten her up.

"You're just too thin. The wind will blow you away." Beth wasn't fat, but she had meat on her. She bloomed health, as did Mary. Both women worked hard, alongside Sarah. The married farmhands ate in their own homes. Their wives took care of their needs, as well as their children. There were eight children on the farm, ranging from three to twelve years old. The older children were given chores. The women farm workers helped in the garden along with keeping all the animals. There were no idle hands at Richland Farm.

That said, food was plentiful, and meals were loud with laughter. Their first lunch had been a solemn affair, since Cliff had asked Flynn and Xandra to tell everyone of their time after the virus struck. Everyone had been shocked, especially at the lack of people and the lack of help from the government or military.

"I honestly don't think there is anyone left to help," Flynn said.

"My goodness, I'm so thankful we didn't leave the farm when this whole mess started. How did Claus seem?" Sarah asked.

"As far as I could tell, healthy and fine. His people were inside the house, but there were a few of them. I figure anyone who stayed away from the public survived," said Flynn.

"Perhaps I'll take Jake and Randy and go visit our neighbors. Stop by to see Claus," Cliff speculated aloud.

"I'd go armed, sir. It's a different world out there and perhaps because everyone is so separated, more survived in this farming community. Just be careful of strangers," Flynn warned. There was a general hum of solemn agreement.

Cliff and his sons had left the farm, Xandra had heard secondhand from Sarah and Flynn. There were several Amish farms affected by the virus. The surviving Amish farmers were absorbed by other Amish families if they were unable to run their own farms. One of Cliff's neighbors, the Ziegler Farm, had lost everyone. There were no survivors. The others were fine and suffered no loss of life. They too had isolated themselves when the virus showed up. That had saved them. Now, months later, it would seem they were all in the clear.

Xandra shut off the water and grabbed a towel. It felt good to be clean every day. She showered in the morning and again at night. She never felt clean enough. She'd put on weight and was happy about that. It was difficult not to pile her plate up, but she was encouraged to eat seconds if she was so inclined. Most of the time she did. The fear and the worry for food were gradually fading.

Wrapped in a thick robe, she walked into the living room where Flynn was reading a book.

"What'cha reading?"

"Stephen King's *11/22/63*. It's good."

Sitting beside him, she leaned into him. He had not initiated any physical advancement on her since they'd been there. He was kind and sweet, but she knew he was waiting for her to initiate something intimate. He'd told her early on he would not take advantage of the situation, that she owed him nothing. He didn't want her to feel like she *had* to have sex with him. She was falling in love with him because she had not been pressured. She loved Flynn for who he was, someone who was honest, caring, and hardworking. He'd put her needs before his.

She placed her hand over his and he gaped at her, surprise in his eyes. She smiled sweetly at him and leaned in to kiss him. She almost laughed when he tossed the book away and took her into his arms. He cradled her damp hair and she wrapped her arms around his neck. Then she drew away.

"Let's go to bed, dear," she said with a wide smirk.

He laughed and got up. He lifted her in his arms and carried her to their bedroom.

Ж

Casper lay in the park, leaning against the large fountain. He was dying and he knew it. He didn't want to die in a building, he wanted the sun on his face. Javier and Ramon had already died. There were many bodies scattered on the sidewalks and street. It wasn't food poisoning. He didn't know what it was, but nearly all of the people who'd been saved were dead. His body was beyond the cramping, diarrhea, and vomiting. There was nothing left, and his body was a husk.

Where was his long-lost friend, Flynn? Was he dead? He remembered Flynn wanted to leave and he eventually had. Casper futilely attempted to imagine what would have happened if he'd gone with him. He'd never know now. He was alone, all the others having taken what they could and left. He hadn't been able to stop them, nor did he care anymore.

He heard the grunting of a lion. It was near. He wasn't worried about the lion killing him. Actually, he wished it would. The lion would end his suffering quickly. However, he suspected his body was too corrupt, too diseased to be edible. He moaned feebly. Though it was mid-day, he was unable to feel the warmth of the sun. The image of Rachael came to his mind's eye and a weak grimace creased his thin face.

It seemed the sun was disappearing, and it was growing darker. He could no longer see the buildings. Only the lion heard Casper's last breath.

BJ rolled down the window and the two people on horses ahead of him slowed down. He lifted a hand in greeting, wanting to be as nonthreatening as possible. Paadi held her Sig Sauer, hidden under a bag. BJ had his Glock in his lap. He wasn't sure he had the ability to drive and shoot, but he didn't want to face these people without the gun within reach. He hoped he wouldn't shoot himself in the crotch.

"Howdy, how are you two doing? It's been a while since we've seen anyone," BJ said, his tone light and friendly.

A man about his age was sitting on a light brown horse. He nodded, his features guarded, though not hostile.

"Howdy yourself." The rider dipped his chin to Paadi. "Ma'am."

"Just peachy. How do you do? Good to see another person. We thought we were the last on Earth," Paadi chirped.

The rider stared at her with a peculiar look on his face, then his lips twitched and he grinned. BJ bit his lips and tried not to laugh. Paadi's Boston accent was so strong it was sometimes startling. It was a great ice breaker.

"It is good to see someone else. I'm Jeff Simmons, this is my brother Bradley." Jeff leaned forward and shook BJ's hand.

"Good to know you. I'm BJ Hamm and this is Paadi Sullivan, by way of Boston." He smiled.

"You folks living near here?" Bradley asked, his body relaxed and easy in the saddle. These men knew horses.

"Yep. We're living over at Halfway Lake, in Winter State Park. There are a couple of others over there. We've settled there, made it our home."

Bradley laughed.

"We're about a mile and a half up the road. We have a large spread there with our families," said Jeff.

"It's good to know we have neighbors. Hey, just be aware, there's a group of three men. Me and another of our group found them about five miles northwest of our camp. They've got ATVs, and from what we gathered, there's a lot of drinking and drugs going on." BJ wanted to warn these folks. There was no telling how many people were in the area, but they should know of the threat.

"Good to know. Thanks for the info. You mind if we stop over for a visit in a few days? Bring the wives?" Bradley asked.

"That would be nice. It's good to know there's someone else here. Are there any other folks close by?" BJ asked.

"Yep. One other group that we know of. We just came from visiting them. They're east of here, about six miles that way." Jeff thumbed behind him. "They're a mix of folks, kids, and animals. Seven adults—four men and three women. Seem to be good people. They're living in structures situated by a six-acre pond."

"That's wonderful. Just knowing we have neighbors is a good feeling," said Paadi.

"It is. Most of our other neighbors didn't make it. Very sad. Well, we'll let you two get on your way. Please stop on by when you can." Jeff shook BJ's hand.

The horses stepped to the far side of the road and BJ drove carefully past.

"Awesome. It's so good to know there are others out there, near enough that should something happen, we're not completely alone!" Paadi's eyes sparkled with delight.

"Yeah, I suspect Emma and Brian will be happy to know that there are others. They're a distance from us, but at least we know. That would be nice to have the ability to trade information and goods, later on down the line." BJ entered the park using their normal route.

"Absolutely. And if they have children, there's hope for our own kids when they grow up. They won't be alone. They'll have others out there."

Paadi was a brilliant mother. BJ liked that about her. She had endless patience with the children and a childlike joy.

"We'll raise them to be strong, with the knowledge to survive this new life." BJ smiled when Paadi reached over and patted his forearm.

He drove the secondary road and they pulled into the parking area. Brian and Emma were working on the insulated storage shed for their preserved food, putting tongue-and-groove pine siding along the sides. The shed was neat and well built, and the shelves would hold a hell of a lot of canning jars. They'd started storing the eggs in there and had built up quite a batch. The surplus of eggs helped supplement the dog food.

There was still plenty of dog food, but since Daisy was pregnant, she was given a little bit more. They wanted healthy pups. Brian and Emma stopped working and the kids came running. It had become a pleasure and mini celebration to unload the truck. There was always something new.

BJ chuckled when Dillan ran behind, determination on his face. He'd started calling BJ Daddy and it had melted his heart. He caught Dillan in his arms when the boy launched himself. He lifted the child above him, laughing, then brought him in for a hug.

"We just met our neighbors, nice folks," BJ said, putting Dillan on his shoulders.

"Really? Tell all," Brian said, a smile blooming.

"Out the rear entrance, a couple miles down the road, they have a farm. They were on horseback. They said they'd met another group about six miles east of us," BJ said.

"Seemed like good folks then?" Emma asked, coming up behind.

"Yeah, got a real good feeling about them. They said the other folks were good people. Like us, they seemed like they got together to survive. I'm glad we're not totally alone," Paadi said, Hailey glued to her side.

BJ knew it bothered her quite a bit to think they were all alone and so isolated. He too worried about it, but not for himself, for the children. In twenty years, these children would be grown, and with so few people left in the world, he'd hate to think of them so isolated. Knowing there were other good people close by was a blessing. It eased his heart and his mind.

He swung Dillan down to carry a bag.

"Wow, this is a nice haul. Thanks for getting all the material," Emma squeaked happily, carrying several bolts of cloth in her arms.

"I tried to get a variety and heavy cottons. There are a few lightweight cotton fabrics, figured those would be good for summer. I chose some simple patterns, figured we teach each other how to make clothing. We can start with the children," said Paadi.

"You're not going to let Paadi near a pair of scissors, are you? Isn't that dangerous?" BJ laughed, earning him a punch in the arm from Paadi.

Paadi leered. "I don't need a pair of scissors to be dangerous, young man," she said in mock threat.

"Guess we're going to have to dig a root cellar after all, BJ. The temp inside the cool storage is at about fifty-five. For the canned foods it's fine. If we want to store smoked meat, we're going to need it cooler than that." Brian said.

"I was afraid of that. I'd hoped we might get away with it," BJ said. He was not a fan of digging.

"I have an idea," said Brian. "I saw it in one of the videos before the power went out. Some people were digging on the north side of their homes, up against their house. They dug the hole deep enough to put a chest freezer in, then drilled vent holes and put PVC pipe in the holes. Sealed it and put a tight mesh over the PVC so mice and crawly things couldn't get into the freezer. We can then cover it with a plastic sheeting along with bundles of rigid insulation. That way, it stays watertight and the top has insulation. We can store our meat in there."

"That sounds a hell of a lot easier than trying to build a structure underground. We can run to Lowe's tomorrow. That's a great idea," said BJ.

It was a relief to construct several modified root cellars behind the building, instead of building a whole structure from scratch. Work smarter, not harder.

"If we get a couple of chest freezers, we should use one to store meat and the other to store vegetables, like the fresh cabbages, carrots, and potatoes," Emma said, excitement in her voice. "I've been reading one of my food preservations books and read we can keep a lot of the root vegetables in the ground. We just have to put some kind of insulation on top of them, like straw. One method suggested filling big black bags with leaf litter. Place those bags over the root veggies you don't want to dig up yet. Even if it snows, the veggies will be safe underground. We can keep potatoes in the chest freezer, but a lot we can keep in the ground."

"That's a great idea!" said Paadi. "We have a ton of potatoes. I was kind of worried that a lot of them would rot if we dug them all up."

"You Irish and your potatoes. Honestly, Sullivan, do you think of anything else?" BJ giggled and was rewarded with another punch to the arm. He laughed at Paadi and got another punch.

"We'll put two large chest freezers, plastic sheet rolls, and several boxes of large black plastic bags on our list. I want to go hunting soon," said Brian. "I'd like to get a boar. I've seen tracks and spoor about three miles south of here. I want to try the smoker out with the hickory wood. Maybe get some nice hickory bacon going."

"Oh, if we could have that, I'd be your very bestest, best friend," BJ practically drooled.

"Oh, heck yeah. Bacon and eggs. I haven't had bacon in months," Emma said dreamily.

Paadi shook her head. "I thought all that would give you a heart attack? You're supposed to be a nurse."

"It'd be worth the risk, for *bacon!*" Emma crowed, causing the group to laugh.

Dillan laughed hard as well, though he had no clue what he was laughing at. This caused them all to laugh harder.

"Here, take these movies to the RV, I got you a few ABC videos, champ." BJ handed Dillan a bag of educational videos for toddlers.

"Thank you, Daddy!" Dillan squealed, clutching the bag to his chest, his large dark blue eyes sparkling. He ran to the RV. Amanda helped him open the door and they disappeared inside.

"When do you want to go hunt that pig?" Paadi asked.

"I'm thinking after we get the root cellars put in. I'd feel better about storing the meat after we smoke it," said Brian. "It should do fine in the canning shed for the short term."

"I want to come with you. You're going to need help bringing that pig home," BJ said.

"I hate to leave you gals here without one of us," Brian said. With his hands on his hips and a worried expression, he kicked a rock.

"Paadi is the best shot here. I don't think we have to worry," BJ said, noting the storm brewing behind Paadi's glasses.

"That's true. Sorry, Paadi, and you, Emma. I didn't mean it to sound like because you are women you can't handle things. I know you can. It's just that if those assholes see two women alone, I'd be afraid they'd be more likely to strike." Brian scrubbed his hands across his face.

Paadi snorted and patted her Sig Sauer at her hip. "Those bastards show up, I've got a bullet or two to cure their ills."

"I've gotten pretty darn good at shooting. Don't worry, I'll shoot first, ask questions later," Emma assured the men.

Ж

Brian paused in his digging to drink some cold water. It was hot as hell and the sun was blazing. They were close to finished with the two holes. He and BJ had gotten two fifteen cubic foot freezers and had started digging two days ago, against the north side of the building.

There were squeals and splashes in the lake, and it was an inviting sound. When they were finished digging, he and BJ were planning to line the bottom of the holes with gravel and pea gravel for good drainage. They'd agreed to leave a four-inch lip above the hole for the freezers. No need in having dirt and water go into the chests.

"I'm guessing my pit is about ready for the gravel," BJ said, eyeing the tape measure.

"How did you get your hole dug so quick? I've got about another hour's worth of digging," Brian grumbled, wiping the sweat from his face with a bright blue bandana.

"Fewer rocks on my side. Seems like you should build a chimney with all your rocks," BJ laughed.

"No kidding. Hell, just about every time I shoveled, I hit a rock. Digging is no fun in this confined space. Let me help you put the gravel in, and we can get the freezer into the hole and get it filled in."

They'd already put the venting piping on the sides of the chest freezers. The pipes went up three feet, to ensure that even with deep snow, the vents would be clear.

"Sounds good. When we go to put it down, let's have the women help. We can use the straps to lower it down." BJ crawled out of the hole.

The bags of gravels were stacked neatly beside the building. Brian had never worked so hard as he had living here. Everything, every change, every modification took time and brute force. He'd lost weight but had gained more muscle. BJ was the same.

When Brian first met BJ, he was almost puny, though he was tall. These days, BJ was more robust and broader through the chest. Brian noticed his shirts had become tighter across his upper torso. He'd gotten new shirts on one of the outings, though his pants were loose in the waist. He'd been on his way to a paunch before. It had bothered him, but he'd put it down to aging. He'd considered himself fairly fit for a firefighter. Now he was a lean, mean, building machine.

The men filled the bottom of the hole with a layer of gravel, then poured in the pea gravel. Brian walked past the building searching for the women.

Emma was at the cooking table; she had the sun oven out and was making a stew. She'd dug up potatoes earlier that morning and was using canned chicken they'd gotten at the store. It was getting close to lunch and his stomach growled in anticipation.

"Hey, Emma, can you and Paadi come over and help us with the freezer? We're ready to lower one of them."

"Uh, yeah. But lunch is almost ready, so once we do that, why don't you two take a break and come eat?"

"Sounds like a fine idea!" BJ yelled.

"Of course, it does, cause you're a walking gut," Paadi said, rounding the building.

"Hey, that hurt. I'm a hard-working man," BJ grouched good naturedly.

"You're a no-good, lazy, lay-about. You should have been done with that hole two days ago," Paadi teased.

"Never satisfied." BJ laughed and shook his head.

It took a bit of maneuvering, but with the wide moving straps, they were able to lower the freezer into the hole. Brian checked to verify the vent pipes weren't shifted. He'd used silicon to seal them.

"What do you think?" he asked Emma.

"It looks great. We'll have to lay on our bellies to get things out, but I'm okay with that," she said.

"Yeah, we'll keep a couple of cinder blocks on it or keep it locked so none of the little ones open it and fall in," Brian said.

"Shit, good idea," Paadi said seriously, all humor gone.

"I'll go ahead and lock it while we eat lunch," BJ said, and Brian noticed the thought disturbed him.

Brian eyed BJ. "Why don't we head out tomorrow morning, early, see if we can't get us a pig?"

"Yeah, that would be nice. Bacon. Pork chops. Boston butt," BJ said, the last aimed at Paadi.

She shot him a glare over her glasses, her dark, blocky eyebrows raising in a threat. Brian snickered beside him. That boy was going to get clobbered. He inched a few steps away from BJ, he didn't want to be in swinging distance.

TWELVE

Flynn walked the field with Cliff. He was amazed that so much food was in front of him. Well, not food, but biofuel, as well as feed for the animals. Cliff's farm was a self-sustaining island in a world that would be losing everything. In less than five years, whatever population was left would again perish by more than half. Perhaps the Amish, this farm, and other places where people pulled together would survive. Those, like Casper, were doomed to die if they stayed in the city.

"How many acres do you have in corn, sir?" Flynn asked. The corn was up to his chest.

"The farm is seven hundred acres. We have two hundred acres in corn right now, some of that would have been shipped out for biofuel to make ethanol. We use some to make our own biodiesel. Now we'll cut back and keep it up for our own use. You see those silos off in the distance? Those are for our cattle. We store our grain there."

Flynn shook his head in wonder. "I have to say, this is all amazing to me. I never knew what went into running a farm."

"We'll take our wheat to Claus. He has a mill and usually grinds our flour for us. The rest of the wheat was sent to market, but now there is no market. We'll end up planting less of everything, except for the food we grow in our garden for ourselves. That's what I wanted to talk to you about."

235

Fear speared through Flynn. Were he and Xandra going to be sent away because the farm would no longer grow as many crops and so they didn't need the extra farm hands, nor extra mouths?

"Yes sir?" was all he managed. His heart was beating fast in his chest and his ears ringing.

"Beth is a veterinarian. She is, rather, a large animal vet. She's pregnant, and to be honest, I'm not happy about her being near those animals. Son, I'd like you to apprentice with her. Begin doing everything she does. She'll be with you and teach you, but I want you to take over care of all our stock."

Flynn was stunned into silence. He said nothing for a few moments. He'd never worked with animals, never encountered large beasts. Now he was being given a chance at a vital and important job.

He swallowed hard. "I'd...I'd be honored to, sir. I mean that. I don't have a clue, but I'll do my very best and I won't let you down," Flynn sputtered.

"Great. Since we have no doctor, my Sarah and I talked about it, Beth can be a people doctor. She has more training than anyone I know. She can attend to all of our needs and you can attend to our animals. My daughter-in-law is only a couple months along, but I'm hoping you'll be capable of most things by the time it begins to get too risky for her to work with the animals." Cliff scratched his jaw and studied the fields surrounding them.

"Might I suggest, Cliff, that at some point, you go to the nearest veterinary clinic and hospital and snag all the supplies you can? I suspect the supplies are just sitting there, and at some point you'll need them," Flynn said.

Cliff scrutinized Flynn for a long moment, and Flynn held his breath. Cliff reminded him of his father, stern but fair. A smile creaked onto the older man's face and he slapped Flynn on the shoulder.

"That is a damned fine idea, son. If you'd like to come with us, I'll take Beth and Jake."

"You might want to leave Beth here. It is going to be gruesome at the hospitals I imagine, and probably at the vet. I suggest we wear protective gear. In fact, if you just take me and give me a list, I'll go in and get what you need. Especially in the hospitals. No clue if I'm immune, but since you all were sequestered on the farm, you might be susceptible. Please, let me do this for you."

"My god, you might be right. Let me think about it and talk to Beth," Cliff said, the color leached from his face.

Flynn understood; it was a frightening thought. He didn't like the idea of being near that gore again, but he liked it even less if this family somehow got sick because he sent them to a virus infested area.

They headed for the house, both deep in thought. Flynn worried he'd opened up a box that shouldn't have been opened.

"There's a veteran's clinic a few miles from here," said Cliff. "I expect it would be safe to go search there. That was open only a few days a week, I believe. Perhaps we can go to these offices and see if there are any dead there. If not, we can get supplies from there."

They walked up onto the large porch. Cliff opened the door to the house and ushered Flynn in. Flynn zeroed in on the aroma of something very delicious cooking. Dinner would be in about twenty minutes.

He smiled when he spied Xandra in the kitchen with the other women. Beth noticed him and her father-in-law and walked into the living room.

"Did you talk to him, Dad?" she asked, wiping her hands on a kitchen towel.

"I did, Beth, and he's happy to learn. We were talking about getting more supplies from the veterinary clinic and the hospitals. He's worried about the possibility of any remains, you know, of the dead. There might be a possibility of the virus still active and perhaps bringing it here."

Beth's eyes widened and she nibbled her lip. "That's a real concern. There are a couple of veterinary clinics on Main Street. We can go to those. I suggest we use my disposable coveralls and double up on gloves and masks. When we're done we can strip and wash down in a betadine solution, then alcohol."

"I've decided you won't be going, daughter. Flynn has volunteered. You can give him a list of what you think you might need."

"Don't forget the tractor supply store, they have a lot of over-the-counter meds for the livestock there," Jake said, coming up behind his wife.

"Okay. We'll get a list and I'll take Flynn out tomorrow," Cliff said.

Beth regarded Flynn, worry in her hazel eyes. He smiled at her and tried to keep his mouth from

238

trembling. It was a scary thought to go back out there, but it was important they have these medical supplies.

"If we can hit ambulances, there may not be any dead people inside. We'd get a lot of supplies from those," Flynn suggested, brightening at the least deadly concept.

"That's actually a good idea. But if you open the ambulance doors and you see anything but a pristine ambulance, close the doors," Beth said.

Flynn nodded. "Count on it."

Ж

Brian was getting ready to head out to hunt his boar. BJ was about to jump out of his skin. He'd never hunted pig before, and they all were excited for bacon. Both freezers were in the ground now, locked up tight with heavy fourteen mil plastic over the top of each chest. Brian placed several cinder blocks over the plastic, so it wouldn't blow away in high winds.

The children were still asleep. Dillan had been allowed to sleep over with Cooper because Brian and BJ were leaving so early. The boys played half the night and Brian was feeling the effects. Emma and Paadi were planning to make pancakes and eggs for breakfast. Each woman sat in their camp chairs with a cup of coffee, staring bleary-eyed into the fire. It was a humid morning, though relatively cool.

"Who in the hell suggested we get up this early?" Paadi groused.

"I thought you cops were up and at 'em like daisies." BJ smirked at Paadi.

She narrowed her eyes threateningly. "You seriously want to start in on me this early?" she growled.

BJ snickered and put his hands up in surrender.

The group heard the distant clopping of horses, several, and looked toward the parking lot.

"I'd bet Jeff and Bradley are here. Guess we won't be going on a hunt this morning," said Brian.

"Damn, they're up even earlier than we are. Glad I'm not a farmer," Paadi said.

A few minutes later the horses came into view. There were four riders, two men and two women.

Brian stood and the rest followed, walking toward the coming horses. Buddy shot past the house with Daisy in pursuit. Neither barked, however, taking their cue from the humans. Brian smacked his leg and Daisy came over to sit beside him, watching.

"Welcome," Brian said. He held out a hand to Jeff.

"Good morning," Jeff said. "Figured we'd swing by this morning since it's gonna be a hot one. That humidity is going to rise so we wanted to get out early."

"Come on over and have some coffee," Brian invited.

BJ ran to the storage shed, pulled out four camp chairs, and carried them to the firepit. The group dismounted and followed Brian.

"Brian, this is my wife Barb, and that's Bradley's wife Ester," Jeff said.

The women tipped their heads.

"Ladies, I'm Brian, and this is BJ, Emma, and Paadi. Please, everyone, sit."

"This is a nice place. You folks have done a lot to it. Ester and I were here last summer," Barb said.

"I agree, this was a wonderful choice. The garden you planted is large and impressive," Ester added.

"I'd planned on living at one of the cabins, but when Cooper and I arrived, it just made sense to make the Beach House our home," said Brian.

"Looks like you were going hunting," Jeff said, eyeing the hunting rifles and backpacks sitting by the camp chairs. "Sorry we interrupted you."

"No, that's fine. If what you say about the weather is true we can wait a day. I don't want to try to bring anything home if it's too hot. The meat would spoil quickly. We were going to hunt boar. I found some indications a couple miles south of here." Brian gave his guests coffee mugs.

"Nice. We've got pigs at our place. You know, we'd be more than happy to trade with you," Jeff said.

"Really? That would be great. I've got a smoker that I'm wanting to use. Make some bacon," Brian proposed.

"Alright. Give me a couple days and we'll get you some meat. Would you want a whole hog? Roughly four hundred pounds," Bradley put in.

"Four hundred *pounds*?" Paadi asked, a stunned expression on her face.

"That might be a bit much, how about half that? That way Emma and Paadi will be able to can some of the meat," Brian suggested.

"Sounds good. I'll bring it by early in the morning. You'll want to work on it when it's cool like this," Jeff said.

"Great! What can we trade?" Emma asked.

"Well, that coffee smells great and we're getting low. We had planned to make a run to get more, but we've been so busy we haven't had time. How about some coffee?" Jeff asked.

Brian tipped his head; it was down to business. Between him and BJ, they'd taken damned near every can and box of coffee in all the stores they hit. The ones in airtight bags were buried underground. They'd snagged a food-saver machine, which vacuumed the air out, and a box of mylar bags and oxygenators at a hardware store. Brian guesstimated they had three hundred pounds of coffee squirreled away, if not more, and that wasn't counting instant coffee.

"Okay, how about ten pounds of ground coffee, five pounds of instant coffee, and ten pounds of sugar. Do you need powdered creamer?" Brian asked.

Smiles rippled across his guests' faces.

"We've got a couple cows." Jeff glanced at his wife, who responded with a wide grin.

"Done." Jeff shook Brian's hand to seal the deal.

Cooper came from the house toward them, still half asleep. He was in Batman pajamas and his hair was sticking straight up. He walked to Brian and crawled up into his lap.

"I'm hungry, Daddy," he said sleepily, then noticed the new people. He buried his face into Brian's chest. Brian knew Cooper was shy with strangers and liked being protected.

"This is my son Cooper," Brian said, noting the surprise rippling through his guests.

"I'll make him a pancake. How does that sound, Coop?" Emma was rewarded by a bobbing head beneath Brian's large hand. She grinned, her eyes crinkling.

"We've acquired several orphans and they've adopted us as their parents," BJ explained, smiling serenely.

"Oh dear, that's so sweet. I guess I didn't think about all the children left behind when the virus struck. The other group has children, but I'm not certain if they are their own children or not," Barb said tenderly, her eyes softening, and Brian detected sorrow behind them.

"We feel pretty lucky to have them. They've been a joy for us," said Paadi.

Emma lifted a questioning brow at the guests before she poured the batter of the pancake mix.

"Oh goodness, no, we've already eaten breakfast. Please, don't let us stop you," Ester said shyly.

Emma poured the batter onto the griddle, which caused a satisfying sizzle. The whoosh of the glass doors from the building announced Dillan. The boy staggered out like a drunken sailor, made his way to BJ, and crawled up in his lap. BJ kissed the chaotic hair and held the boy in his arms. Dillan's stuck his thumb in his mouth and closed his eyes. Brian smiled when Barb and Ester cooed, their hearts melting.

"I'm impressed with your camp, it's well organized," said Bradley. "Are those sheds new?"

"Yes. We've all been working to make this place a home. We've put in two inground root cellars — we used chest freezers. We have one set up for meat and the other for the vegetables. We plan to put milk crates with straw into the freezer and put the veggies and fruit in them. We have that shed over there that we've stocked with the canned goods. The building is well insulated," Brian said.

"Well, it certainly shows. Were you a builder in your previous life?" Bradley asked.

"No, I was a firefighter. BJ's the carpenter. Emma is a nurse and Paadi was a Boston police officer." Brian grinned, his eyes crinkling. He took the plate that Emma handed him and fed Cooper. Like a baby bird perched on his lap, the boy opened his mouth wide and ate the food.

"A nurse, wow, that's great. Would you mind, keeping the coffee and we'll trade on visits to see Emma?" Barb asked.

Jeff gave her a pained expression and Brian laughed.

Emma snickered. "Keep the coffee. And come by any time. I don't mind. It will be nice to have company."

"Deal. Next visit, I'll bring my applesauce cake and some cheese. We have goats and I make cheese," Barb said.

The tightness in Brian's chest eased. He liked these people. They now had friends and others to trade with.

"We have powdered and canned milk for the kids, but at some point next year, do you think perhaps it will be possible to trade for a milking goat and a lesson on cheese making?" Paadi asked.

"Absolutely. We've got several. We can bring one of them by on the next visit. You'll need to build her an enclosure and keep her on a sturdy chain though. You don't want her getting into your garden, she'll eat it all," Barb laughed.

"Thank you, thank you so much! It will be nice for the kids to have fresh milk," Emma said.

Brian got up and handed Cooper over to Emma.

"I want to show them the place," Brian said, and the men stood. Emma eyed Brian and he winked, guy stuff.

He, BJ, Bradley, and Jeff poured more coffee, and strode about the camp with their mugs, Bradley was impressed with the structures and how well they were built and said so.

"You guys do precision work. This is nice. The interior is actually cool," Bradley said after standing inside the canning shed. The cool air washed over them when they opened the door and the air rolled from the shed. It was holding the chill very well. Being located in the shade of the trees helped a great deal.

Jeff bent over at the waist, checking out the underside of the structure's bottom. "I like the way you used the tree stumps as supports for the floor. It keeps it well off the ground and I'd say that will go a long way in keeping the rotting down."

"We wanted it built into the trees. This way it keeps it well within shade and the sun off it. There are so many trees, we cut them down and figured we'd used the stumps as structural support for the buildings," BJ explained.

An hour later, the girls got up and came outside. Their guests were getting ready to leave. Hailey and Amanda were enchanted with the horses, who snuffled their outstretched hands. They sent their guests off with handshakes and hugs.

"Wow, that was so nice," Emma breathed, walking to the firepit.

"It'll be nice to have a goat and fresh milk. That will be better for baking instead of the powdered milk," Paadi mentioned.

"I'm glad they're nice people. You never know anymore, and I'm sorry to say that I'm very paranoid about meeting new people," BJ said. All agreed.

Emma prepared breakfast. The children were fed first and then were off playing. Brian was slightly disappointed about not going hunting, but he was excited about two hundred pounds of pork. He was definitely going to use that smoker.

A week later Jeff was good to his word and brought half a hog, early in the morning. He was driving his truck, an angry goat trussed up in the bed. Barb had come along and had even brought a long chain and a metal stake so the goat could be kept away from the garden.

"Until you're about to smoke it, I'd keep the carcass in the lake to keep it cool," Jeff advised.

Brian set up cold smoking for the bacon, using hickory chips to flavor it. It took longer but would preserve the meat longer. Both he and BJ hovered by the smoker, tending it. They had used BJ's refrigerator for the soaking part of the process. A week was spent freezing water in baggies to put into the freezer once the meat was done. This ensured the temperature was low in the freezer. The smell was tantalizing, and Brian chuckled when he spied Emma and Paadi standing near the smoker.

Brian wanted to go hunting again. He'd heard wild turkeys earlier that morning and thought roasted turkey would be an unexpected treat. BJ offered to keep an eye on the smoker, while the women were canning much of the pork. They'd set up the gas camp stove and had a propane bottle hooked up, using one pressure canner at a time. The kids were swimming and playing at the shore.

"I'm heading out," Brian said. "Wish me luck. Hopefully I'll get a turkey."

"That would be nice. Early Thanksgiving," said Emma.

Ж

Emma and Paadi set up a processing station by the firepit. The worktable was situated in place and there was a good breeze blowing off the lake. They placed a tub with a lid in the water to keep the meat cool until they cut it up and processed it.

"The next batch we make, I think we should spice it with cumin, along with the salt and pepper," Paadi suggested.

"Yum! That sounds amazing. We can fix it with canned tomatoes or fresh if we have them, along with the jalapeno peppers, onions, and bell peppers. We can make flour tortillas and have a burrito or fajita night." Emma wiped sweat from her face. They had found several cases of Tattler canning lids. The Tattler lids were reusable and because all they had was all they would ever have, it meant that they had the ability, in theory, to keep canning indefinitely.

"The cilantro has been growing like crazy, along with the basil and thyme. I reckon we can make a nice salsa to go with it," Paadi said.

Emma chuckled. "Dang it, now I'm hungry."

"That bacon sure smells good," BJ said.

"How's the ice coming? Is it staying frozen in the chest freezer?" Paadi asked, sipping coffee.

"It's coming. I'm glad we started a few days ahead, it takes time for it to freeze, and the more I add to the chest freezer, the longer it stays frozen. By the time the bacon is done, I'll have a lot of ice in there. If we keep trading out the thawing ice and refreezing it, that freezer should stay nice and cool. During the winter, it will be nice to store a lot of meat in there. It should last us all winter." BJ poured himself more coffee.

"It certainly feels good to have this meat. If we can stock up this fall, I'd like to can venison," Emma declared.

"How is Daisy doing? And the pups?" BJ asked.

Daisy had delivered six large puppies the night before. They'd put her in the storage room away from the children, who were making her nervous. They'd been warned to leave her alone. Two puppies were stillborn and buried. No one told the children. Buddy was at Emma's feet and had fretted and sniffed and worried over the puppies. Emma brought him out to give Daisy a break.

"She's doing better," Emma replied. "Between Buddy and the kids, she wasn't very happy. I checked on her earlier and she was a lot calmer. The four babies are nursing well."

"That's good. In a few weeks, those puppies will be ruling the roost," BJ laughed.

Paadi glanced at her watch. "It's time to cut the fire off the canner. We can let it sit for twenty minutes and then let it cool the rest of the way. That will give us enough time to process the next batch of meat and use the spices."

Emma switched off the fire and the rocker reduced its insistent noise. It got a bit quieter after the loud hiss of the pressure canner stopped. Emma and Paadi washed their hands in a bowl of soapy water.

"Can you get us another propane tank, BJ? We've been using this one for quite a long time." Paadi dried her hands with a towel. "It's feeling light, nearly empty. If it runs out and the canner is on, we'll need to switch it out right away so the pressure doesn't go down too far."

BJ rolled his eyes and bowed.

"Take Buddy with you," said Emma. "He needs a romp in the woods to get some of that anxiety worked out. Daisy snapped at him and I imagine he's feeling a little abused."

"You got it. We boys know when we're not wanted, don't we, Buddy?" BJ said in a singsong voice and the dog's tail wagged excitedly.

"So glad you figured it out, chowderhead." Paadi laughed at the expression on his face.

BJ smirked. Emma suspected that the two were actually flirting. She'd seen over the last weeks that the two were getting closer, spending more time together, with the two children they'd adopted. Both were surely still grieving over their loved ones, but Emma noted a spark between the two. She was glad. They suited each other. BJ was calm and easygoing, and Paadi, well, Paadi was Paadi. A handful.

Paadi helped Emma bring the container with meat from the lake. Brian had deboned it for them, and they'd used the bones for a hearty stew with potatoes and onions from the garden and canned carrots from the store. The carrots weren't as good as fresh, but the stew was delicious. Emma tossed fresh spinach and chives into the mix and they'd made cornbread in the sun oven. It was a wonderful dinner. Cooking and eating outdoors was nice. The house had a dining table inside, but it was hot.

Emma brought up the possibility of putting in a few extra windows. Brian and BJ were dubious about the work vs reward. After much discussion, the conclusion was that they had the fans and the large tent out front for hot nights. During the winter, the house would stay much warmer without excess windows. Since their front door was all glass, there would be a lot of heat loss via that. So that matter was put to rest.

The women cut the meat into one-inch chunks. The All-American pressure canners each held up to nineteen quart jars in each batch. They would process large batches at a time. Once they had the meat cut up, they put the large container into the water. They spiced the meat, ensuring it was coated, and then they loaded the clean jars. Paadi washed her hands and toted the still hot canner to the table. Once they got the other canner loaded, they'd start the process of canning all over again.

"My oh my, isn't this just nice? Two beautiful women," a man's voice said.

Emma and Paadi jerked and spun. Emma's mind went blank for a moment then she blanched. It was Mole and Pirate, the two men Brian and BJ had warned them about. She looked around desperately for the children, her heart slamming frantic and hard into her chest. Paadi cursed under her breath. They'd been caught with their guard down. *Damnit.* Where were BJ and Buddy? She cursed herself for a fool.

"Smelled that wonderful food and figured we'd come check you out. Good thing we did, ain't that right, Jeri?" Mole laughed, scratching his gut.

He was filthy and Emma smelled him from fifteen feet away. His breath was redolent of beer and serious halitosis. The man had rotten teeth. The bastard was gag worthy and she wasn't certain she wouldn't vomit there on the spot.

"You got that right, Riley. Damn fine women *and* food. Seems like you girls need a couple of men with all them brats you got." Jeri pointed to the children, who were now huddled by the water. Amanda was clutching the others to her.

"You need to leave here now," Paadi snarled. "You're not welcome here."

"Don't think about reaching for that gun, I'd hate to hurt one of them kids." Riley sneered nastily, aiming the shotgun their way.

Emma's blood turned cold.

"Yeah, that's right, you got it. Now here's how this is gonna work. You're gonna go with my friend Jeri, miss big mouth. He's gonna take you in for a little bump and grind. You cooperate and we'll leave the kids alone. You don't and we'll hurt you all. You got me?" Riley asked in a smug voice.

"Shit, I ain't had a woman in a long time. Girl, I'm gonna get you *goooooood*. Let's go!" Jeri hooted with malicious glee.

The sensation of ice water flowing through her body nearly buckled Emma's knees. Her brain screamed for the safety of the children.

THIRTEEN

His heart hammering hard, Flynn was trying not to hyperventilate. The mask he wore didn't help. Sweat dripped uncomfortably under his arms. He gripped the list Beth gave him, and he and Cliff had hit the ambulances. They were a gold mine. Like Beth had suggested, if the ambulance wasn't pristine, he didn't go in. Luckily, there were windows on the ambulance and he hadn't had to open the doors. He'd found only one ambulance that was left in a bloody mess.

He snagged every last bit of the sterile gauze, tubing, instruments, IVs, and oxygen tanks. He pushed the gurney out and loaded it into the bed of the truck. Cliff gave him a look and he shrugged. The gurney was perfect; it was adjustable and would hold a patient. He figured Beth might appreciate it. There were syringes, pediatric needles, and a portable suction machine.

There were various sized catheters and he took all those, as well as essentially everything he touched. He figured Beth would go through it and she'd know their uses. He'd emptied out each of the ambulances, filling bag after bag.

They'd gone to the veteran's clinic and had found all kind of medical paraphernalia. He'd been given orders to find the pharmacy and remove all the pills, leaving anything that was in a fridge. If he spotted a PDR, a *Physician's Drug Reference,* and several other books she listed, he was to take those. Luckily, he'd found the PDR at the veteran's clinic.

He stood before the hospital's emergency bay doors. They were halfway open, and he was hit by the stench. This was their last stop before they hit up the CVS pharmacies.

Cliff set up the cleaning station away from the truck. Flynn would strip down completely to clean up when he exited the hospital. He was naked beneath the disposable coveralls. Cliff gave him a nervous thumbs-up and grimaced anxiously. Flynn strode hesitantly forward, between the opened doors, careful not to touch them. He watched where he placed his feet. He was wearing an old pair of shoes, which were to be thrown away.

He spied the first lump of bones and shivered. It was covered with clothing, but the clothing was stiff and black with dried blood. He averted his eyes and kept walking. The reception area was clear. He stepped to one of the curtained rooms, which had the curtain drawn closed. Blood covered the floor and was splashed onto the curtain. He didn't want to go near that. He walked to the next area; the exam table was bloody, with black blood-crusted sheets, but there was no body.

Thank God.

He moved to the cabinets with multi drawers. Careful of any blood spatter, he opened each drawer and emptied the contents into the large black bag. He didn't even check what he was getting, he simply dumped each tray into the bag. His hands were shaking so badly he dropped one tray. He left it. It landed in a black puddle of dried blood.

"Get a grip, Flynn, don't freak out," he hissed at himself.

He took a deep breath and coughed it out, regretting the stench he'd just breathed in. He swallowed hard and closed his eyes. Trying to shake off the creeps, he resumed his work. Once he'd emptied the cabinets, he headed to the next bay. This one was clean, and he breathed easier. His hands shook less, and he quickly dumped the contents. He marched from room to room, avoiding the lumps of bones and dried blood. His body was saturated with sweat and he was nauseated from the heat that was trapped in the hospital.

It took him over an hour to go through the rooms and offices. Some offices he didn't enter, seeing a body or two within. It just wasn't worth the risk. When he was finished, he headed outside. There was a bottle of betadine sitting outside waiting for him. He squirted and sprayed the plastic bags. It was probably overkill, but he didn't care. Then he took the bottle with alcohol and spritzed off the betadine. Cliff watched him from the truck, which was twenty feet away, fear and worry reflected on his face. Flynn well understood. This was dangerous work, and not taking it seriously could kill people.

He stripped off the coveralls, mask, gloves, and shoes, standing naked in the bright sunlight. He was self-conscious and quickly sprayed himself with the betadine. Although he'd been covered head to toe with the coveralls, he sprayed himself completely. He resembled some kind of gory ghoul. The betadine pooled at his feet. He spritzed himself with the alcohol spray. He had to hold his breath; the smell of the alcohol took his breath away. The breeze was cooling his body and it was good. He carried the bags to the truck and put them in the bed, tying them together so they wouldn't fly out.

There was an old towel on the tailgate, and he dried himself off then tossed the towel away. They wouldn't take it home. He got dressed and felt human again. Climbing into the truck, Flynn stared at Cliff.

"You alright?" Cliff asked, scanning him up and down.

"Yeah. I'll tell you, I was scared to death. I didn't touch anything or get near any blood." Flynn snagged a bottle of water and drank it down.

"Good. Once we hit the CVSs, we'll head home. Sarah will have fixed the cottage up for us, with plenty of food." Cliff tried to smile, though it trembled a bit.

They'd all agreed that after the run, Flynn and Cliff would go into quarantine for a week. If he or Cliff got sick, they'd stay in the cottage, and when they died, the cottage would be burned to the ground with all the equipment and supplies they'd gotten today. Flynn thought it was very brave of Cliff, because Flynn was fairly confident he was immune, but Cliff hadn't been exposed, nor had the people on the farm.

Cliff drove off and headed for the first CVS pharmacy. When Flynn walked into the store, there was no sign of death. The air was stale. He walked out and over to Cliff.

"This store has a ton of coffee. You want me to do a bit of gathering?" Flynn asked, a mischievous grin on his lips.

"Heck yes! Thanks," Cliff replied, his face more relaxed.

Flynn hurried in and cleared out all the medications and creams in the storage room of the pharmacy. He figured Beth would know what it was all for. He zoomed through the store pilfering the cans of coffee. As he was leaving, he grabbed a handful of candy bars. Xandra would like those.

The other stores with the pharmacies were just as easy. The last one he'd had to break the glass door since it was locked.

They headed home. Cliff wasn't driving fast, so Flynn took the opportunity to scrutinize the homes lining the road. The yards were overgrown and garbage blew across the road. It was desolate and lonesome.

"It's like a ghost town here," Cliff whispered, a catch in his voice.

"It is. My recommendation is we shouldn't leave the farm for a while. Maybe not until you go to see Claus. When do you think you'll go?"

"Not for another three months. I believe you're right, we'll stay put for a while. Thank you again for doing this, Flynn. My family and I appreciate it. I don't know what the future holds, but with these medical supplies, Beth will be able to take care of most anything that may happen. We owe you."

"No you don't, Cliff. Xandra and I are so grateful you took us in, took a chance on two strangers. We know what's out there and what it takes to survive. We wouldn't have if it hadn't been for you and your family's kindness. So no, you don't owe me anything, you've paid me in full."

Cliff chuckled. "All right, we'll call it square."

Clive drove to the rear of the property where there was a cottage, more like a miniature bunkhouse. It had a bathroom, galley kitchen, and three bunkbeds. They took the bags into the bunkhouse and left the gurney in the bed of the truck. Flynn spotted a walkie-talkie on the counter and glanced at Cliff questioningly.

"We use that when we're out in the fields," said Cliff. "Cheaper than cellphones."

He picked it up and spoke into it.

"We're all set in the bunkhouse, Sarah. Thanks, honey, for the food and for the fridge." Cliff let the talk button go.

There was ear splitting static, a crackle, and then Sarah's voice.

"Figured you boys would like a few beers. We'll drop food off at the truck. You'll be getting paper plates, not my best China."

"Okay, darlin', I'll be in touch." Cliff set the walkie-talkie on the counter.

"I'm going to take another shower." Flynn went to get the clean clothes sitting on the bunk. He grinned when he noticed the Stephen King book he'd been reading sitting atop the pile of clothing.

Emma's mouth was dry and her body was shaking. They were trapped, and the men were using the children as hostages for their good behavior. Tears filled her eyes and the man in front of her blurred.

"Move. Now!" Jeri screamed.

Emma jerked and glanced at Paadi, who was frozen in place. The color had leached from her face and she was a sickly gray. She spun away from Emma and started walking in jerky movements. Emma heard the children crying and stared at Riley, who was watching Jeri and Paadi.

Emma edged her hand to the gun tucked at the base of her spine. Just as her fingers curled on the grip, an explosion jerked her body, as though she'd been shot. She saw a blur her mind couldn't process. For a horrifying moment, she thought she was shot. She gaped at Riley, who had a shocked expression on his face, his chest blossoming in brilliant red. Buddy grabbed the downed man by the neck and was shaking him wildly. The dog made no sound. Another boom and Emma saw BJ, all the blood gone from his face, and then she glanced at Paadi.

Jeri was on the ground and Paadi pulled her weapon. She aimed it at the downed man's face and shot him three times. BJ was running, and as he went by Riley he called Buddy off the man. Riley wasn't moving anymore. Buddy's muzzle was bloody. He sat beside the dead man and waited for a command. Emma patted her leg and the dog ran over to her. BJ ran to Paadi, grabbed her, and dragged her away from the dead Jeri. He held her in his arms and the children ran to him and Paadi.

Emma ran over and threw her arms around them all and they were all crying hysterically. She wasn't sure when they stopped crying. Dillan clung to BJ, and Hailey was glued to Paadi. Emma held Cooper and her free arm encircled Amanda, rocking both children.

"Is everyone okay?" BJ croaked, tears sliding down his face.

"I think so. We need to get these kids into the house and get those bodies out of here," Emma said, wiping her eyes.

"Get the kids in, I'll take care of the bodies," BJ panted, pushing them all toward the house.

They entered the house and went to the large couch. BJ held Paadi's face in his hands and stared into her eyes.

"You sure you're, okay?" he asked. Paadi nodded jerkily. BJ leaned forward and kissed the top of her head, kissed each of the children and then Emma, then he was gone.

"What do you think happened to the third man?" Emma asked, her voice shaking.

"Hopefully dead. I'll suggest that Brian and BJ go and search for him, verify he's dead. If he isn't, then kill him," Paadi snarled, her eyes hard as black diamonds.

Ж

Brian ran through the forest. He'd heard the distant gunshots; multiple shots. His long legs ate up the distance and he rushed past trees and low bushes. Was it the three men he and BJ found? Someone else? Were the children okay? Emma?

Lord, why can't I run faster?

His breath came in gasps and his mouth was so dry he was unable to swallow. It was an agonizing run; time was standing still, and he seemed to be running against a molasses tide. When he broke through the trees he saw nothing on the beach but the cooking equipment. Then he spotted BJ bent over a body. He was tying a rope onto the legs of a man. As Brian drew closer, he realized it was Mole. His heart fell into his stomach. BJ spun, drawing his Glock, when he heard Brian. When he saw his friend he holstered his weapon. Brian noticed BJ was pale as death.

"Everyone okay? The kids? Emma and Paadi?"

When BJ nodded, Brian's breath came out all at once and he damned near buckled with relief.

"What happened?" Brian gasped, trying to catch his breath. He bent over at the waist and spat. He spotted Emma at the doors and waved. Her lips quivered and she disappeared into the house.

"I was getting a tank of propane. Buddy was with me. When I was returning I saw Pirate leading Paadi to the house. Mole had his shotgun pointed at the kids on the beach. When he was distracted watching Pirate, I shot the son-of-a-bitch. Buddy finished him off. Then I shot Pirate and Paadi finished him off." BJ's eyes were haunted.

Brian stared at Mole. His throat was ripped open, his dead eyes wide in shock. Pirate lay beside him, three holes in his head.

"Now that you're here, you can help me load them into the truck? I didn't want the women trying to lift these bastards."

"Yeah. After we dump them let's go and find Crackhead. I'm sorry we just didn't shoot them right then and there. I'm glad you were here. If we'd have gone hunting, this might have ended differently." The very thought made Brian weak in the knees.

BJ untied the dead man's feet and it took a bit of hoisting, but they got both bodies into the truck bed. The men drove about five miles away and then took a utility road. Driving in about a half mile, Brian maneuvered so the bed was pointing to the side of the road. Then he and BJ rolled the bodies out.

"Thanks again, BJ. You saved our family," Brian said, slapping BJ on the back.

BJ smiled wanly.

"Don't punish yourself. From now on, anyone who seems like a threat, we shoot. No questions asked, no guilt. We can't take another chance like that," Brian said, his voice hard.

"I agree. I'll never let another piece of shit walk away," BJ said.

The two men climbed into the RAM and headed home. When they arrived, the women were outside at the pressure canner. Brian exhaled when they pulled into the drive. When he got out, the children gathered around him. He hugged each of them and whispered reassurances. Then he went to Paadi and hugged her hard.

"Sorry we didn't end them the first time," he whispered into her hair.

"I doubt you'll make that mistake again," she said, a sardonic lift to her lips.

Brian shook his head. "No, no I won't." He drew Emma to him. He rocked her, her body vibrating in his arms. He leaned away and gazed into her eyes.

"You sure you're alright?" he asked gently.

She gave a shaky exhalation and bobbed her head. "I am, but honestly, I believe a hell of a lot of gray hairs sprung up, not to mention ten years off my life." She laughed shakily.

He hugged her tight then let her go. "We're gonna go find the other one. We'll make certain he doesn't make it another step closer to this place."

Brian and BJ left the camp and headed into the woods. They moved quickly and with purpose. Brian's mind kept returning to when they'd first discovered the men and he repeatedly kicked himself for not killing them that first time. That was the old world pushing in on the new world. He had to forget the old ways of thinking. Letting someone like that live these days was a liability that could end up costing them all. It wasn't a price he was willing to pay.

As a firefighter, he was used to saving lives, not taking them. Each killing took a small piece of him. The alternative, however, to lose his new family to pieces of shit like them, would kill him. He had to change his way of thinking or none of them would survive. He was thankful they'd all kept in practice with their weapons. He couldn't imagine what he'd have come back to if they hadn't.

The topography changed and he and BJ started on a decline. They detected the odor of the camp and measured their descent until it came into view. It was still nasty and reeked. Crackhead was sitting in his chair drinking a beer. Brian and BJ tiptoed toward him, both holding their Glocks. Brian stepped on a twig and it snapped loudly, like a gunshot. The man's head jerked up. He was sluggish, either drunk, high, or both. His eyes widened at the sight of two men aiming guns at him.

He started to get up, feeling for the shotgun at his feet. Brian was the first to fire and then BJ's weapon went off. Brian hit him twice, as did BJ. It was overkill, but Brian thought it was satisfying, knowing that the lowlife wouldn't get a chance to hurt or kill anyone ever again. They walked down into the camp where the fire was blazing away. He and BJ kicked dirt over the fire, amazed that these men hadn't started a forest fire. They searched the camp.

"You think we should take these ATVs?" BJ asked.

"No. They can't carry much and in a few months, gas won't be worth anything. Neither they nor the trucks will run. It would be junk scattered about."

"True. I don't see anything in this camp worth salvaging," BJ said, peering into the filthy tents. Nothing but bottles and cans littered the ground. It would get covered eventually by vines and bushes. The body would rot into the ground. Brian didn't think anything would eat it, so poisoned it was by drugs and booze. They strolled away from the camp, neither regretting their actions.

Ж

Flynn stepped into the cottage. Xandra was on the couch, trying her hand at knitting. She glanced up and cried out happily, throwing the yarn and needles aside.

"I'm so glad you're home. No problems in the cabin?" she asked. Her eyes were bright and she encircled Flynn with a hug.

"Only that Cliff snores like a damned train," Flynn laughed, hugging her to him.

It was good to be home with Xandra after the weeklong isolation. It was late afternoon and Xandra would be heading to the main house later to start dinner preparations.

"Ah, well, tonight you'll sleep peacefully," she said, a wide grin on her blushing face.

"How was your day?" he asked, sitting on the couch and pulling her onto his lap.

"Oh, you know, the same. Weeded the garden and we started canning. Man, that's some hot work. Sarah has a stove outside in a small kitchen shed. She said they do their summer canning out there. Just standing near the canner was hot. But it was so amazing, learning how to can all the things we grew. We were doing tomatoes today. We had to scald them to get the peels off. Then I was in charge of squishing them. That was kind of fun. There were a ton of quart jars we filled. Sarah has a whole shed full of jars, lids, and rings," Xandra gushed.

"That's awesome. My day was boring as hell. I did finish the book though," he said.

Soon, the couple found something else to do, other than work.

Ж

At dinner a couple of weeks later, the whole family and some of the farmhands were at the dinner table. Flynn was enjoying the company of them all. There was talking and laughter and remarkable homemade food. For years, it had only been himself and his father. Then a roommate here or there. Then he was living alone. His world had consisted of work, home, bars. Though it was an okay life for him then, he never imagined doing anything but living and working on a farm now. He'd begun working with the large animals and Beth was showing him the way of it. He'd begun to feel a connection with the animals he handled.

Xandra's cheeks were pink with good health, and her face was filling out as she gained back the weight. She'd lost that hollow-eyed, haunted appearance. Her dark hair was glossy and healthy. When he looked in the mirror now, he saw a tan, strong man reflected. A man who was satisfied. No, more than satisfied with his life. It was like he'd discovered his purpose, his calling. He'd never even known it. Before, he was just existing, going through the motions. Now he was truly living.

Ж

The air had a crisp bite to it. Fall was officially here. The leaves began their change from green to gold and crimson. Emma and Paadi labored hard every day to can the produce coming ripe. Brian and BJ were gearing up for another hunt. They had gotten a boar, smoked it, and made jerky out of it. It was a juvenile, so it wasn't that big. Their larder was full and they had cheese

Emma made. The goat was pulling her weight, keeping the grass cut and eating leftover veggies. Today Jeff and his group were coming by. They were going to have a cookout.

Jeff's group had slaughtered a cow and were bringing beef to Brian and his group. They were trading it for two of the pups when they got just a little older. The women had talked about canning much of the beef, and BJ had voted that they smoke some.

Brian walked into the shed that held all their canned foods. There were hundreds of neatly lined up jars. He was amazed at what the women had accomplished. It was hard to believe they'd grown that much food, but they had. Emma and Paadi were saving the seeds of the biggest and best vegetables to be used the next year. Barb was bringing different seeds to add to their variety. There were boxes of shelled beans drying and they would store those for soups and chilis, and for next year's planting.

The children were gathering wood, even Dillan. The puppies were following, pulling at the children's pants. Brian laughed. He walked over to where they'd planted the fruit trees and touched one of the apples. It wasn't big, but it looked delicious. His fingers itched to pluck it, but Emma or Paadi would skin him alive. They had plans for the apples.

Since Emma had no peaches, she was using canned peaches from the store to make a peach cobbler for the gathering using the sun oven. He coughed a chuckle when he saw BJ following Paadi. Her mouth was going faster than a runaway horse, and BJ was sniggering at something she was saying. Brian beheld a romance in their future.

On the beach, Daisy and Buddy were laying by the water. Waterfowl were skimming along the surface and diving down. The adult dogs had chased the puppies earlier and they were pooped.

Emma walked up to him and nudged him with her elbow. "You alright?"

"Yeah. Just looking around and checking things out. I feel a chill in the air. Winter isn't far off," he said.

"Yep. I woke up this morning and had to put a pair of socks on. It'll be nice though. The leaves have started changing color and it will be pretty. We've got plenty of food put away now, so we don't have to worry. The hen has gone broody again, so I suspect we'll have a few more babies."

"Hmm, maybe next year we'll have enough chickens to have a baked chicken from time to time," Brian said, liking the idea.

"That's what we're aiming for. Barb said they were going to clear more land and start planting wheat, so that way we can barter for flour."

Emma seemed happy. Brian grinned down at her. She was always thinking about cooking or making food. She'd made goat butter and goat cheese, and both were good.

"That's good to know. We just don't have the land for planting that. We do have a bumper crop of potatoes though and I'm looking forward to french fries today," he said, rubbing his hands.

"Oh yeah! We'll get that done. I've made potato salad. The shed really keeps things cool and that's where I keep the mayo. It helps having that small refrigerator. Barb has a recipe for mayonnaise, so I might be trying that next," Emma enthused.

Unable to help himself, Brian hugged her.

"What was that for?" she laughed.

"Just for being wonderful. For taking good care of all of us. I mean that. You and Paadi do so much. You keep us whole."

Emma hugged him hard. "Hey, you started this rodeo, remember? When I got here you'd already started it all. Thanks to you, we've all come together and made a home, made a life, and made a future. We now have hope, where once we had only the prospects of an extinction and a life alone," she said, tears shining in her eyes.

Brian's eyes stung with tears. She was right, they now had a future and hope. He was under no illusions it would be an easy future. There were certainly threats out there. Their isolated location was a large factor in their safety, along with the dogs and their resolute determination. No. Not an easy future, but one he was certain might hold joy and hope.

EPILOGUE
FOUR YEARS LATER

Brian swung the ax down and split the wood cleanly. Cooper stepped in and sat another block of wood on the stump. He took the split wood and stacked it on the wood pile.

"When can I start chopping wood, Dad?" Cooper asked.

"I'd say in a couple years. It takes precision not to chop your foot off." Brian grinned at his son, for son he was. Cooper was growing tall. In a few more years he'd be a teenager. That broke Brian's heart. The children were growing up so fast. Amanda was now a teen and acting like a woman. Emma was having a time, but Amanda was a sweet girl. Emma was teaching Amanda the art of healing and nursing, and the girl was showing a great aptitude.

Emma walked toward them carrying two-year-old Hope. Brian laid the ax down and reached for his daughter. He held her up and elicited a squeal.

"I think she's cutting a molar. She's been grumpy all morning," Emma said. She wrapped an arm about Cooper's neck. The boy giggled as Emma squeezed.

"Poor rabbit. Hey, I was thinking we take a ride over to Jeff's later. What do you think?" Brian asked, kissing Hope and then handing her to her mother.

"That's a great idea. I've got a suspicion Amanda has a crush on Johnathan," Emma laughed.

Johnathan was Jeff and Barb's middle son, who was fifteen. It would be something to keep an eye on. One of the last items that Brian and BJ had gotten were bicycles, along with extra parts, pumps, and patches. They acquired two bike trailers. Once the gas went, they didn't have the ability to go far on foot. With the bikes, they could ride to Jeff and Barb's farm to visit and trade. Now the trailers carried the babies, along with trading items. All the children had a bike. Though Dillan's legs were still too short to ride, he was growing fast. Cooper was tall and lanky and so had learned to ride the bike that spring. Dillan rode on the fender of BJ's bike, holding onto his father's waist.

"Yeah, we need to watch those two," Brian grumbled, causing Emma to laugh. He bent and kissed his wife on the cheek.

"I'll go check the bikes to make sure the tires aren't flat." She walked away with Hope. Brian waved bye to his daughter and lifted the ax up.

Ж

BJ came out of the camper, Paadi behind him. She was six months pregnant and plodding along, instead of at her normal speedy pace.

"Emma said Brian's up for a visit over to Barb's. I was thinking of staying here. Mathew isn't feeling well," Paadi said as they walked toward the beach. Three-year-old Mathew was sitting with Dillan, and the boys were playing in the sand. Ten-year-old Hailey was helping them make sandcastles.

"I'll stay here with you," BJ offered. "Hailey, did you want to go with Brian and Emma? They're going to see Jeff and Barb."

"Heck yeah, Dad. I want to ride their horses again." Hailey jumped up and down in excitement.

"Can I go?" Dillan asked.

"Why don't you stay here with me and Mommy? Maybe we can put on a movie," BJ said.

Dillan's body slumped. "Okay," he said, not entirely happy.

BJ winked at Paadi, who rolled her eyes. Mathew climbed up into BJ's lap and laid his head on his chest.

BJ touched the child's head. "No fever," BJ said. He kissed Mathew on his dark head.

"I'm thinking it is growing pains. He's been eating a lot. He said his knees hurt this morning," Paadi said.

Amanda walked down and sat beside the couple.

"You going with your folks over to the Simmons'?" Paadi asked and BJ hid a smile, knowing that Amanda would be going.

"They're going? Oh, I better go change and get cleaned up!" Amanda exclaimed and ran to the house.

BJ guffawed.

"Predictable." Paadi rolled her eyes.

"She's a chowderhead," Mathew said, his thumb in his mouth.

BJ narrowed his eyes at Paadi, who snorted.

Ж

Flynn withdrew the file from the horse's mouth. He'd had to file down a back molar. It was his last task of the day and he'd be heading in to get cleaned up for dinner. He patted the horse on the neck and walked out of the barn. The sun was beginning to sink lower. It had been a long day, but he had good news for Cliff. Two of the dairy cows were pregnant and seven of the beef cows were pregnant. That was good, the herd was increasing. Sadly, the year before, they'd lost three calves. He hoped this year would be better.

He walked into the cottage and gazed lovingly at Xandra. She was changing two-year-old Joey. The child squealed when he spied his father. His fat legs kicking excitedly. Xandra laughed and got up.

"Okay, go get Daddy." The boy shot off the couch and into Flynn's arms.

Flynn held his son to him and snuggled. No matter how hard the day or how tired he was, Joey and Xandra made him feel like the king of the world. He laughed and hoisted the child up.

"What did you do today?" he asked the child and received a squeal.

"He was carried by Beth's daughter," Xandra said then laughed.

"How? She's not bigger than a minute and Joey's close to as tall as she is!" Flynn laughed.

"Well, his feet were dragging the floor, but he didn't seem to mind."

"Goober." He smirked at his son and gave him his wooden horse. The child stuck it in his mouth and gnawed with slobbery glee.

"Let me get showered and we'll head over," Flynn said.

"Take your time, we're having roast. I've already done the mashed potatoes. They're waiting on the bread to finish," said Xandra.

Flynn went into the bathroom that Cliff and the farm hands had built onto their cottage. There were two additional bedrooms, the kitchen was extended, and a stove and large refrigerator were added. Xandra cooked a lot of their meals here, but more often than not they joined the family. Cliff adopted them into their own family and loved them as his very own. He'd taken to Joey and Joey called Cliff PaPap, as did all the other grandchildren.

They'd gone three days prior to retrieve the flour and maze Claus had milled for them. Flynn was amazed at the amount of flour. There were sacks and sacks of it. Jake normally went with Cliff, but Flynn didn't have any animals that needed tending and so had gone. He'd wanted to take a look-see. He rarely left the farm. There wasn't much to see. Claus reported seeing no one for years now. It was the same at the farm. It was as though there were only a few tiny islands of humanity. Life was going on, though at an unhurried pace with millions fewer humans.

Flynn stood under the spray of hot water. He was hot and sweaty from working with the animals. He was happy too. His tiny family was happy and healthy, as was his extended family. He was amazed at how fast time was passing and the joy he experienced in his life. The horrors of before were fading into the distant past. Sometimes his friend Cramer came to mind. Deep down, Flynn knew his old friend was dead.

There was no kind of life in that dead city or any other city. Only those who broke away and found a way to survive were the ones to make it. He and Xandra did just that. There was hope for his small family and for others too. There was a future. It was a simple and largely uncomplicated future. They worked hard to survive, protect what they had, and appreciated each day.

Made in the USA
Middletown, DE
14 October 2023

40789485R00156